D1187258

Hans
Andersen's
Fairy
Tales

Retold by
Vera Gissing
Illustrations by
Dagmar Berková

First published 1979 by

Octopus Books Limited

59 Grosvenor Street

London W1

Translated by Vera Gissing

Graphic design by Jiří Schmidt

This edition © Artia 1979

Illustrations © Dagmar Berková

ISBN 0 7064 0649 4

Printed in Czechoslovakia by Svoboda

1/19/03/51-01

CONTENTS

The Constant Tin Soldier

Once upon a time there were twenty-five tin soldiers. All of them were brothers, for they had all been made from the same old tin spoon. They held rifles in their hands and every one of them looked alike with their lovely uniforms of red and blue. The very first words they heard in this world, when the lid was taken off the box in which they lay were, 'Tin soldiers!' It was the cry of a small boy, as he clapped his hands; he had been given the tin soldiers because it was his birthday. Straightaway he stood every one of them on the table.

They were like peas out of the same pod, the very image of one another, all that is except one, who was slightly different; he had only one leg, for he was the very last to be made and there was not quite enough tin left. But he stood on his one leg just as firmly and steadfastly as the others did on two. And it was this very soldier who met the most unusual fate.

There were many other toys scattered on the table where the little soldiers had been put, but by far the most attractive one was a magnificent paper castle. Through its tiny windows one could see right into the rooms. In front of the castle stood some little trees round a small mirror, which was made to look like a lake. Some wax swans swam on the lake, and were reflected in it.

It was truly very pretty, but prettiest of all was a little doll who stood in the open doorway of the castle. She, too, had been cut out of paper, but she wore a dress of the softest muslin, with a narrow blue ribbon round her shoulders like a shawl. In the middle of the ribbon sparkled a glittering coin the size of her face. The little maiden was stretching out both her arms, for actually she was a dancer, and one of her little legs was raised so high that the little tin soldier could not see it at all, and thought that she, like himself, had only one leg.

'That would be the wife for me!' he thought. 'But then she is too high and mighty. She lives in a castle, whereas I live in a box and, to top it all, there's twenty-five of us in it—that would be no proper home for her! Still, I am going to try to get to know her.' Then he stretched right out to his full height behind a snuff-box which also stood on the table. From there he had a perfect view of the little maiden, who stood persistently on one leg without losing her balance.

Later that evening, all the other tin soldiers were put back in the box and the people of the house went to bed. That was when the toys really began to play—at visiting, at fighting wars, and at having parties. The tin soldiers rattled in the box, for they wanted to play too, but they couldn't push the lid off. The nut-cracker turned somersaults and the slate pencil raced about on the slate. They all made such a noise that the canary woke up and joined in, chatting away in verse! The only two who never moved were the little tin soldier and the little dancer. She stood so erect on tiptoe, both her arms stretched out and he, too, stood steadfast on his one leg, without taking his eyes off her for a moment.

The clock struck twelve, and with a bang, the lid of the snuff-box sprang

open. But there was no snuff inside, oh no, just a little black goblin. A Jack-in-the-box full of tricks!

'Tin soldier!' the Jack-in-the-box called out. 'Kindly keep your eyes to yourself!'

But the tin soldier pretended not to hear.

'Very well then, just you wait till morning!' threatened the Jack-in-the-box.

In the morning when the children got up, they put the little tin soldier on the window-ledge. Who knows if it was the fault of that Jack-in-the-box, or the wind, but all of a sudden the window flew open and the little tin soldier fell head first from the third floor to the ground. It was a fearsome fall for he hit the ground with his cap and lay with his one leg in the air, his bayonet stuck between the paving stones.

The maid and the little boy ran down straightaway to look for him. But though they very nearly trod on him, they did not see him. If only the little soldier had cried out, 'Here I am!', they would have found him, but he didn't think it dignified to call out loudly when he was in uniform.

Then it started to rain and the drops fell faster and faster, till there was a real downpour. When it was over, two small boys came along.

'Look at this!' cried one of them. 'It's a tin soldier! Let's give him a sail!'

They made a little boat out of newspaper and put the tin soldier in it. Away he sailed down the gutter by the pavement with both boys running alongside, clapping their hands with glee. My word, what enormous waves there were in that gutter and what a current—but then, what a downpour! The little paper boat rocked up and down and every now and then it twirled right round, making the little soldier quite giddy. But he remained steadfast, never moving a muscle, never flinching, eyes forward, his rifle clasped to his side.

All at once the boat was swept under a covered drain where the soldier found it was as dark as his own box.

'Where am I going?' he wondered. 'It's all that Jack-in-the-box's fault! Oh, if only my little maiden was sitting here beside me, I wouldn't care if it was twice as dark!'

Just then, a large water-rat that lived in the drain appeared.

'Have you a passport?' asked the rat. 'Show me your passport!'

But the little soldier said not a word and clutched his rifle tighter than ever. The boat sailed on, with the rat following. Ugh! How it gnashed its teeth and shouted to the sticks and the straws, 'Stop him! Stop him! He hasn't paid the toll! He hasn't shown his passport!'

But the current grew stronger and stronger. The little soldier could already see clear daylight ahead, where the drain ended but he also could hear such a roar, loud enough to frighten the bravest of men. Just imagine, that drain ended in a great canal! Falling into it was as dangerous for the tin soldier as sailing down a mighty waterfall would be for us.

He was already so very near, he could not stop. The little boat flew like the wind, and the poor little soldier held himself as erect as he knew how. No one could call him a coward! The boat spun round three or four times, and filled with water right to the brim; surely it must sink! The little soldier was now up to his neck in water and the little boat sank deeper and deeper still. The sodden paper was falling apart more and more. Now the water closed over the soldier's head and he thought of the pretty little dancer whom he would never see again. In his ears rang the old song:

'Onward, onward, warrior!
Forward to your death!'

The paper fell apart completely and the tin soldier fell down, down and then he was swallowed by a large fish. It was so dark inside! It was even worse than the drain and no room to move at all. But the tin soldier remained undaunted, stretched out to his full length, clasping his rifle.

The fish flung itself about in a frenzy, twisting and turning horribly. At last it stopped and was perfectly still. Then suddenly, it seemed as if a streak of lightning flashed through it. A light shone brightly, and some-one called, 'Here is the tin soldier!' The fish had been caught, taken to market, sold and brought into the kitchen, where the maid had cut it open with a large knife. Picking the tin soldier up by his waist with two fingers, she carried him into the sitting-room, where everyone was most curious to see this very remarkable little man, who had travelled the world inside the fish's tummy. But the little tin soldier wasn't one to boast—it was a mere trifle to him.

They stood him upon a table and there... well, fate plays a strange hand in life sometimes... the little tin soldier found himself in the very same room in which he had lived before. He saw the same children and the same toys still standing on the table, and the magnificent castle with the prettiest little dancer. She was still balanced on one leg, with the other high up in the air, for she too was very steadfast! The tin soldier was so touched, he almost burst into tin tears, but this wouldn't have been the proper thing to do. So he gazed at the dancer and she gazed back at him, but neither spoke.

All at once, one of the small boys picked up the tin soldier and threw him straight into the stove—for no reason at all. That Jack-in-the-box must have most definitely had a hand in that!

The tin soldier now stood in the fiery glow and felt the fearsome flame, but he couldn't really tell whether it was the flame of a real fire, or the flame of love. His colour was all gone, but who knows whether he lost it during his travels, or through grief. He looked at the little dancer and she looked back at him, and he felt himself melting but still he remained steadfast as he clutched his rifle. Suddenly the door opened and the draught caught the little dancer. She flew like a fairy straight into the stove to the tin soldier. Instantly she was ablaze, and was gone. The tin soldier melted into a shrivelled lump and, when the maid cleared the ashes the following day, she found his little tin heart. But all that was left of the dancer was the shiny coin, and that was as black as a cinder.

The Red Shoes

Once upon a time there was a little girl, delicate and pretty, but as she was poor, she had to walk barefoot in summer and, in winter, she had to wear hard wooden clogs. In time her little feet grew awfully sore and red.

In the centre of the village lived the old mother of the shoemaker. One day she made a pair of little shoes out of some old pieces of red cloth. They didn't look very nice, but she meant well, and she gave them to the little girl, whose name was Karen.

In fact, she was given the red shoes on the very day her mother was being buried, and that was the first time she wore them. They were not, of course, suitable for mourning, but she had no others and so she walked in them, her legs bare, behind the simple coffin.

Just then, a large old carriage rode by, with a large old lady in it. Seeing the little girl, she pitied her and said to the priest, 'Why don't you let me have the little girl. I shall look after her well!'

Karen thought that her red shoes were responsible for all this but the old lady said they were ugly, and burnt them. Karen was dressed cleanly and neatly and she was taught to read and to sew. People told her how pretty she was but her mirror said, 'You are more than pretty, you are beautiful!'

One day the Queen happened to travel through that part of the country, with her little daughter, the Princess. People rushed to the palace where they were staying and so did Karen. The little Princess, dressed in white, was standing at the window for everyone to see. She wore neither train nor golden crown, but had on her feet a pretty pair of red morocco shoes. They were indeed much prettier than those the shoemaker's mother had made for little Karen. Nothing in the world could be compared to these red shoes.

Karen was now old enough to be confirmed. She was given a new dress and was also to have a pair of new shoes. The rich shoemaker in the town measured her little foot. He did this in his own workroom, where there were large glass-fronted cupboards with dainty shoes and shining boots. They were all very beautiful but, as the old lady's sight was poor, she did not get much pleasure from looking at them.

Among the shoes was a pair of red ones, just like those worn by the Princess. How pretty they were! The shoemaker told them that they had been made for the count's daughter, but they had not fitted her.

'This must be polished leather!' said the old lady. 'See how they shine!'

'Yes, they shine beautifully!' Karen cried, and, because they fitted her well, the old lady bought them, not realizing that they were red, for she would never have allowed Karen to go to confirmation in red shoes. And yet this did happen.

All the people kept looking at her feet, and when she walked from the nave to the chancel, it seemed to her that even the old portraits of priests and their wives, with their stiff ruffs and long black robes, had their eyes fixed upon her red shoes. She thought only of the red shoes as the priest laid his hand upon her head and spoke of holy baptism, the covenant of God, and told her that now she was a true Christian. Then the organ

played ceremoniously, the children's sweet voices rang out and the old school-master sang too, but all Karen thought of were her red shoes.

That afternoon the old lady had been told by many people that Karen had worn red shoes for her confirmation and that this was not the correct thing to do. It was in fact quite unsuitable, and that whenever Karen went to church in the future, she would have to wear black shoes, even if they were old.

Next Sunday there was holy communion and Karen was to receive it for the first time. She looked first at the red shoes, then at the black ones, then at the red ones again — and put them on.

It was a beautiful, sunny day. Karen and the old lady walked along a path through the cornfields and it was rather dusty.

An old soldier stood at the church door. He was on crutches and had a magnificently long beard, more red than white — in fact it was red. He bowed right to the ground and asked the old lady if she would permit him to wipe the dust off her shoes. Karen put her little foot out, too.

'Oh, what pretty dancing shoes!' said the soldier. 'Grip tight when you dance!' And he struck the heels with his hands.

The old lady gave the old soldier a coin and then entered the church with Karen.

Again all the people in the church looked at the red shoes and all the portraits gazed at them too. When Karen knelt before the altar and put the golden chalice to her lips, all she could think of were her red shoes. It seemed to her that they were floating before her eyes. She forgot to join in the singing of hymns and she forgot to say the Lord's Prayer.

Then all the people came out of church and the old lady climbed into her carriage. Karen was just lifting her foot to follow, when the old soldier, who was standing at her side, exclaimed, 'Oh look, what pretty dancing shoes!'

Karen could not help herself, she had to make a few dance steps, and once she started, her feet danced on and on, just as if the shoes had been given power over them. She danced round the church and could not stop. The coachman had to run after her and catch her. He lifted her into the carriage, but her feet went on dancing, so she kicked the kind old lady most cruelly. At last the red shoes were taken off and her feet were still.

At home they put the shoes away in a cupboard, but Karen could not stop herself from looking at them.

The old lady lay in bed, for she had become ill. They said she would not get well again. It was necessary to nurse her and look after her, and who was there more suited to this than Karen? But in town a grand ball was being held and Karen was invited. She looked at the old lady, who could never get better. Then she looked at the red shoes, and it seemed to her it would be no sin. So she put on the red shoes, there was no harm in that. And then she went to the ball and began to dance.

But when she wanted to move to the right, the shoes danced to the left, and when she wanted to dance up the room, the shoes danced down the room, down the stairs, through the streets and out through the gates of the town.

Dance she did and dance she must straight into a dark wood.

Suddenly something shone through the trees and she thought it must be the moon's bright face. But it was the old soldier with the red beard. He sat there, nodding his head and saying, 'Oh look, what pretty dancing shoes!'

She grew very frightened and wanted to take off the red shoes, but they wouldn't come off. She tore her stockings, but the shoes gripped her feet tight.

Dance she did and dance she must over fields and meadows, in rain and sunshine, by night and by day—by night was the most horrible!

She danced into the lonely churchyard, but the dead were not dancing; they had more important things to do. She wanted to sit down on the poor man's grave, where bitter tansy grew, but for her there was neither rest nor respite. And as she danced to the open church door, she saw an angel clad in long white robes, with wings that reached from his shoulders right to the ground. His face was grave and stern and in his hand he held a broad, shining sword.

'Dance you will!' he said. 'Dance in your red shoes, till you are pale and cold, till your skin shrivels and your bones stick out! Dance you shall from door to door, and wherever proud, vain children live, there you will knock, so they may hear you and be afraid. Dance you shall, dance —'

'Mercy!' cried Karen. But she could not hear the angel's answer, for the

shoes were carrying her on through the gate, out into the fields, along highways and byways. And all the time she had to dance.

One morning she danced past a door she knew well. She heard psalm-singing from within, and soon a coffin was carried out, strewn with flowers. Then Karen realized, that the kind old lady was dead, and she felt deserted by all mankind and accursed by the angel of God.

Dance she did and dance she must, even through the dark nights. The shoes bore her over thorns and briars, till her limbs were torn and bleeding. She danced over the heath to a small lonely house. She knew the executioner lived there. She tapped on the window with her fingers and cried:

'Come out! Come out! I cannot come to you, for I am dancing!'

And the executioner replied, 'Don't you know who I am? I cut off the heads of wicked men but I see my axe is sharp and keen!'

'Don't cut off my head!' Karen cried, 'for then I could no longer repent of my sins. But cut off my feet with the red shoes!'

And then she confessed to him her sins and the executioner cut off her feet with the red shoes. But even then the little shoes with the little feet danced on across the field into the deep forest.

Then the executioner made her a pair of wooden feet and crutches too, and he taught her the psalm which is always sung by sinners. And Karen, kissing the hand which had held the axe, went on her way across the heath.

'Now I have suffered enough for the red shoes!' she said. 'I will go to church, so people can see me once more!'

And she went as fast as she could to the church door, but as she approached it, the red shoes danced in front of her, and she, growing frightened, turned back.

All that week she was terribly sad and shed many, many bitter tears, but when Sunday came round again, she thought, 'By now I must have suffered enough, and endured enough. I think I must be as good as many of those who sit and kneel in church!'

She went there with courage, but as she neared the gate, she saw the red shoes dancing in front of her again, and she turned back in great terror, repenting more deeply than ever of her sins.

Then she went to the pastor's house and begged to be allowed to serve there. She would work hard and do all she could. She did not care what wages they gave her, only a roof over her head and a home with good people.

The pastor's wife had pity on her and took her into service and Karen was hard-working and grateful. Every evening she sat and listened to the pastor reading the Holy Bible. The children all loved her but whenever they talked of dressing up and finery and how wonderful it must be to be a queen, she would shake her head.

The following Sunday all the household went to church and they asked if she would like to come too. But she sighed and looked sadly, with tears in her eyes, at her crutches. So the others went to listen to the word of God, while she went alone into her little chamber. It was barely big enough for a bed and a chair and there Karen sat down with her prayer book. As she read, the wind brought her the sound of the organ and she lifted her tear-stained face and prayed, 'Oh God, help me!'

Then the sun shone so very brightly and an angel of God in his white robe stood before her, the same whom she had seen that awful night by the church door. He no longer held the sharp-edged sword but carried instead a lovely green bough, full of roses. With this he touched the ceiling, which lifted to a great height, and a bright gold star sparkled in the spot where he had touched it. Then he touched the walls, and they widen-ed and parted and Karen saw and heard the organ, which was playing. She saw the old portraits of priests and their wives. The congregation sat in the ornate pews, praying and singing.

The church itself had come to the unfortunate girl in her narrow little chamber, for she too had come into it. She was sitting with the rest of the pastor's household, and when they finished their prayers and rose, they nodded to her and said:

'You did well to come, Karen!'

'This is mercy!' said she.

And the organ played again, and the children's voices sang out sweetly and beautifully. The bright sunlight shone warmly, pouring through the windows upon Karen's pew. Her own heart was so full of sunshine, of peace and of gladness, that it burst.

And her soul flew upon a sunbeam to God in heaven, and no one there asked about the red shoes.

Little Ida's Flowers

'My poor flowers are quite dead!' sobbed little Ida. 'Only last night they were so pretty and now all the petals are drooping. Why?' she asked the student who was sitting on the sofa. She happened to be terribly fond of this student, for he could tell stories and could cut out the loveliest pictures: hearts with little dancing ladies in them, flowers and huge palaces with doors that you could really open. He was such a jolly student! 'Why do the flowers look so poorly today?' little Ida asked once again, pointing to the whole withered bunch.

'Do you know what's wrong with them?' said the student. 'These flowers went to a ball last night, and that's why their little heads are drooping!'

'But flowers surely can't dance!' little Ida protested.

'Oh yes they can,' said the student. 'When it grows dark and the rest of us are asleep, they dance about to their heart's content. They have a ball almost every night!'

'Are children allowed to go to those balls?'

'They are,' said the student. 'Tiny daisies and lilies of the valley.'

'Where do the prettiest flowers dance?' asked little Ida.

'Have you not often been beyond the gate of that great palace where the King lives in summer—where there's such a beautiful garden filled with flowers? You must have seen the swans—they always swim near when you throw them crumbs. I bet you anything that's where they hold the ball!'

'I went to that garden only yesterday with my mother,' said Ida. 'But all the leaves had dropped from the trees and there wasn't a flower to be seen. Where are they all? In the summer I saw so very many!'

'They are in the palace!' said the student. 'You see, after summer as soon as the King with his courtiers moves back to town, the flowers rush out of the garden into the palace and have a merry time. If you could see them! The two most beautiful roses sit on the throne and are King and Queen. The scarlet cockscombs line up at their side and stand and bow. They are the royal pages. Then all the prettiest flowers arrive and the ball begins. Blue violets play the part of little naval cadets, and they dance with hyacinths and crocuses, and call them young ladies! Tulips and the large yellow lilies are old ladies; they keep their eye on things, making sure that everyone behaves and everything goes off nicely.'

'Doesn't anybody punish the flowers for dancing in the King's palace?' asked little Ida.

'No one really knows anything about it!' answered the student. 'It is true that sometimes at night the old caretaker who looks after the palace comes along with his enormous bunch of keys. But the minute the flowers hear the keys jingling, they stand as still as statues and hide behind the long curtains, with only their little heads peeping out. "There are some flowers here," the old caretaker will mutter. But he can't see them.'

'How lovely!' cried little Ida. 'Could I see the flowers?'

'Of course you can,' the student announced. 'Next time you go to the palace, just remember to look in at the window, and you'll see them for sure. I did so today and just imagine, there was a tall yellow daffodil stretched out on the sofa. It was a lady-in-waiting.'

'Can the flowers from the Botanic Gardens go there too? Can they make such a long journey?'

'They certainly can,' said the student. 'For they can fly when they want to. Surely you've noticed those pretty butterflies—the red, yellow and white ones—that look like flowers? That is exactly what they have been. They jump off their stalks high into the air, flap their little leaves as if they were wings, and off they fly! And because they are very well behaved, they are allowed to fly in daytime too, and don't have to go back home and sit still on their stalks. So in the end, those leaves turn into real wings. You've seen it for yourself! It is quite possible, of course, that the flowers from the Botanic Gardens have never been in the King's palace and that they don't even know that it is such a merry place at night. But I'll tell you something, it will be quite a surprise for the professor of botany, who lives right next door to the Botanic Gardens—I think you know him! Next time you go into his garden, tell one of the flowers that a grand ball is taking place at the palace. It will pass the word to the others and they'll fly off. When the professor goes into the garden, there won't be a single flower left, and he will be quite baffled as to where they have gone!'

'But how can the flower tell the others? After all, flowers can't talk!'

'That they can't,' replied the student. 'But they make themselves under-stood by signs. Surely you've noticed, whenever a breeze blows, how they bow and move all their little green leaves? To them it is just as plain as talking!'

'Does the professor understand their language?' Ida asked.

'Why, of course! One morning he went into his garden and saw a big stinging-nettle moving its leaves and paying court to a beautiful scarlet carnation. It was saying, 'You are so pretty and I like you so very much!' But the professor won't put up with things like that. He smacked the stinging-nettle's leaves, for they are really its fingers, but he stung himself and from that day he doesn't dare touch a single nettle.'

'How funny!' laughed little Ida.

'Do you think it is right to stuff the child's head with such nonsense?' said the disapproving, surly councillor, who was paying a visit and was sitting on the sofa. He didn't like the student, and always grumbled when

he saw him cutting out those funny or fascinating pictures. Sometimes it was a man hanging on the gallows, clutching a heart in his hand, for he was the stealer of hearts. Sometimes an old witch, flying on a broomstick, carrying her husband on her nose. The councillor didn't like this at all and he would say, as he was saying now, 'Is it right to stuff the child's head with such nonsense? What silly imagination!'

But all the same, little Ida found everything the student told her most amusing and most entertaining and she kept on thinking about it. The flowers were drooping because they were tired after dancing right through the night—they must surely be ill. Ida took them to her other toys which were standing on a pretty little table. The table drawer, too, was full with lovely things. Ida's doll Sophie was asleep in a doll's bed, but little Ida said to her, 'You must get up now, Sophie, and make do with the drawer for a bed tonight. These poor little flowers are ill and so must lie in your bed, then perhaps they'll get better!' She lifted the doll from her bed, but the doll looked grumpy and said not a word, for she was very cross at being turned out of her bed.

Then little Ida placed the flowers in the doll's bed, covered them with a blanket and told them to lie nice and quiet, that she would make them some tea, so they could get well and be up again in the morning. She drew the curtains by the bed, so the sun would not shine in their eyes.

All that evening she thought of nothing else, but what the student had told her. And when it was time for her, too, to go to bed, she peeped behind the curtains hanging in front of the windows where her mother's lovely flowers stood, hyacinths and tulips. She whispered to them so very softly, 'I know you're going to the ball tonight!' The flowers pretended not to understand and never moved a petal but they didn't fool little Ida.

When she was tucked up in bed, she thought for a long while how lovely it would be to see the pretty flowers dancing in the King's palace. 'I wonder if my flowers have really been there?' she thought, and fell asleep. During the night she woke up again. She had been dreaming about flowers and the student, and of the miserable councillor who was cross with the student for stuffing her head with nonsense. There was complete

silence in the bedroom where little Ida lay. A night-light was burning on the table and her father and mother were asleep.

'I wonder if my flowers are still in Sophie's bed?' little Ida said to herself. 'I would so like to know!' She sat up in bed and gazed at the half-opened door, and could just see all her toys and the flowers. She listened hard, and it seemed to her that a piano was being played, but softer and more beautifully than she had ever heard before.

'I'm sure all the flowers are dancing in there now!' she said to herself. 'How I'd love to see them!' But she didn't dare get up, for fear of waking her father and mother. 'If only they would come in here,' she thought. But the flowers did not come and the music sounded so wonderful. At last little Ida could bear it no longer, it was all too beautiful. She slid out of her little bed, crept to the door and peeped into the next room. Oh, what a pretty sight she saw there!

No night-light was burning in that room, yet it was brightly lit; the moon was shining through the window right into the centre of the room. All the tulips and hyacinths were standing in two long rows on the floor; not a single one remained in the window, all that was left were their empty pots. The flowers were dancing on the floor so gracefully round one another, turning and holding one another by their long green leaves. Sitting at the piano was a large yellow lily, which little Ida was sure she had seen that summer, for she remembered that the student had said to her, 'Good gracious, doesn't it look like Miss Lina!'—one of little Ida's friends. Everyone had laughed at him then, but now little Ida also saw that the lily was very like her friend and that whilst playing the piano, it behaved like her too—turning its long yellow face first to one side, then to the other and nodding in time to the lovely music.

Nobody noticed little Ida.

Now she saw a large blue crocus jump right on to the centre of the table, where all the toys were, walk right up to the doll's bed and pull aside the curtains. There lay Ida's poorly flowers but they got up straightaway, and nodded to the others as if to say they wanted to dance, too. An old chimney-sweep doll, whose bottom lip was broken off, stood up and bowed to the pretty flowers. They didn't look sick at all now, but jumped about with the others and were very merry.

Suddenly it sounded as if something had fallen off the table. Little Ida looked to see. It was her carnival rod jumping down among the flowers for it seemed to think it was one of them. It was actually very pretty, and on its top sat a little wax doll with a wide-brimmed hat exactly like the one worn by the councillor. The carnival rod hopped to the flowers on its three red legs and stamped about heavily, for it was dancing the mazurka. The other flowers couldn't stamp.

All at once the little wax doll on the carnival rod started to grow big and tall, twisting round above the paper ribbons, shouting loudly, 'Is it right to stuff the child's head with such nonsense! Its all that silly imagination!' Just then he looked the very image of the councillor in his wide-brimmed hat for he was just as yellow and just as grumpy. But the paper ribbons on the rod whipped his skinny legs, so he cowered and shrank back, turning into a tiny wax doll again. What fun it all was! Little Ida couldn't stop herself laughing. The carnival rod went on dancing and the councillor had to dance with it. It made no difference whether he grew big and tall, or whether he shrank back into a yellow wax doll with the wide-brimmed hat. At last, some of the flowers pleaded for him, especially the ones who had lain in the doll's bed, and so the carnival rod stopped dancing. Just then, a loud knocking was heard from inside the drawer, where Ida's doll Sophie lay together with lots of other toys. The chimney-sweep ran to the edge of the table and lying on his tummy, he stretched and managed to pull the drawer slightly open.

Sophie stood up and gazed round her wonderingly. 'You're having a ball!' she cried. 'Why wasn't I told!'

'Will you dance with me?' asked the chimney-sweep.

'As if I would dance with a fellow like you!' she said and turned her back on him.

Then she sat on the drawer, hoping that at any moment one of the flowers would come and ask her to dance. But nobody came. So she coughed, 'A'hem, a'hem, a'hem!' But still nobody came. The chimney-sweep danced by himself and made a good job of it, too!

As none of the flowers seemed to notice Sophie, she tumbled from the drawer on to the floor, with quite a bang. Now all the flowers crowded round her, asking if she had hurt herself, and they were all so very kind to her, especially the ones which had lain in her bed. But Sophie hadn't hurt herself one little bit. All Ida's flowers were thanking her for the lovely bed,

and were making such a fuss of her. They led her to the centre of the room, where the moon was shining, and danced with her, with the other flowers forming a circle round them. Sophie now was truly happy! She announced they could keep her bed, that she didn't mind sleeping in the drawer one little bit.

But the flowers said, 'We thank you most sincerely, but we cannot live much longer. Tomorrow we shall be quite dead. But tell little Ida, that we would like to be buried in the garden where the canary already lies. Then in the summer we'll grow again and will be prettier than ever!'

'Oh, you mustn't die!' Sophie said, kissing the flowers.

At that moment the door opened and a crowd of flowers came dancing inside. Little Ida couldn't make out where they had come from—and told herself they must surely be the flowers from the King's palace! Right in front were two lovely roses with little gold crowns on their heads. They were the King and the Queen. Next came beautiful violets and carnations, greeting everyone around. They brought music with them. Big poppies and peonies had pea-pods for instruments and they blew them till their cheeks were red. Bluebells and little white snowdrops tinkled like real bells. It really was lovely music. Many other flowers followed, and they all danced together, the blue violets with the red daisies, ragged robins with lilies of the valley—and they all kissed each other. It was such a delightful sight!

Then at last the flowers bade each other good night and little Ida, too, crept back into bed, where she dreamed of all she had just seen.

When she got up in the morning, she rushed to her little table to see if the poorly flowers were still there. She drew aside the curtains by the doll's bed. All the flowers were still there, but they were quite withered; much more so than the previous day. Sophie lay in the drawer where she had been put, looking very sleepy.

'Do you remember what you're supposed to tell me?' asked little Ida. But Sophie just looked stupid and didn't utter a word.

'You are not nice at all,' said little Ida, 'and yet everyone danced with you!'

Then she picked up a little cardboard box, on which pretty little birds were drawn, and opening it, she placed the dead flowers inside. 'This will be your beautiful coffin,' she said to them. 'And when my cousins arrive, they will help me to bury you in the garden, so that you will be able to grow again next summer, prettier than ever!'

Ida's cousins were two bright boys called James and Adolphus. Their father had given them each a new bow and arrow and they had brought them to show to Ida. She told them about the poor flowers and how they had died, and asked the boys to bury them. The two boys walked in front, their bows over their shoulders, and little Ida followed with the dead flowers in the pretty box. They dug a small grave in the garden. Ida kissed the flowers, then laid them, with the box, in the ground. And Adolphus and James fired their arrows over the grave, for they did not have a shotgun, or a cannon.

Thumbelina

Once upon a time there was a lady who dearly wanted a little baby, but she had no idea how to find one. So she went to an old witch and said, 'I want a little baby so very much! Could you please tell me where I can get one?'

'That can be easily arranged!' said the witch. 'Here is a corn seed; it is different from those which grow in the farmer's field and which are fed to the chickens. Plant it in a flower-pot and see what happens!'

'Thank you!' said the lady and gave the witch a gold coin.

Then she went home and planted the corn seed, which straightaway grew into a big, beautiful flower. The flower looked exactly like a tulip, except that its petals were tightly closed, as if it was still a bud.

'What a lovely flower,' said the lady and kissed the beautiful red and yellow petals. No sooner had she kissed them, when there was a little popping sound and the flower opened.

It was a real tulip, that was quite obvious, but on the green stamen right in the centre of the flower sat a tiny girl, so pretty and so sweet. She was in fact no bigger than a thumb and that is why they called her Thumbelina.

She was given a magnificent, brightly varnished walnut-shell for a cradle, blue violet petals for mattresses and a rose petal for a cover. She slept there at night, but during the day she played on the table, where the lady had placed a plate of water with a ring of flowers round it. A large tulip leaf floated on top of the water and on this Thumbelina was allowed to sit and sail from one edge of the plate to the other. Two white horse hairs were given to her for oars. It really was a pretty sight! She could sing, too, oh, so sweetly and so prettily, that no one had ever heard such wondrous sounds.

As she lay in her pretty little bed one night, an ugly toad came hopping in through the window, where one of the panes was broken. The toad was such a hideous thing, huge and horribly wet, and she jumped straight on to the table where Thumbelina lay fast asleep beneath the scarlet rose petal.

'What a lovely wife she'd make my son!' said the toad and took the walnut-shell with Thumbelina asleep inside it. Then she hopped away through the broken window pane into the garden.

A large, wide stream flowed through the garden, its banks were swampy and muddy. This was the home of the toad and her son. Ugh! He was every bit as ugly and repulsive as his mother. 'Croak, cro-ak, brekeke-keksh!' was all he could say when he saw the beautiful little girl in the walnut-shell.

'Don't talk so loud, or she'll wake up!' said the old toad. 'She could run away from us, for she's as light as a swan's feather! Let's sit her on a broad water-lily leaf in the stream. She is so light and so tiny, it will seem like an island to her! She won't be able to escape from there, and we shall have time to build a castle down under in the mud, where you two will live together!'

There were many water-lilies growing in the stream with wide green leaves, which appeared to float on the water. The leaf farthest out was bigger than all the others. The old toad swam to this leaf and placed upon it the walnut-shell in which Thumbelina still lay fast asleep.

The poor little girl woke up early the next morning, and seeing where she was, she cried and cried, for there was nothing but water all round the great big leaf and no way for her to get ashore.

The old toad sat down below in the mud, decorating her room with rushes and yellow water-lily buds, so it would look really pretty for her new daughter-in-law. Then she swam with her hideous son to the leaf upon which Thumbelina was standing. They wanted to carry her tiny little bed into the bridal chamber, before she arrived herself.

The old toad curtsied deeply into the water and said, 'Take a look at my son here. He is to be your husband, and you are both going to live happily together down in the mud!'

'Croak, cro-ak, brekekekekeksh!' was all her son could say for himself.

Then they took her lovely little bed and swam away with it, whilst Thumbelina sat all alone crying on the green leaf, for she did not wish to live with the horrid toad and to marry her son.

The little fishes, swimming down in the water, had seen the toad and had heard what she said, so now they poked their heads upwards to have a look at the little girl. The moment they saw her, they liked her and felt very sorry indeed that she should have to go and live with the ugly toad. No, such a thing must never happen! They gathered in the water round the green stalk which held the leaf, and nibbled through it with their teeth. Then the leaf sailed off down the river, with Thumbelina on top, far away, where the ugly toad could not reach it.

Thumbelina floated past many towns and villages, and the little birds, sitting in the bushes, sang out the moment they saw her, 'What a beautiful little maiden!'

The leaf floated on and on until at last Thumbelina came to a foreign land. A lovely white butterfly fluttered round her and settled down on the leaf, for it liked Thumbelina very much. Thumbelina was so happy now for the old toad could not get to her and everything she saw, as she sailed, looked so beautiful. The sun shone down on the water, and looked like sparkling gold. Thumbelina took off her sash and tied one end to the

butterfly and the other to the leaf which now sailed much faster, with the butterfly for a sail.

At that moment a big cockchafer flew by and having seen her, it immediately fastened its claws round her slender waist and flew off with her into a tree. The green leaf sailed on down the river with the butterfly flying with it, for it was tied to the leaf and could not get away.

Goodness gracious! how scared poor Thumbelina was when the cockchafer flew up into the tree with her! She felt sorrier still for the beautiful white butterfly which she had fastened to the leaf, for if it could not get loose, it would surely starve to death. But the cockchafer did not care about that. He settled with her on the largest green leaf in the tree, fed her with the sweet juices of flowers and told her that she was very pretty, though not in the least like a cockchafer.

Soon all the other cockchafers, who lived in that tree called to pay her a visit. They looked Thumbelina up and down and one young cockchafer lady said, shrugging her feelers, 'Why, she only has two legs, the poor little thing.' 'Neither has she any feelers!' said another. 'She has such a skinny waist, ugh!, and she looks like a human! Isn't she ugly!' said a third.

That is how all the lady cockchafers talked about Thumbelina who really was so pretty! The cockchafer, who had carried her away, thought so, too, but when everyone else kept saying how ugly she was, he began to believe it. In the end he did not want her at all, and told her to go wherever she wished.

They flew down with her from the tree and sat her on a daisy. There she sat and cried, because she thought she was so ugly that even the cockchafers did not want her, though in truth she was the most beautiful creature anyone could imagine, as gentle and fresh as the prettiest rose petal.

That summer poor Thumbelina lived all alone in the big wood. She wove a bed from blades of grass and hung it under a large burdock leaf, which kept off the rain. She lived on sweet juices which she sucked from the flowers, and drank the dew which she found each morning on the petals.

So summer and autumn passed by, but then winter followed, the long, cold winter. All the birds, which had sung to her so melodiously, had flown away, trees and flowers withered, the big burdock leaf, under which she lived, shrivelled up and only a yellow, dry stalk remained. Poor

Thumbelina was so cold, so dreadfully cold, for her dress was in shreds and she herself was so tiny and delicate, that she very nearly froze to death. It started to snow, and each snowflake that fell on her was like a whole shovelful would be to us, for we are big and she was no bigger than a thumb. So she wrapped herself in a dead leaf, but she just could not get warm, and shivered with cold.

Near the wood in which she had lived, there was a big field, but the corn had been taken away and only bare stubble stood up from the frozen ground. To Thumbelina it seemed like a huge forest through which she had to pass, and oh, how bitterly cold it was! She came to the door of a field-mouse, who had a small hole under the stubble. There the field-mouse lived in warmth and away from the wind. She had a roomful of corn and a nice kitchen and a larder. Poor Thumbelina stood by the door, just like any other poor beggar-girl, and begged for a few grains of corn.

'You poor little thing!' said the field-mouse, who was really a kind old field-mouse. 'Do come into my warm room and have a meal with me!'

The field-mouse liked Thumbelina and later on she said, 'If you like, you may stay here all winter, but you must keep my little room clean and tidy and you must tell me stories, for I like to hear them very much.' So Thumbelina did what the kind old field-mouse asked of her, and they lived comfortably together.

'I think we shall have a visitor today,' said the field-mouse one day. 'My neighbour calls on me every week. He is even better off than I; he lives in great halls and goes about in a magnificent, black velvety fur coat. If you had him for a husband, you'd be well cared for. But he can't see. You must tell him the very nicest stories you know!'

But Thumbelina did not bother. She did not want to marry the neighbour, because he was a mole. He called on them in his black velvet coat; he was terribly rich, just as the field-mouse had said. His house was more than twenty times as big as the house of the field-mouse and, sure enough, he was most knowledgeable. But, as he could not see the sun and the beautiful flowers, he spoke nastily about them.

Thumbelina had to sing, and she sang 'Mole, mole, come out of your hole!' and 'Ladybird, ladybird, fly away home'. The mole fell in love with her because of her beautiful voice, but he didn't say anything for he was indeed a most dignified man.

He dug a long underground passage from his house to theirs, and he allowed the field-mouse and Thumbelina to walk there as they pleased. But he told them not to be scared of the dead bird which lay in the passage. The bird was all in one piece, with its beak and its feathers. It could not have been dead long, since winter was just beginning and he had been buried in the very place where the mole built his passage. Then the mole put a piece of rotten wood in his mouth and it shone like a light in the dark. He walked in front to light up the long, dark passage. When they came to the spot where the dead bird was, the mole turned his wide nose upwards against the soil, pressing it hard, till there was a large hole for the light to shine through.

There in the middle of the floor lay a dead swallow, its beautiful wings pressed tightly against its body, its legs and head tucked under its feathers. The poor bird must surely have died of cold. Thumbelina felt so terribly sorry for it; she loved all birds, for they sung and chirped for her so beautifully all through the summer.

But the mole poked the swallow with one of his short legs and said, 'This won't chirp no more! It must be a miserable fate to be born a little bird! Thank goodness this hasn't happened to any of my children. Why, such a bird hasn't a thing except its twitter, and what's more its fate is to starve in winter!'

'Yes, you've spoken as a wise man,' said the field-mouse. 'What has a bird to show for all its chirping, once winter comes? It cannot help but starve and freeze, and that, if you please, is all very grand!'

Thumbelina remained silent, but when the other two turned their backs to the bird, she bent over it, parted the feathers which covered its head, and kissed its closed eyes.

'Maybe this is the very one which sang to me so sweetly in the summer,' she thought. 'What pleasure it gave me, this dear, lovely bird!'

Then the mole filled the hole which let in the light, and escorted the ladies home.

That night Thumbelina just could not sleep. She rose from her bed and

with some hay wove a large, lovely rug, which she spread on the dead bird down in the passage. Then she tucked soft cotton wool, which she found in the field-mouse's room, all round it, so the bird would keep warm on the cold ground.

'Goodbye, beautiful bird!' she said. 'Goodbye, and thank you for your lovely song this summer, when all the trees were green and the sun shone upon us so warmly!'

With that she lay her head on the bird's breast, and at once was startled, for it seemed to her as if something inside was beating. It was the little bird's heart. The bird was not dead, only stiff and faint with the cold, and now it was warm it had revived.

In autumn all swallows fly to warmer lands but, if one stays behind too long, it gets so cold, that it drops down as if dead and stays where it falls and becomes covered by snow.

Thumbelina was filled with terror because the bird was so big compared to her, for she was, after all, only as big as a thumb. Then she plucked up her courage, pressed the cotton wool tighter still round the poor swallow, and brought a mint leaf, which she herself was using for a blanket, and placed it on the bird's head.

The following night she crept back along the passage, and by then the bird was completely recovered. But it was so very faint, that it could only open its eyes for a brief moment and look at Thumbelina, who stood there with a piece of rotten wood in her hand, for she had no other light.

'Thank you, you beautiful little girl!' said the sick swallow. 'I am nicely warm now and soon my strength will come back and I will be able to fly again outside in the warm sunshine!'

'Oh,' said Thumbelina, 'it is bitterly cold outside. It is snowing hard and freezing! Stay here in your cosy little bed and I will take care of you.'

Then she brought some water for the swallow in a petal. The swallow drank it and told her how he had damaged his wing on a bramble bush and could not keep up with all the other swallows who were flying away to warmer regions. How eventually he had fallen to the ground. He could remember no more, not even how he had got to where he now lay.

The swallow stayed underground all winter and Thumbelina was most kind to it and grew very fond of the bird. She told neither the mole, nor the field-mouse about all this, for they did not like the poor unfortunate swallow. Soon, spring arrived and the sun warmed the earth. The swallow bade Thumbelina goodbye, and she opened up the hole made earlier by the mole.

The sun shone down so beautifully upon them. The swallow asked Thumbelina to fly away with him; she could sit on his back and together they would fly far away into a green forest. But Thumbelina knew that the field-mouse would be very upset if she were to leave her.

'No, I can't come!' said Thumbelina.

'Goodbye, then goodbye, you dear, beautiful girl!' said the swallow and flew away into the sunlight.

Thumbelina gazed after him, her eyes brimming with tears, for she was very fond of the poor swallow.

'Tweet, tweet!' sang the bird as he flew away to the green forest.

Thumbelina was terribly sad. She was never allowed out into the warm sunshine. The corn, which had been sown in the field above the field-mouse's house had grown so high, that it was like a dense forest to the poor little girl.

'Now,' said the field-mouse to her one day. 'You must get your wedding clothes ready.' Their neighbour, the boring mole in the black velvet coat, had asked Thumbelina for her hand. 'You must have both woollen and linen clothes, in fact everything that's needed, if you are going to marry the mole!'

Thumbelina had to work the spindle, and the field-mouse hired four spiders to spin and to weave night and day.

The mole called on them every evening and talked of nothing else but how, when the summer was over, the sun would no longer shine so warmly, for just then it was so baking hot, the earth was nothing but dry dust. Yes, once the summer was over, the wedding between him and Thumbelina would be held. But she did not look forward to this one little bit, for she did not like the boring mole at all. Every morning, as the sun rose, and every evening, as it went to bed, she crept out through the door and, when the wind ruffled the ears of the corn, she could see the blue sky and she would think how bright and lovely it was out there, and would yearn with all her heart to see the dear swallow once more. But he never came back. He must have flown far away into the beautiful green forest. When autumn came, Thumbelina's trousseau was ready.

'In four weeks from now your wedding will be held!' the field-mouse said to her.

But Thumbelina cried and said she would never marry that tiresome mole.

'Stuff and nonsense!' said the field-mouse. 'Stop making such a fuss, or I'll bite you with my white teeth! Why, you're getting such a handsome husband! He has a black velvet fur coat, the likes of which even the Queen herself has not! His kitchen and cellar are filled to the brim. You should count yourself lucky!'

At last the wedding day arrived. The mole came to take his bride away. She was to live with him deep under the earth and never come out into the warm sunlight, for the mole detested the sun. The poor child was terribly unhappy. Now she had to say goodbye to the sun, which she was at least allowed to watch through the doorway whilst living with the field-mouse.

'Goodbye, bright sun!' Thumbelina cried, stretching her arms high into the air and at the same time, stepping farther away from the field-mouse's house. For here the corn had been harvested and only the dry stubble remained. 'Goodbye, goodbye!' she cried. throwing her little arms round the scarlet flower which grew there. 'Give my love to the dear swallow, if you should see him!'

Suddenly, 'Tweet, tweet!' sounded over her head. She looked up and saw the swallow, which was just passing by. The bird was delighted to see her and Thumbelina told him how she was being forced to marry the miserable mole, and how she would have to live deep down under the earth, where the sun never shone.

'The cold winter is just about to start,' said the swallow. 'I shall fly off far from here to warmer lands. Would you like to come, too? You can sit on my back! Just tie yourself to me with your sash and we shall fly away from the tiresome mole and his dark room, far from here, across the mountains to where the sun shines more brightly still than here, where there's always summer and lovely flowers. Do fly away with me, dear, sweet, tiny Thumbelina, who saved my life when I lay frozen!'

'I will come with you!' cried Thumbelina. Then she sat astride the bird's back, her legs on the outstretched wings, and tied herself with the sash to one of the strongest feathers. Then the swallow flew high into the air, and over forests and seas, high over great mountains, where snow always lies. The cold air made Thumbelina shiver, so she snuggled into the bird's warm feathers, with only her little head peeping out, so as not to miss any of the beauty beneath.

So they came to the warm regions of the South. There the sun shone more brightly than it does here and where the sky seemed twice as high above the earth. There, magnificent green and blue grapes grew on terraces and trellises. Lemons and oranges hung in the woods and the scent of myrtle and mint was everywhere, and such pretty children ran about in the road, playing with huge, colourful butterflies.

The swallow flew farther still, and the farther he flew it seemed that everything grew more and more beautiful. At last they came upon magnificent green trees by a blue lake and there stood a shining white marble palace which had been standing there since ancient times. Grape-vines twined up its high pillars and on the very top were many swallow nests one of which was the home of the swallow who was carrying Thumbelina.

'This is my house!' said the swallow. 'But if you prefer to choose one of the lovely flowers which grow on the ground, I will put you down there, and I am sure you'll be as happy as can be!'

'Isn't it lovely!' cried Thumbelina, clapping her little hands.

Lying on the ground was a big, white marble pillar, which had fallen down and broken into three pieces. Between these pieces grew the loveliest white flowers. The swallow flew down with Thumbelina, and sat her on a large petal.

What a surprise she had! In the centre of the flower sat a little man, so white and so transparent, it was as if he were made of glass. On his head he wore the prettiest golden crown, and on his shoulders he had a pair of magnificent, translucent wings. And he was no bigger than Thumbelina.

He was the angel of flowers. There was such a little man or such a little woman in every flower, but this one was the King of them all.

'My word, he is so handsome,' Thumbelina whispered to the swallow.

The little man had quite a fright at the sight of the swallow, for, compared to him, it was a giant of a bird, he himself being so small and so dainty. But when he saw Thumbelina, he was delighted, for she was the prettiest maiden he had ever seen. Then he took the golden crown off his head and, placing it on hers, asked what her name was and whether she would like to be his wife, for then she would be Queen of all the flowers!

Here was a real man, totally different from the son of the toad and the mole with the black velvet fur coat. So she said, 'yes', and at once from every flower came a lady or a gentleman, each one of them so lovely and dainty, they were a pleasure to behold. Everybody gave Thumbelina a gift, but the best of them all were a pair of beautiful wings from a big white fly. They were fastened to Thumbelina's back and now, she too, could fly from flower to flower.

There was much rejoicing and the swallow, sitting above in its nest, sang to them with all its might. But his heart was heavy and sad, for it loved Thumbelina very much and would never have parted from her.

'You cannot be called Thumbelina any more,' said the angel of flowers. 'It is an ugly name, whilst you are so very pretty. We'll call you Maia!'

'Goodbye, goodbye!' said the swallow, and flew away once again from the warm regions, far away back to us.

And here he built a little nest over the window where lives the man who knows how to tell fairy-tales. To him it sang 'tweet, tweet!' And that is how we came to hear this whole story.

The Swineherd

Once upon a time there was a poor Prince. He had a very small kingdom, but it was still big enough for him to marry on, and to marry he wished.

Yet it was rather bold of him to dare to say to the Emperor's daughter, 'Would you like to marry me?' But the Prince did dare, for his name was quite renowned everywhere. Hundreds of Princesses would have been only too glad to say 'yes', but let us hear what the Emperor's daughter did.

On the grave of the Prince's father a rose bush grew. It was such a beautiful rose bush! It flowered only once every five years, and even then it had only one bloom. But that rose was so sweetly scented, that whoever smelt it forgot all his sorrows and worries.

The Prince also had a nightingale, which sang as if all the loveliest melodies were held in his throat. The rose and the nightingale were just right for the Princess. And so the Prince put them into silver caskets and sent them to her.

The Emperor had them carried before him into the great hall where the Princess was amusing herself with her maids of honour by playing 'visitors' — they never did any work. When she saw the silver caskets with the presents, she clapped her hands for joy.

'If only it was a little pussy-cat!' she said. But out came the rose.

'Isn't it prettily made!' said the Emperor. 'It is exquisitely made.' But when the Princess touched it, she could have cried.

'Ugh, daddy!' she shouted. 'It isn't an artificial one, it's real!'

'Ugh!' cried all the maids of honour. 'It's real!'

'Let's take a look at the second casket before we start getting cross!' suggested the Emperor.

Out came the nightingale. He sang so beautifully, that it was not possible to find any fault.

'Superbe! Charmant!' cried all the court ladies, for they all babbled in French — one worse than the other.

'How this nightingale reminds me of the greatly lamented late Empress's musical box!' said an old courtier. 'Yes, yes,—it has the very same tone, the very same eloquence!'

'Yes,' sighed the Emperor, bursting into tears like a child.

'I can hardly believe it's real!' retorted the Princess.

'Oh yes, it's a real bird!' said the men who had brought it.

'Let it fly off then!' said the Princess and flatly refused to let the Prince in.

But the Prince wouldn't be deterred. Smearing his face black and brown, he pulled his cap down over his eyes and knocked.

'Good morning, Emperor!' he said. 'Can you find a job for me, here at the palace?'

'People come thick and fast asking for work!' the Emperor replied. 'But let me see — I could do with somebody to see to the pigs. We've got a fair number of them.'

So the Prince was employed as the imperial swineherd. He was given a poor little room near the pigsty, and there he had to live. But he worked at something all day long, and by evening he made a pretty little cooking pot, with little bells all round it and whenever the pot started to boil, the bells tinkled prettily, ringing out an old melody:

'Ah, my dearest Augustine,
All is gone, gone, gone!'

But the strangest thing of all was, that if you held your finger in the steam which escaped from the pot, you would smell straightaway everything that was being cooked on every stove in town. Now this was something quite different altogether from a rose!

The Princess was walking past with all her maids of honour. Hearing the melody played by the pot, she stopped. She looked really pleased, for she too knew how to play 'Ah, my dearest Augustine' — it was the only tune she could play, and then only with one finger.

'I can play that tune!' she cried. 'That must be a well-bred swineherd! Listen, go and ask how much he wants for that instrument!'

One of the maids of honour had to run there and ask, but she put her clogs on first.

'How much do you want for that pot?' she asked.

'I want ten kisses from the Princess!' said the swineherd.

'Good gracious me!' said the horrified maid of honour.

'I shan't let it go for less!' insisted the swineherd.

'Well, what did he say?' asked the Princess.

'I can't even tell you!' answered the maid of honour. 'It's too dreadful!'

'Whisper it then!' And the maid of honour whispered it.

'What a saucy fellow!' said the Princess and walked away at once. But she had gone only a little way, when the bells rang out again so very prettily:

> 'Ah, my dearest Augustine,
> All is gone, gone, gone!'

'Listen,' said the Princess, 'ask him if he'd like ten kisses from my maids of honour!'

'No thank you!' replied the swineherd. 'Ten kisses from the Princess, or the pot stays mine!'

'How annoying!' said the Princess. 'But you must all stand round me, so no one may see!'

And the maids of honour all stood round her, spreading their wide skirts and the swineherd got his ten kisses and the Princess got her pot.

What fun they had! That pot had to boil all evening and all day. There wasn't a single stove in the whole town but they knew what was being cooked on it, from the chamberlain to the cobbler. The maids of honour danced and clapped their hands in delight.

'We know who is to have soup and pancakes! We know who is to have cutlets and rice pudding. It is so interesting!'

'Frightfully interesting!' said the lady of the wardrobe.

'But not a word to anyone, for I'm the Emperor's daughter!'

'We wouldn't dream!' they all cried.

The swineherd — or rather, the Prince, but then they all thought him to be a real swineherd — the swineherd never let a day go by without making something. Now he made a rattle. When he swung it round, it played all the waltzes, jigs and polkas which have ever been heard since the creation of the world.

'Oh, it is *superbe!*' cried the Princess, as she passed by. 'I've never heard prettier compositions! Listen, go and ask him how much he wants for that instrument! But mind, there'll be no kissing!'

'He wants a hundred kisses from the Princess!' said the maid of honour, who had been sent to the swineherd.

'The fellow must be quite mad!' said the Princess and she walked off. But after going a little way, she stopped. 'We have to encourage the arts!' she said. 'I am, after all, the Emperor's daughter! Tell him he'll get ten kisses, the same as yesterday and the rest he can collect from my maids of honour!'

'Oh, but we shouldn't like that at all!' objected the maids of honour.

'What nonsense!' said the Princess. 'If I can kiss him, so can you. Remember I feed you and pay you!'

And so the maid of honour had to return to the swineherd.

'A hundred kisses from the Princess,' announced the swineherd, 'or we both keep what we've got!'

'Stand round!' ordered the Princess, and the maids of honour stood round and the swineherd got on with the kissing.

'What's all that commotion by the pigsty?' wondered the Emperor, when he stepped out on to the balcony. He rubbed his eyes and put on his spectacles.

'Those maids of honour must be up to something! I'd better go and inspect!' He pulled up his slippers at the heel, for they were trodden down.

My word, how he rushed!

When he came into the courtyard, he went about on tiptoe. The maids of honour were engrossed in counting the kisses to see fair play, to make sure the swineherd wouldn't get too many, nor too few. So they didn't even notice the Emperor. He drew himself up on tiptoe.

'Well I never!' he cried, seeing the kissing pair, and he hit them over the head with his slipper, just as the swineherd was getting his eighty-sixth kiss. 'Out!' screamed the Emperor, for he was furious. And the Princess and the swineherd were turned out of his kingdom.

And there stood the Princess weeping, with the swineherd scolding, and the rain pouring down.

'Oh, poor me!' cried the Princess, 'if I had but taken that handsome Prince! Oh, how unfortunate I am!'

The swineherd went behind a tree, wiped the black and brown off his face, took off his filthy rags and stepped forth in all his princely splendour. He looked so handsome, the Princess couldn't help but curtsy before him.

'I've learnt to despise you!' said the Prince. 'You wouldn't have an honest Prince! You couldn't appreciate a rose nor a nightingale, but you kissed a swineherd for a simple toy! Serve you right!'

With that he went back to his own kingdom, slammed the door and bolted it. The Princess was left standing outside singing in earnest:

'Ah, my dearest Augustine,
All is gone, gone, gone!'

The Real Princess

Once upon a time there was a Prince, who wanted to marry a Princess, but then she had to be a real Princess. He travelled the world in hopes of finding such a Princess, but there was always something not to his liking. There were plenty of Princesses, of course, but he could never be sure if they were real Princesses or not, there was always something which wasn't quite right. And so he returned home and was terribly sad, for he wished so much to have a real Princess for his wife.

One evening the weather was terrible. There was lightning and thunder and the rain came down in buckets. Then somebody knocked at the city gate, and the old King himself went to open it.

Before the gate stood a Princess. But, dear me, what a state she was in with that rain and that wind! Water trickled down from her hair and from her clothes, it seeped in through the toe of her shoes and seeped out again at the heel—but she said she was a real Princess.

'We'll find out soon enough,' thought the Queen, but she said not a word. She went into the bedroom, took all the bed-clothes off the bed, and put one single pea on the bedstead. Then she took twenty mattresses and laid them all on top of the little pea, and put twenty feather-beds filled with ducks-down on top of the mattresses.

This was the bed the Princess was to sleep on.

The following morning she was asked how she slept.

'Terribly badly!' she complained. 'I hardly closed an eye all night long. Goodness knows what was in that bed! But I laid on something hard, and I am black and blue all over. It was simply awful!'

Now it was perfectly plain to them that this must be a real Princess, if she could feel the one little pea through twenty mattresses and twenty feather-beds! None but a real Princess could have such a delicate skin!

The Prince took her for his wife, for now he was sure he had found a real Princess. And the pea was put in a museum, where you can still see it today, provided that nobody has stolen it.

Don't you agree that this was a real fairy-tale!

The Tinder-Box

A soldier came marching along the high road—left, right, left right! He had a knapsack on his back and a sword by his side, for he was returning home from the wars. And on the road he met an old witch; she was awfully ugly, with a bottom lip hanging right down to her chest. 'Good evening, soldier!' she said. 'What a nice sword you have, and what a large knapsack! You're a real soldier to be sure! Now you'll get as much money as you want!'

'Thank you very much, old witch,' said the soldier.

'Do you see that big tree?' asked the witch, pointing to a tree standing close by. 'It's quite hollow inside. Climb up to its top and you'll see a hole, through which you can slip right down deep into the tree. I'll tie a rope round your waist, so I can pull you up again when you give me a shout!'

'And what am I to do inside that tree?' asked the soldier.

'Why, fetch money from there!' said the witch. 'To be sure, when you get right down to the bottom, you'll find yourself in a big passage, which will be brightly lit, for there are over a hundred lamps burning there. Then you will see three doors, which you'll be able to open, for in each lock there is a key. When you enter the first room, you'll see a large chest in the middle of the floor, with a dog sitting on top of it. His eyes are as big as tea-cups, but don't mind that! I'll give you my blue-checked apron, just spread it on the floor. Then go over to the dog, take him and put him down on this apron, open the chest and help yourself to all the money you want. It contains only copper. If you prefer silver, go into the next room. Only there you will find a dog with eyes as big as mill-wheels but don't mind that. Just sit him down on my apron and help yourself to the money! But if perhaps you prefer gold, you can have as much as you can carry, if you go into the third room. The dog who sits on that money-chest has such eyes, each one as big as a tower. Imagine, what a dog! But don't mind that! Sit him down on my apron, then he won't harm you.'

'That doesn't sound too bad,' said the soldier. 'But what am I to give to you, old witch? You'll want something from me, to be sure!'

'Not at all,' said the witch. 'I don't want a single coin! Just bring me the old tinder-box my grandmother forgot there when she was last down.'

'Very well then,' agreed the soldier. 'Tie the rope round my waist!'

'Here it is,' said the witch, 'and here is my blue-checked apron.'

With that the soldier climbed up the tree, dropped down the hole and found himself, exactly as the witch had said, in the large passage where hundreds of lights were burning.

He opened the first door. Brrr! There sat the dog with eyes as big as tea-cups, glaring at him!

'What a fine fellow you are!' said the soldier, putting him down on the witch's apron and helping himself to as many copper coins as his pockets would hold. Then he closed the chest, put the dog back on it and went into the next room. And there, to be sure, sat the dog with eyes the size of mill-wheels.

'Don't stare at me like that,' said the soldier, 'You could strain your eyes.' And he sat the dog on the apron. But when he saw the heap of silver coins in the chest, he threw away all the coppers and filled his pockets and his knapsack with the silver. Then he went into the third room. Oh, what a horrid sight it was! The dog in there really did have eyes as big as towers.

'Good evening!' said the soldier, lifting his cap in salute, for he'd certainly never seen such a dog. He examined him for awhile, but then thought, enough is enough, and sat him on the apron and opened the chest. Gracious me! What a lot of gold! For that he could buy the whole town and all the sugar pigs in the cake shop and all the tin soldiers, and whips and rocking-horses in the world! This certainly was money! The soldier threw away all the silver, which filled his pockets and knapsack, and stuffed them with the gold instead. In fact his pockets, his knapsack, his cap and boots were all so full, he could scarcely walk! Now he had money! He sat the dog back on the chest, slammed the door and shouted,

'Pull me up again, old witch!'

'Have you got the tinder-box?' asked the witch.

'Why, to be sure, I clean forgot about that,' said the soldier, and went back to get it. The witch pulled him up, and there he was, back on the road, with his pockets, boots, knapsack and cap full of money.

'What are you going to do with that tinder-box?' asked the soldier.

'That's none of your business!' snapped the witch. 'You've got your money! Now give me my tinder-box!'

'Stuff and nonsense!' said the soldier. 'You tell me right now what you want it for, or I'll draw my sword and cut off your head!'

'I shan't!' cried the witch.

So the soldier cut off her head. And, as she lay there, the soldier tied all the money in her apron, slung the bundle over his shoulder, put the tinder-box in his pocket, and set off for the town.

It was a grand town and the soldier went into the very best inn, where he ordered the very best room and his favourite food—for he was a rich man now, with all that money.

The servant who cleaned his boots thought, of course, how ridiculously shabby old boots they were for such a rich gentleman, but then he hadn't bought any new ones yet. The next day he had new boots and also smart new clothes! Now the soldier had become a grand gentleman and people

were telling him of all the wonderful sights in the town, about the King and what a pretty Princess his daughter was.

'How can I see her?' asked the soldier.

'She isn't to be seen,' was everyone's reply. 'She lives in a big copper castle, which is surrounded by lots of walls and towers! Nobody but the King is allowed in, because it has been foretold that she will marry a common soldier, and our King wouldn't like that.'

'I'd most certainly like to see her,' thought the soldier, but see her he could not, for it wasn't allowed.

From now on he lived a merry life, going to the theatre, driving through the royal park, and giving away lots of money to the poor, which was nice! But then he well remembered from days of old how hard it was to be without a penny! Now he was rich, and well-dressed, and had lots of friends, who all said what a fine fellow and a true gentleman was he. The soldier loved hearing that! But, as he was spending money each day in this manner and never getting any back, in the end he was left with nothing

but two coins. He had to move from the magnificent rooms into a tiny little attic right under the roof; he had to clean his own boots and mend them with a darning-needle and none of his friends bothered to visit him, for so many steps led to that room of his!

Once, when it was a really dark evening and the soldier couldn't even buy himself a candle, he suddenly remembered that there was still a bit of a candle left in the tinder-box which he had taken from the hollow tree, with the help of the witch. He took out the tinder-box and the candle-end, but the moment he struck a light and the sparks flew from the flint, the door burst open and, before the soldier stood the dog with eyes as big as two tea-cups whom he had seen in the tree, and he said:

'What are my master's commands?'

'Well I never!' wondered the soldier. 'What a funny tinder-box this is, when I can get whatever I like with it! Find me some money!' he ordered the dog, and in a flash the dog was gone! And in a flash he was back again, a big bagful of coppers in his mouth.

Now the soldier knew what a magnificent tinder-box it was! If he struck once, in ran the dog who sat on the chest of coppers; if he struck twice, in ran the one who had the silver money, and if he struck three times, in ran the one who had the gold.

And so, the soldier moved back into his splendid rooms, dressed himself in fine clothes and soon all his friends began to know him again and to love him once more.

One day the soldier thought, 'It really is rather ridiculous, that nobody is allowed to see the Princess! Everyone says how beautiful she is! But what good does it do her, when all the time she has to sit in that big copper palace with all those towers! Am I never to see her? Now where is my tinder-box!' He struck it once and there stood the dog with eyes like tea-cups.

'I know it's the middle of the night,' said the soldier, 'but I so dearly want to see the Princess, if only for a moment!'

The dog was out of the door and, before the soldier knew what was what, there he was again, carrying the Princess. There she sat, fast asleep on the dog's back and she was so beautiful that it was plain to see at once she was a Princess. The soldier couldn't help himself, he had to kiss her hand. Then the dog ran back again with the Princess.

In the morning, when the King and Queen were drinking tea, the Princess said she had such a strange dream that night, all about a dog and a soldier. She was riding on the dog's back, and the soldier had kissed her.

'That's a fine carry-on,' exclaimed the Queen. And she ordered one of the elderly ladies-in-waiting to sit by the Princess's bedside the next night to see whether it really was a dream, or what was the meaning of it.

The soldier longed terribly to see the beautiful Princess again, and so the dog appeared in the palace, took the Princess and ran off with her for all he was worth. But the elderly lady-in-waiting put on a strong pair of boots and ran after him just as fast. And, when she saw the dog and the Princess disappear into a big house, she said to herself, 'Now I know where it is!' and with a piece of chalk, she drew a big cross on the gate. Then she returned home and went to bed, and the dog with the Princess returned, too. But when the dog saw the cross chalked on the gate of the house where the soldier was living, he took a piece of chalk and drew a cross on every gate in town. This indeed was a clever idea, for now the lady-in-waiting would never find the right gate.

Early the next morning the King and Queen came to see where it was the Princess had been that night, and the lady-in-waiting and all the court officials went with them.

'Here it is!' exclaimed the King, when he saw the first door with a cross on it.

'Oh no, dear man, it's over there,' said the Queen, seeing another door with a cross on it.

'But here's the cross, and here's another!' they all cried, for no matter where they looked, there were crosses on the gates. Now they realized that all the looking in the world wouldn't help them.

The Queen, however, was a very clever woman, who could do more than ride about in a coach. She took a big pair of golden scissors, cut up a large piece of silk and made a nice little bag from it. This bag she filled with fine buckwheat seed and fastened it to the Princess's waist. When this was done, she snipped a little hole in the bag, so the seed would trickle out, leaving a trail wherever the Princess went.

That night the dog re-appeared, put the Princess on his back and ran off with her again to the soldier, who loved her terribly and wanted so very much to be a Prince, so he could marry her.

The dog did not notice the grain trickling out of the bag all the way from the palace to the soldier's window, which he reached by running up the wall with the Princess on his back. So, in the morning, the King and the Queen saw quite plainly where their daughter had been, and they took the soldier and put him in jail.

There he now sat. Brr, how dark and boring it was, and to top it all, they said, 'Tomorrow you'll hang.' These were not glad tidings and what's more, the soldier had left the tinder-box at his lodgings in the inn. In the morning he could see through the iron bars of the little window, how all the people rushed out of town to see him hanged. He heard drums and saw soldiers marching. Everybody was running, even the cobbler's apprentice in his leather apron and slippers. He was running so fast that one of the slippers flew off, landing right by the wall where the soldier sat behind the iron bars, looking out.

'Hey, cobbler boy, not so fast,' said the soldier. 'It won't start before I appear! But wouldn't you rather turn round and run to my old lodgings and bring me my tinder-box? I'll give you four coins. But you'd better run like the wind!' The cobbler's boy was always glad of a copper or two, so he dashed away for the tinder-box, gave it to the soldier and, well now, let's wait and see!

Outside the town big gallows had been erected and round it stood soldiers and hundreds of thousands of people. The King and the Queen sat on magnificent thrones facing the judges and the whole Council.

The soldier was already standing on the ladder, but as they were about to put the rope round his neck, he said that it was always the custom of the court to grant the offender one simple, harmless wish, before carrying out the punishment. He would so love to smoke his pipe once more for, after all, it would be his very last smoke here on earth.

The King didn't want to refuse such a wish, and so the soldier took out his tinder-box and struck it once, twice, three times—and straightaway all the three dogs were there, the one with eyes as big as tea-cups, and the one with eyes like mill-wheels, and the one with eyes like towers.

'Help me now from being hanged!' said the soldier, and with that the dogs flew at the judges and all the councillors, seizing some by the leg, others by the nose, tossing them high up into the air, so that when they hit the ground again, they were smashed to pieces.

'Not me!' objected the King, but the biggest dog seized him and the Queen and threw them up after the others. The soldiers grew frightened and the people all shouted, 'Good soldier, you shall be our King and you shall marry our beautiful Princess!'

Then they put the soldier into the King's carriage, and all the three dogs danced in front shouting 'hurrah' and the boys whistled through their fingers and soldiers saluted in his honour. The Princess left the copper palace and was made Queen, which was much to her liking! The wedding lasted eight days and the dogs sat at the table with the rest, eyeing it all with wonder.

The Emperor's New Clothes

Many years ago there lived an Emperor so very fond of fine new clothes, that he spent all his money on dressing himself up. He didn't care for his soldiers, he didn't care for the theatre or for rides to the forest, he cared only, but only for showing himself off in new clothes. He had a robe for every hour of the day and, just as it is said about a King, that he is 'in council,' it was said of him, 'The Emperor is in the dressing-room.'

The big city, where the Emperor lived, was a very busy one, and every day many strangers came to it. One day, two swindlers arrived. They pretended to be weavers, saying they could weave the most magnificent cloth imaginable. Not only were the colours and patterns exceptionally beautiful, but any clothes made from this material had the magic power of being invisible to anyone unfit for his job, or terribly stupid.

'These would be fantastic clothes,' thought the Emperor. 'If I wore them, I would find out who in my kingdom is unfit for his post; I could tell the clever ones from the dim-witted! Oh yes, that cloth must be woven for me at once!' And he paid the two impostors a lot of money in advance, so they could commence their work.

The swindlers set up two looms and pretended to work, but the loom was quite, quite bare. They brazenly asked for the finest silk and the richest gold thread. This they pushed into their own sack.

'I would really like to know how far they've got with that material!' thought the Emperor, but a queer feeling gripped his heart at the thought that anyone stupid or unfit for his post wouldn't be able to see the material. Though he was quite convinced that he didn't need to worry about himself the slightest bit, he thought it best to send someone else first to see how it looked. All the people of the town knew of the strange power of the material, and they were all eager to see how unfit or stupid their neighbour was.

'I'll send my old honest minister to the weavers,' the Emperor decided.

'He's the best one to judge that cloth, for he has plenty of sense and no one carries out his job better than he!'

So the old honest minister went off to the hall where the two swindlers sat, working away at the empty looms.

'Gracious me,' thought the old minister, his eyes rolling, 'I can't see a thing!' But aloud he said nothing.

Both the swindlers asked him to step nearer, and enquired how he liked the lovely pattern and the beautiful colours. Then they pointed to the empty loom and the poor old minister opened his eyes wider than ever, but he still couldn't see a thing, for of course there was nothing there.

'Goodness me!' thought he. 'Am I that stupid? I never thought I was, and nobody must find out! Am I unfit for my post? No, it would never do for me to admit I can't see the cloth!'

'Well, why don't you say something?' said one of the weavers.

'Oh, it's a wonderful cloth! Truly magnificent!' said the old minister, peering through his spectacles. 'Such pattern and such colours! Yes, I'll certainly tell the Emperor how exceptionally nice it is!'

'We're happy to hear that!' said the two weavers and they named the colours and the special pattern. The old minister listened most carefully, so he could repeat it all to the Emperor upon his return. And this he did.

The swindlers now asked for more money, more silk and gold thread, saying they needed it for weaving. They put the lot into their own pockets, not a single thread reached the loom and they went on weaving, as before.

A little later, the Emperor sent another worthy official to see how the weaving was progressing and if the cloth would soon be ready. He fared the same as the minister. He looked and looked, but as there was nothing there but the empty looms, he saw nothing.

'Well, don't you think this is a beautiful piece of cloth?' asked both the swindlers, pointing at and explaining the magnificent pattern which of course wasn't there at all.

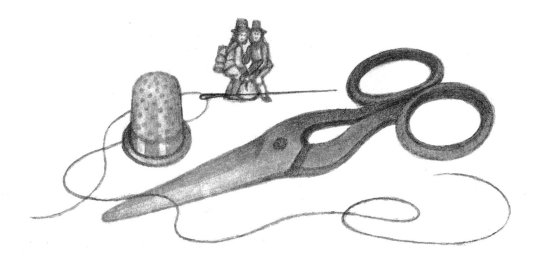

'I'm not stupid!' thought the official, 'could it be then that I'm unfit for my office? That would be most strange! I mustn't let anyone see!' And so he praised the cloth, which he couldn't see at all, assuring them of his pleasure from seeing the lovely colours and the magnificent pattern. 'Yes, it is truly exquisite!' he told the Emperor.

The whole town was talking about the magnificent material.

Now the Emperor wished to see it, while it was still on the loom. He left with a whole group of selected men, the two elderly, experienced officials among them, to visit the two crafty weavers who were weaving away for all they were worth without a single thread on the loom.

'Isn't this material truly magnificent?' asked the two worthy officials. 'Just look at that pattern, Your Highness, and those colours!' and they pointed at the empty loom, for they assumed that the others could see the cloth.

'What's this?' thought the Emperor. 'I can't see anything! Oh, this is terrible! Am I stupid? Am I, perhaps, unfit to be an Emperor? That would be the very worst fate which could befall me! — Why, this material is truly beautiful!' he said aloud, 'I give it my official approval!' and he nodded his head with satisfaction, while he looked at the empty loom. He didn't want to admit he couldn't see a thing.

All his followers looked and looked, with no more result than the rest. All the same, they said, like their Emperor, 'Oh, it's truly beautiful!' and advised him to wear clothes made from the magnificent material for the first time in the grand procession which was soon to take place. 'It is fantastic, exquisite, magnificent!' were the words that passed from mouth to mouth and one and all were most delighted with it. The Emperor gave each of the swindlers a knight's cross for his button-hole and the title of Court High Weaver.

Before the morning of the procession the swindlers sat up all night by their looms, with more than sixteen lights burning. People could see for themselves how busy they were to finish the Emperor's new clothes. They pretended to take the cloth off the loom, they snipped the air with their big scissors, they sewed with a needle without thread and, in the end they said, 'There, now at last the clothes are ready!'

The Emperor came there in person with his noble gallants, and both the swindlers raised one hand as if holding something, and said, 'These are your trousers! Here's the coat! Here's the cloak!' and so on. 'They are as light as gossamer! You would almost think you haven't a stitch on, but that's the very beauty of them!'

'How very true!' nodded all the gallants, but they saw nothing, for there was nothing to see.

'Your Imperial Highness, be gracious enough to take off your clothes now!' said the swindlers. 'We shall dress you in the new ones, over there, please, in front of that large mirror!'

The Emperor took off all his clothes and the weavers pretended to dress him in all the individual garments they were supposed to have made, and they held his waist as if fastening something round it. That was supposed to be the train. And the Emperor turned and twisted before the mirror.

'Oh, how they suit you! What a perfect fit!' everybody cried. 'What a pattern! What colours! What exquisite robes!'

'The canopy which is to be carried over Your Highness in the procession is waiting outside,' the master of ceremonies announced.

'Very well, I am ready,' said the Emperor. 'They fit me well, don't you think?' And he turned round in front of the mirror just once more, for he wanted everyone to think he was looking at the magnificent robes.

The chamberlains who were to carry the train, fumbled about on the floor, pretending to pick up the train. They walked along, their empty hands in the air, not daring to show that they couldn't see a thing.

And thus the Emperor marched in the procession under the beautiful canopy, and all the people in the street and at the windows said, 'Oh, how wonderful are the Emperor's new clothes! What a magnificent train he has to his robe! How splendidly they fit!' Nobody wanted to admit that he couldn't see anything, for then he would have been unfit for his post or would have been awfully stupid. Never had the Emperor's clothes been such a success.

'But the Emperor hasn't got anything on!' cried a little child.

'Dear God, listen to the voice of the little innocent!' said the father, and it was whispered from man to man what the child had said.

'He hasn't anything on, that's what a little child says, that he hasn't anything on!'

'Why, he hasn't a thing on!' all the people shouted at last. And the Emperor went all goose-pimply, for he knew they were right, but he thought, 'I have to last out till the procession is over.' And so he marched on even more proudly, while the chamberlains walked behind him, bearing the train that wasn't there at all.

The Ugly Duckling

It was so lovely in the country! It was summer; the wheat was yellow, the oats were green, the hay was stacked up in the grassy meadows, while the stork paraded about on his long red legs, chattering away in Egyptian, for this was the language he had learned from his mother. Thick woods spread all around the fields and meadows, and deep lakes were in the middle of the woods. It was indeed beautiful in the country! The warm sunbeams fell upon an old manor-house surrounded by a deep moat and, from its walls all the way down to the water's edge, large burdock leaves grew—they were so tall that little children could stand upright under the largest ones. This spot was as wild as any in the densest forest. And this was the place a duck had chosen to build her nest. She was doing her best to hatch little ducklings, but she was tired of sitting on the eggs, for it was taking so terribly long and she rarely had visitors. The other ducks preferred swimming along the canals to climbing up to see her for bit of gossip under a burdock leaf.

At last the eggs started to crack, one after another, with a cry of 'peep-peep!' All the eggs were coming to life, with little heads popping out.

'Quack, quack! Quick, quick!' said the mother duck encouragingly, and the baby ducklings hurried as best as they could, peering under the green burdock leaves on all sides. Their mother allowed them to look as much as they wished, for green is so good for the eyes.

'What a big place the world is!' wondered all the ducklings, now that they had so much room to move about.

'So you think this is the whole world?' the mother instructed them. 'The world stretches a long way past our garden, all the way to the parson's fields! But I have never been there. Are you all here now?' And she got up. 'Oh no, you're not all here yet. The largest egg is still there. How much longer is this one going to take? I am really sick to death of it!' And with that she settled down again in the nest.

'How are you getting on?' asked an old duck, who came by for a visit.

'This one egg is taking simply ages!' complained the nesting duck. 'It is not even trying to crack. But just look at the others; they are the prettiest ducklings I've ever seen! They all take after their father, that scoundrel of a fellow — he doesn't even drop in to see me!'

'Let me see the egg which doesn't want to crack!' said the old duck. 'Believe me or not, it's a turkey egg! They played the same trick on me once. When I think of the trouble and bother I had with those youngsters; imagine, they were afraid of water! I couldn't get them to go in, though I squeaked and quacked and hissed and snapped — nothing was the slightest bit of use! Show me that egg! Yes, quite definitely it's a turkey egg! Leave it alone and teach your other children to swim instead!'

'I think I'll sit on it a while longer!' the duck announced. 'I've sat on it for so long now, I'll last out a bit longer!'

'As you like!' said the old duck, and waddled away.

The big egg burst open at last. 'Peep, peep!' cried the newly born as he tumbled out. He was huge and ugly. The duck looked at him closely. 'How awfully big that duckling is!' she wondered. 'He's not a bit like the others! Could it be a young turkey-cock after all? We'll know soon enough! He'll get in the water, even if I have to push him in myself!'

The next day the weather was beautiful. The sun shone down on all the burdock leaves lining the wall. The mother duck waddled with all her family behind to the canal. Splash! and she was in the water. 'Quack, quack!' she cried, and one duckling after another jumped in. At first, the water closed over their heads, but they came straight up again and swam quite easily. They all floated merrily along, even the ugly, grey duckling.

'That's no turkey!' the mother duck said to herself. 'Just look how nicely he uses his legs, and how erect he holds himself! He's my baby! Come to think of it, he isn't at all bad-looking, when one takes a closer look! Quack, quack! Come along now with me, I'll lead you into the world and introduce you to the duck-yard. Take care to keep close to me, so nobody treads on you, and keep a look-out for the cat!'

They came into the duck-yard. The noise there was deafening, for two duck families were fighting over an eel's head — and the cat got it in the end.

'You see, such is the way of the world!' said the mother duck, licking her beak, for she too fancied the eel's head. 'And now on your feet!' she ordered. 'Show me how quick you can be and go and bow to that old duck over there! She's the most distinguished of all the ducks here. She is of Spanish blood, that's why she is so plump. As you see, she has a red rag round her leg — that is exceptionally beautiful and the greatest distinction any duck can have. It means that they would hate to lose her, and so she must be easily recognisable to everybody, animals and people! Hurry now, and don't turn your feet inwards! Well brought up ducklings always place their feet well apart, like father and mother! Like this! Bow nicely now and say "quack, quack!"'

The little ducklings did as they were told. But the other ducks eyed them up and down, quacking loudly, 'Oh no, not another bunch! As if there wasn't enough of us already! And fie! How ugly that duckling is! We shan't put up with him!' And one of the ducks flew straight at him and bit him in the neck.

'Leave him alone!' cried the mother duck. 'He's doing no harm!'

'But he's far too big and far too conspicuous!' said the duck that had bitten him. 'So we'll go on nipping him!'

'You have pretty children, mother!' said the old duck with the rag round her leg. They are all pretty but one, and that hasn't turned out well at all! I wish you could remake it!'

'That is impossible, your ladyship!' said the mother duck. 'He may not be handsome, but he has a kind heart and he swims beautifully, like any of the others, in fact a little better than the rest. I am confident he'll grow into a beauty, or that in time he'll at least not look so big. But he was so long in that egg, it must have affected his figure!' She scratched the duckling fondly behind his neck and stroked his feathers on his back. 'Besides,' she added, 'he's a drake, so looks don't matter that much! I just hope he grows big and strong to fight through life.'

'The other ducklings are so charming!' praised the old duck. 'Make yourselves entirely at home, and if you come across an eel's head, do bring it along to me!'

And they made themselves at home.

But the poor little duckling, who had been the last to hatch and who was so ugly to look at was nipped and pecked and teased by ducks and hens alike. 'He's such a monstrous fellow!' they all said. And the turkey-cock, who had been born with spurs on and so fancied himself as an emperor, puffed himself out like a ship in full sail, and made straight for the duckling, gabbling away till his face turned scarlet. The poor little duckling hardly knew what to do, or where to turn. He was upset because he was so ugly and the laughing-stock of the whole duck-yard.

That is how it was the first day and things grew worse and worse. Everybody was against the poor duckling, even his brothers and sisters were unkind to him, and said, 'If only the old cat would get you, you ugly creature!' And even his mother sighed, 'I wish you were far away!' The ducks bit him, the hens pecked him, and the maid who fed the poultry kicked him.

So the little duckling fled, flying over the hedge. The little birds in the bushes were frightened and flew up in the air, and the duckling thought, 'That is because I am ugly!' He closed his eyes and ran on. And so he came to some wide marshes, where wild ducks were living. He stayed there all night, for he was tired and weary.

In the morning the wild ducks flew up and saw the newcomer. 'Who are you?' they asked. The duckling turned in all directions, greeting everyone as nicely as he knew.

'You really are uncommonly ugly!' said the ducks. 'But what does it matter, if you don't want to marry into our family!'

Poor duckling! He had not even thought of marrying! All he wanted was to be allowed to stay among the reeds and drink a little marsh water now and then. For two whole days he lay there. Then two wild geese came along, or to be more precise, two wild ganders. Not much time had passed since they pecked their way out of their egg-shell, so they were somewhat impertinent.

'Look here, friend!' they called to the ugly duckling. 'You're so ugly that we quite like you! Come with us, and be a bird of passage, like us! A stone's throw away from here, on a neighbouring marsh, there are a few adorable, beautiful wild geese, all maiden young ladies, and they are calling, "Hiss! Hiss!" You might be quite a success, in spite of your ugliness!'

Bang—bang! it echoed suddenly from above, and both the ganders fell dead into the reeds. The water turned blood-red. Bang—bang! it echoed once again and whole flocks of wild geese soared upwards from the reeds. And shots rang out again. There was a grand shoot on. The hunters had circled the marsh, some in fact were sitting in branches of trees, which stretched right over the reeds. Blue smoke drifted in little clouds between dark trees, rolling far out over the water. The hounds hurtled through the mud — splash! splash! The reeds and rushes were swaying in all directions. It was terrifying for the poor duckling. He turned his head to hide it under his wing, but just then an enormous dog appeared right by his side. His tongue was hanging right out and his eyes were gleaming. He thrust his open jaw right towards the duckling, barred his sharp teeth and snap!—he was gone, gone without even touching him.

'Thank heaven!' sighed the duckling. 'I am so ugly that even the dog doesn't want me!'

And he lay there quite still, while the shots whistled through the rushes.

Not till much later in the day did silence reign again. But the poor duckling did not dare to get up even now. He waited several hours more before he looked around and then he hastened away from the marsh as fast as he could. He ran over fields and meadows but the wind was strong and only with difficulty could he fight his way forward.

Towards evening he came to a shabby little cottage. It was so wretched that it couldn't make up its mind on which side to fall, and that is the only reason it remained standing. The wind swept round the little duckling so fiercely that he had to sit tight on his tail, so as not to be blown right over. And all the time it grew worse. But then the little duckling noticed that the door of the cottage had come off one of its hinges, and was therefore hanging so crookedly that it was possible to slip through the gap inside.

In the cottage lived an old woman with a tom-cat and a hen. The tom-cat, whom she called Sonny, could arch his back and purr; he also knew how to make sparks fly, but you had to stroke him the wrong way first. The hen had tiny short little legs and was therefore called Chickatiny Shortie; she laid some beautiful eggs, and the old woman loved her as her own child.

The next morning they noticed the strange duckling at once and the tom-cat began to purr and the hen to cackle.

'What's going on?' asked the old lady, looking round. But her sight was rather poor and so she mistook the duckling for a plump duck, who had gone astray. 'What a valuable catch!' she said. 'Now I shall have duck eggs—that is if it isn't a drake! We must test it out.'

So the duckling was taken in on trial for three weeks, but no eggs appeared.

Now the tom-cat was the master of the house and the hen the mistress and they always used to say 'we and the world', for they believed they were half of the world—and the better half at that! The duckling thought it possible to have a different opinion, but the hen would not stand for this.

'Can you lay eggs?' she asked.

'No.'

'Shut your beak then!'

And the tom-cat asked, 'Can you arch your back till your fur stands on end? Can your purr and make sparks fly?'

'No.'

'In that case keep your opinion to yourself when sensible people are talking!'

So the duckling sat in a corner, feeling thoroughly sad at heart. Then he remembered the fresh air and the sunshine. He felt a strange yearning to float on water and in the end he just couldn't help himself and had to confide in the hen.

'What's the matter with you?' she asked. 'You don't have any work to do, that's why you have such fancy ideas in your head! Lay some eggs or purr, and you'll get over it!'

'But it is so wonderful to float on water!' said the duckling. 'It is so wonderful when the water closes over your head while you dive to the very bottom!'

'Sounds most delightful, I'm sure!' said the hen. 'Are you quite mad? Ask the tom-cat, he is wiser than anyone I know, if he likes to float on water, or dive under! I don't even want to speak about what I think! Ask the old woman, our mistress, in all the world there's no wiser creature than she! Do you think she longs to float and to duck her head under water?'

'You don't understand me!' complained the duckling.

'If we don't understand you, who would understand! Surely you don't

think yourself wiser than the tom-cat and our old lady, without mention-
ing myself at all! Forget those fancies, my child, and thank the Creator for
all you have been given! Haven't you arrived in a warm room, where
there's company you can learn a lot from? But you're a muddler and it's
not particularly entertaining having to put up with you! But you should
believe me, for I mean well. I am telling you unpleasant facts, but that's
how to tell true friends. Now set to work and lay some eggs and learn to
purr or make sparks fly!'

'I think I will go out into the wide world,' said the duckling.

'Very well then, go!' replied the hen.

And off the duckling went. He floated on water and dived, but all the
animals ignored him, because of his ugliness.

Autumn came, the leaves in the woods turned yellow and brown, and
the wind caught them and sent them dancing; there was a wintry chill in
the air. The clouds were heavy with hail and snow and on the fence sat
a crow who croaked 'Ow, ow!' from sheer cold. Brr, the very thought of the

winter was enough to give one the shivers! The poor duckling was certainly not very comfortable.

One evening, just after sunset, a whole flock of large, beautiful birds flew out of the bushes. The duckling had never seen anything so beautiful before. They were dazzling white, with long graceful necks. They were swans; they gave out the strangest of cries, spread their magnificent, long wings and flew away from the cold regions to warmer countries, across the immense, open sea. They rose high, so high, and the ugly little duckling's heart was gripped with the strangest feeling. He spun round and round on the water, straining his neck high after them and letting out a cry so loud and so strange that it frightened even him. He could not forget the beautiful, lucky birds! When they were lost from sight he dived straight to the bottom. When he came up again, he was almost beside himself. He didn't know what they were called or where they were flying to, yet he loved them as he had never loved anybody before. But he wasn't envious, not in the least—for how could he even think of wishing such beauty for himself—he would be happy just to be accepted by the other ducks—he, the poor ugly creature!

The winter was cruel, bitterly cruel. The duckling had to swim to and fro on the pond, to keep it from freezing up altogether. But every night the hole in which he swam grew smaller and smaller, and a crust of ice formed on it, too. The duckling was forced to keep his little legs going all the time to prevent the gap from closing altogether. In the end, faint with exhaustion, he lay perfectly still and froze fast in the ice.

Early the next morning a farmer was passing by. Seeing the duckling, he went down to him, broke the ice with his clog and took him home to his wife. There he revived.

The children wanted to play with him, but the duckling was afraid they wanted to hurt him, and in his terror he flew straight into the milk-pan, spilling the milk all over the room. The farmer's wife screamed and waved her hands; the duckling flew into the butter-tub and then into a barrel of flour and then up again. What a sight he looked! The farmer's wife went on screaming, chasing him with a pair of tongs, and the children were falling over one another trying to catch him shrieking and laughing. Luckily for him the door was open. The duckling flew into the bushes into the newly-fallen snow, where he lay in a daze.

It would be too sad to tell of all the misery and suffering the duckling had to endure that cruel winter. When the sun began to shine warmly again, he was lying on the marsh among the rushes, the larks were singing, the beautiful spring had returned!

Then the duckling opened his wings. They were stronger now than before and bore him forwards mightily. Before he realized it, he found himself in a huge garden, where the apple-trees were in full bloom and fragrant lilac hung on long green branches over the winding stream. Oh, how beautiful it all was, how spring-like, how fresh! And out of the thicket right in front of the duckling came three beautiful white swans; they spread their wings and swam lightly, so lightly on the water. The duckling recognised the magnificent birds and was seized with a strange sadness.

'I'll fly over to the kingly birds! They'll peck me to death for daring to go near them when I am so ugly. So what! It's better to be put to death by them than to be bitten by the ducks, pecked at by the hens, kicked by the girl who tends the poultry, and to suffer so in winter!'

And so he flew into the water and swam towards the beautiful swans. They saw him and turned towards him, their wings humming. 'Kill me then!' said the poor creature, and he bowed his head to the surface, waiting for death. But what did he see in the clear water? There, underneath him, he saw his own reflection. No longer was he the clumsy, dirty-grey bird, ugly to all — he was a swan!

It matters not if one is born in a duck-yard, if one has been hatched out of a swan's egg!

The young swan was truly happy now after all his hardships. The big swans swam round him and stroked him with their beaks.

Some little children came into the garden. They threw bread and grain into the water, and the smallest one of them cried, 'There's a new swan!' And the others chanted, 'Yes, a new swan has come!' They clapped their hands and danced about and ran to fetch their father and mother. Bread and buns were thrown into the water and everybody said, 'The new swan is the prettiest! It is so young and so lovely!' And the old swans bowed before him.

The young swan was suddenly overcome with shyness. He tucked his head under his wing, not knowing what to do. He was so very happy, but not at all proud, for a good heart is never proud. He recalled how he had been laughed at and cruelly treated. Now everyone was saying he was the loveliest of all these lovely birds. The lilacs bent their branches right down to him and the sun shone warmly and brightly. The wings of the young happy swan were suddenly humming and with his slender neck stretched out the swan cried joyfully, with all his heart, 'I never dreamt of so much happiness, when I was the ugly duckling!'

The Darning-Needle

There was once a darning-needle so fine that she thought of herself as a sewing-needle. 'Now take good care of what you're holding,' she said to the fingers that picked her up. 'Don't drop me, please! If I fall on the floor, you may never find me again, I am so fine!'

'You're not all that fine,' said the fingers, gripping her tightly.

'Look, I come with my train!' said the darning-needle, pulling after her a long thread, but without a knot in it.

The fingers guided the needle straight to the cook's slippers, the uppers of which had split and had to be sewn together.

'This is vulgar work,' said the darning-needle. 'I'll never get through that leather, I'll break, I'll break!' And break she did. 'Didn't I tell you,' she went on. 'I'm much too fine!'

The fingers now thought the needle to be useless, but they had to hold her tight while the cook dropped some sealing-wax on her and pinned her to her scarf.

'See, I have now turned into a brooch,' said the darning-needle. I knew my worth would be recognized in the end; if you really are somebody, you're sure to become something!' And then she laughed, but only to herself, of course, for a darning-needle never shows outwardly that she is laughing. And there she sat in the scarf as proud as a peacock, as if she was sitting in a coach, looking round in all directions during the ride.

'May I take the liberty of asking you whether you are of gold?' she asked the pin who was her neighbour. 'You look so splendid, and you have your own head, though it is somewhat small! You should get it to grow, for it is not everybody who can be stuck up with sealing-wax!' With that the darning-needle drew herself up so proudly that she fell out of the scarf straight into the sink, just as the cook was emptying it.

'Now I am off on my travels,' said the darning-needle. 'I only hope I shan't get stuck!' But that is what she did.

'I am too fine for this world!' she said, as she lay in the gutter. 'However, I have my self-respect and that's something to cheer up any man!' And the darning-needle held herself erect and did not lose her good humour.

All sorts of things swam over her—sticks, straws, scraps of newspaper. 'Just look how they sail along,' said the darning-needle. 'They have no idea what is stuck underneath them! It is I, and I am sticking where I am! Take a look at that splinter swimming on, I bet he hasn't a single thought in his head which isn't about splinters such as he! And there goes a straw, see how it turns and twirls! Stop thinking so much about yourself! Or you'll go bump against the pavement! And those newspapers! Everyone has long forgotten what is in them, yet they are throwing themselves about! I sit here quietly and patiently! I know what I am, and I'll stay what I am!'

One day something appeared near the needle which was so shiny that she took it for a diamond. But it was only a glass-splinter from a bottle, and as it glittered so brightly, the darning-needle spoke to it, introducing herself as a brooch! 'Surely you're a diamond!' 'Yes, something of that

sort!' And so each believed the other to be very precious indeed, and they started talking about the haughtiness of the world.

'Well, I used to live in a box belonging to a young lady,' said the darning-needle, 'and that lady was a cook. On each of her hands she had five fingers and I've never seen anything so conceited as those five fingers! Yet she only had them to hold me, to pick me from the box and put me back again.'

'Did they shine at all?' asked the glass-splinter.

'Shine!' said the darning-needle, 'oh no, with them it was pure pride, pride! They were five brothers in all, all from the same family, they held themselves very erect side by side, though they were of different length. The one on the outside, Thumb was the name, was short and fat; he usually wasn't in line with the other fingers and had only one bend in his spine, so he could only bend once. But I heard it said that if he were chopped off a man, that man would no longer be fit for military service. The second finger, Sweet-tooth, poked in sweet and sour things, pointed at the sun and the moon, and it was he who pressed the pen when they were writing. Longfellow was head and shoulders taller than the rest. Ringman had a gold ring round his tummy, and the smallest one, Peer Musician, did nothing at all and was proud of that. Proud they were and proud they'll stay, and so I took to the sink.'

'And now we sit together here and sparkle,' said the glass-splinter. But then more water poured into the gutter and it overflowed its banks and carried the splinter away.

'So now he's got further, he's been promoted,' said the darning-needle. 'And I go on sitting here, for I am too fine, but I am proud of that and my pride deserves respect!' So she sat on, erect, full of her own thoughts.

'I could almost believe I was born of a sunbeam, I am so fine! And it seems to me the sun is always looking for me under the water. Why, I am so fine that my own mother couldn't find me. If I still had my old eye which broke off, I think I'd burst into tears — though I wouldn't! It is not ladylike to weep!'

One day some boys were raking about in the gutter, looking for old nails, small coins and such like. They poked about in the dirt, having fun.

'Ouch!' cried the one who pricked himself on the needle. 'That's a fine fellow!'

'I am a fine lady,' said the darning-needle, only nobody heard her. The sealing-wax had dropped off and she was black all over, but then black is a very slimming colour and so the needle fancied herself finer than ever.

'There floats an egg-shell,' cried the boys and they stuck the darning-needle into the shell.

'White walls and I all in black,' said the needle, 'that is very becoming! Now I shall be noticed! I only hope I shan't be sea-sick, for then I would break!' But she was not sea-sick and she did not break.

'For sea-sickness a good remedy is to have a stomach of steel and always to remember that the likes of us are more than human. I've cured myself! The finer one is, the more one can stand.'

'Crunch!' said the egg-shell, as a waggon rolled over it. 'Oh, how it presses!' sighed the darning-needle. 'Now I'll be sea-sick after all! I'll break, I'll break!' But she did not break, though the waggon had passed over her. She stayed where she was — and we shall leave her there!

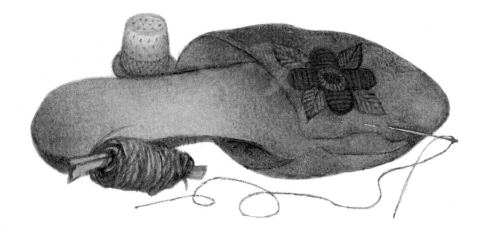

The Wild Swans

Far, far away, in regions where the swallows fly in our winter-time, there lived a King who had eleven sons and an only daughter called Elise. The eleven brothers were Princes and went to school with a star on their breast and a sword at their side. They wrote on golden boards with diamond pens and they learnt everything off by heart and kept the learning in their heads, so it was easy to see they were Princes. Little Elise would sit on a little crystal stool, looking at a picture book which had cost the half of a kingdom.

Oh yes, the children lived happily, but this was not to last for ever.

Their father, the Lord of all the country, married a very wicked Queen, who did not wish the children at all well, in fact there was not even a touch of kindness in her. They felt this the very first day. There was a grand gala at the palace and the children were playing a game called 'visitors'. But instead of getting as always as many cakes and baked apples as they could eat, the Queen gave them only a dishful of sand.

A week later she sent little Elise away to be brought up by a peasant in the country and, before very long, she had told the King so many lies about the poor Princes, that he stopped caring for them.

'Fly into the world and look after yourselves!' said the wicked Queen. 'Turn into great, voiceless birds!' But she was unable to prepare for them the fate as cruel as she intended. Instead they turned into eleven beautiful wild swans and, with a very strange cry, they flew out of the palace windows towards the park and the wood.

It was still early in the morning when they passed over the farmhouse where their sister was sleeping. The swans circled above the roof, stretching their slender long necks and flapping their wings, but nobody saw or heard them. They had to go on, high into the clouds, far away into the wide world; so they turned to the big dark forest which stretched all the way to the seashore.

Poor little Elise stood in the farm cottage playing with a green leaf, for she had no other toy. She made a hole in the leaf with her finger and peeped through it at the sun and it was then she fancied she could see the bright eyes of her brothers. And whenever the warm sunbeams shone on her cheeks, she thought of her brothers' loving kisses.

Day followed day, one like the other. When the wind blew through the big rose bushes in front of the house, it would whisper to the roses: 'Who in the world could be more beautiful than you!' But the roses shook their heads and said: 'Elise!' And on Sundays, when the peasant's old wife sat at the door of her cottage, reading her hymn-book, the wind would turn the pages and say to the book: 'Can anybody be more pious than you?' 'Elise is more pious,' the hymn-book would reply. And what the roses and the hymn-book said was nothing but the truth.

When she was fifteen years old, Elise was to return home. But when the Queen saw how beautiful she was, she hated her all the more. How gladly would she have changed her into a wild swan like her brothers, but she dared not do this straightaway, for the King was anxious to see his daughter.

Early the next morning the Queen went into a bathroom made of marble and fitted with soft cushions and the most exquisite carpets. She took three toads, kissed them and said to one, 'Settle on Elise's head, when she comes into the bathroom, so she becomes lazy like you.' 'Settle on her forehead,' she said to the second, 'so she will be as ugly as you and so that her own father will not recognize her.' 'Settle on her heart,' she bade the third toad, 'so her mind will become evil and will bring torment upon herself!' With that she put the toads into the clear water, which turned green at once, and called Elise, undressed her and ordered her to get into the water. As she went under, one toad settled in her hair, the second on her forehead and the third on her bosom. But Elise did not seem at all aware of this. The moment she rose, three scarlet poppies appeared on the water. Had the toads not been poisonous and kissed by the Queen-witch, they would have turned into three roses. All the same they still turned into flowers because they had rested on her head and her heart. Elise was too pious and too innocent for magic to have power over her.

The wicked Queen, seeing this, rubbed walnut-juice all over the poor maiden, till her skin turned quite brown; then she smeared her pretty face with a nasty-smelling ointment and entangled her long beautiful hair. Nobody could recognize the lovely little Elise now.

When her father saw her he was shocked and said she could not be his daughter. Nobody wanted to have anything to do with her, except the dog and the swallows; but they were only dumb, simple animals and no one paid any attention to them.

Poor Elise burst into tears and thought of her eleven lost brothers. Broken-hearted, she stole away from the palace and wandered the whole day over fields and moors, till she reached a big forest. She did not know where to go, but she was filled with such sorrow and longing to see her brothers, who had surely been driven out into the world like herself, that she determined to seek and find them.

Shortly after she entered the forest, night fell. She lost her way in the dark, and so lay upon the soft moss, said her prayers and leaned her head against a tree trunk. It was so still in the forest, the air was pleasantly mild, and all round her in the grass and in the moss gleamed the green lights of

many hundred glow-worms. When Elise touched one of the branches with her hand, the bright insects flew down to her like falling stars.

All that night she dreamed of her brothers. They were all children again, playing together, writing with diamond pens on golden boards and looking at the picture book which had cost half of a kingdom. But they no longer wrote noughts and strokes on the board; instead they wrote of their most daring deeds and of everything they had seen and done. And in the picture book, everything came to life—the birds sang and men and women stepped from the pages and talked to Elise and to her brothers. But when she turned over the pages, they jumped back into their places in the book, so that the pictures would not get mixed up.

When Elise woke up, the sun was high in the sky. She could not actually see it, for the tall trees entwined their thick branches so closely together that behind them, the rays of the sun trembled like a soft, golden veil. The air was filled with scent and birds perched on Elise's shoulders. She heard the hum of water, for there were several large springs, which merged together into a pool with a lovely sandy bottom. Bushes were growing thickly right round it, but the deer had trodden a path through them and Elise followed this path to the water's edge. The water was so clear that if the bushes and branches had not been moving with the wind, she would have surely thought that they were painted on the smooth surface, so distinctly was each individual leaf mirrored upon it, whether glowing in the sunlight, or lying in the shade.

The moment she saw her own face reflected in the water, she was most startled, so brown and ugly did it look. But when she dampened her little hand and rubbed her eyes and forehead, she could see the gleam of her own white skin. Then she took off her clothes and stepped into the fresh water. In all the wide world there wasn't a royal child more beautiful.

After she had dressed herself again and plaited her long hair, she walked over to the bubbling brook, drank out of her hand and went on farther into the deep forest. She thought of her brothers and of the good God who would surely not forsake her. It was He who made the wild crab-apples grow to feed the hungry. He showed her such a tree, whose branches were bent under the weight of the fruit. Elise had her lunch, then propped up the boughs and wandered on into the deepest part of the forest. Such silence reigned there, that she could hear her own footsteps and each withered leaf which cracked beneath her feet. There was not a bird to be seen, not a single sunbeam to penetrate the thick curtain of the heavy branches. The tall tree trunks stood so close to each other, that when she looked straight before her, she fancied herself entirely surrounded by trellis-work. This was solitude such as Elise had never known.

And the night that followed was so dark! Not a single glow-worm lit up the moss. With sadness in her heart Elise lay down to sleep and then she dreamed that the Angel of God was gazing down upon her with kindly eyes, while little cherubs were peering at her from under his arms and over his shoulders.

In the morning when she awoke, she did not know if it had been a dream, or if it had really happened.

She had walked on only a few steps when she met an old woman carrying blackberries in a basket, and she gave her some. Elise asked the old woman if she had seen eleven Princes on horseback in the forest.

'No,' replied the old woman, 'but yesterday I saw eleven swans with crowns on their heads. They were swimming down the river which is not far from here.'

And she led Elise a little farther to a hillside, at the base of which the river flowed and turned. The trees lining its banks stretched their long leafy branches towards each other, and where the natural growth prevented them from reaching one another, the roots had loosened from the earth and thus the trees leaned towards each other over the water, their boughs intertwined.

Elise bade the old woman goodbye and walked on along the river, till she came to the place where it flowed into the sea.

The beautiful wide sea lay before the young maiden's eyes, but there was not a single yacht or boat to be seen; how was she to go on? She gazed at the tiny pebbles on the shore, which were rounded and smoothed by the waves. Glass, iron, stones, everything that lay there on the shore, had been moulded into shape, and yet the water was far softer than Elise's hand. 'It rolls on tirelessly, and smooths all the corners,' she said. 'I too will go on tirelessly, like the water. Thank you for the lesson, you bright rolling waves. My heart tells me that some day you will carry me to my dear brothers.'

Upon the wet sea-weed, there lay eleven white swan-feathers. Elise collected them in a bunch. Drops of water were on them still though whether they were dew drops or tears, nobody could tell. The shore was empty and desolate, but Elise did not feel lonely. The sea had an ever-changing face, changing more often in a mere few hours than the inland lakes change in a whole year. When a big black cloud appeared in the sky, it seemed as if the sea was saying: 'I too can grow dark.' And then the wind would blow and the waves would fling out their white foam. But when the clouds shone with a scarlet tint and the winds died down, the sea resembled a rose-leaf. Now it was green, now white, yet no matter how peaceful it was, it still stirred lightly by its shores. The water there heaved gently, like the bosom of a sleeping child.

When the sun went down, Elise saw the eleven wild swans with golden crowns upon their heads flying towards the land. They flew one behind the other, like a long flowing white ribbon. Elise climbed down the hillside and hid behind a bush. The swans settled close to her and flapped their large white wings.

The moment the sun disappeared under the water, the swans vanished too, and in their place stood eleven handsome Princes. She gave a loud cry, for though they had altered greatly, she knew that they were, that they must be her brothers. She embraced them and called them each by name and the brothers were so happy when they recognized their little sister, who had grown so tall and beautiful. They laughed and they cried, they talked and soon realized how wickedly their stepmother had treated them.

'As long as the sun is in the sky,' said the eldest brother, 'we fly and swim as swans. But when the sun goes down, we take again our human form. That is why we must always take care to stand on our feet at sunset. For if we were flying at sunset, we would hurtle down the moment we changed to humans. We do not live here; beyond the sea there is another land as beautiful as this, but it is very far away. To reach it, we have to cross the sea and there is not an island on which we can spend the night. But midway, one solitary little rock rises out of the waves. It is just large enough for us all to stand side by side. If the sea is stormy, the waves break and soak us. All the same, we are thankful for this resting-place, for there we can spend the night in our human form; without the rock we should never be able to visit our dear native country, for we need the two longest days of the year for our flight. Only once every year is the visit to our homeland possible, and then we can remain here only eleven days. We always fly over the large forest, where in the distance we can see the palace in which we were born and where our father dwells, and the high tower of the church in which our mother is buried. Here it seems that even the trees and bushes are akin to us; here the wild horses still race over the plains, as in the days of our childhood; here the charcoal-burner still sings the old songs to which we used to dance as children. This is our native land for which we yearn, and this is where we have found you, our dearest sister! We can stay here for two more days, then we must fly again across the sea to a wonderful country, but it is not our motherland. How shall we take you with us? We have no boat nor raft.'

'How can I set you free?' asked Elise.

And they went on talking almost through the night, closing their eyes only for a few hours.

Elise was awakened by the rustling of swans' wings. Her brothers had turned again into swans and at first flew in large circles above her, but then flew away, except one, who was the youngest, who stayed by her side. He laid his head in her lap, and Elise stroked his white wings; they remained thus the whole day. Towards evening the others returned, and once the sun had set, they changed back into their natural form.

'Tomorrow we shall fly away and we must not return for a whole year. But we do not want to leave you! Have you the courage to come with us? My arm is strong enough to carry you all day long through the forest, surely then the combined strength of our wings will be sufficient to carry you across the sea?' said one of the brothers.

'Oh yes, take me with you!' Elise cried.

All that night they spent weaving a mat from the springy willow bark and the tough rushes, and their mat was big and strong. Elise lay down upon it and, when the sun rose and the brothers turned again into swans, they all seized the mat with their beaks and soared high into the clouds with their dear sister, who was still asleep. As the sun shone fully upon her face, one of the swans flew over her head, shading it with his broad wings.

When Elise awoke they were already far from land. She thought she must be still dreaming, so strange did it seem to be flying over the sea, high above the waves. By her side lay a branch of lovely ripe berries and a bunch of tasty roots. These had been picked by her youngest brother and

placed on the mat. Elise thanked him with a smile, for she knew him as the swan who flew overhead, shading her from the fierce sun.

They were flying so high, that the first ship they saw beneath seemed like a seagull, sitting on the sea. Behind them was a huge cloud, a mountain of a cloud, and on it Elise saw the gigantic shadows of herself and her eleven brothers; it was the most beautiful picture she had ever seen. But as the sun rose higher and higher in the sky, and the cloud moved farther and farther in the distance, even the shadowy picture eventually disappeared.

The whole day they continued to fly, like an arrow whizzing through the air, and yet the swans were moving more slowly than usual, for they had their sister to carry. A heavy storm was brewing and evening was drawing near. Anxiously Elise watched the sun drop down towards the horizon, yet there was still no sign of the rock in the sea. It seemed to her that the swans plied their wings with increasing vigour. It was her fault, of course that they were unable to fly faster. At sunset they would take their human form, hurtle into the sea and drown. It was then she started praying most fervently—but there was still no rock to be seen. The black storm-cloud drew nearer and nearer still, violent gusts of wind foretold the tempest, and the clouds joined together, forming a single, frightening wave, which rolled rapidly forwards—and from the cloud one flash followed another.

The sun was now on the rim of the sea. Elise's heart trembled. Then the swans dived downwards, so swiftly that she thought she would fall, but they began to hover. Half of the sun was already under water and, at that moment, Elise dimly saw the little rock below; it seemed no larger than a seal's head sticking out of the sea. The sun was going down so fast, it was now no bigger than a star. Just as her foot touched hard ground, the sun died down altogether like the last spark on a burning piece of paper. She saw her brothers standing tightly round her, linking hands. True enough, there was only just enough room for her and for them. The sea beat against the rock, drenching them like torrential rain. The sky blazed with flashes as if it were on fire and the thunder rolled, one blast after another. But sister and brothers kept firm hold of each others' hands.

By daybreak the sky was clear and the wind had gone and the moment the sun rose, the swans flew away with Elise from the rock. The sea was still very rough and, as the travellers looked down from the sky, the white foam upon the black-green waves seemed like millions of swans swimming on the sea.

When the sun had risen higher, Elise saw in front of her a mountainous land, which appeared to be floating in the air. Glaciers glittered on the mountains and, in the centre, a palace was to be seen, a mile in length at least, where one row of colonnades daringly rose above another. Below, palm groves swayed and rare flowers bloomed, as large as mill-wheels. Elise asked if this was the country to which they were flying, but the swans shook their heads, for what she saw was the beautiful, airy, forever changing castle of the fairy Morgana; the swans were not permitted to bring a human being there. Elise did not take her eyes off the castle; but suddenly the mountains, the forests and the castle disappeared and in their place stood twenty proud churches, all alike, with high towers and pointed windows. She thought she could hear the organ playing but it was only the murmur of the sea. Now the churches were quite, quite near, but all at once they changed into a whole fleet of ships sailing below them. She looked down, but all she could see now was the sea mist passing over the water. The scene before her eyes changed constantly, but at long last the land whither they were flying appeared before them. Beautiful blue mountains with cedar-woods, towns and castles rose into view. Long before sunset Elise was sitting on a little rock in front of a large cave overgrown with delicate green creepers that looked like embroidered drapes.

'We shall see what you will dream of tonight,' said the youngest brother and showed her the little chamber where she was to sleep.

'If only I would dream how to set you free,' said Elise. This thought occupied her constantly, and she begged God most earnestly for His assistance, even in her sleep. Then it seemed to her she was flying high in the air to the airy castle of the fairy Morgana and there the beautiful, radiant fairy came to meet her. All the same she rather resembled the old woman who had given her berries in the forest, and told her of the swans with the royal crowns on their heads.

'It is possible to set your brothers free,' said she. 'But have you sufficient courage and patience? It is true the sea is softer than your delicate hands, and yet it can mould the hard stones to any shape, but the sea does not feel pain which your tender fingers will feel. The sea has no heart, it is not weighed by fear and anxiety which you shall have to endure. Do you see the stinging-nettle I hold in my hand? Many of these grow round the cave in which you sleep. You can use only these or the stinging-nettles which grow on the graves in the churchyard—remember that! You must pluck them, though they will sting your hand. You must trample on them with your feet, and get yarn from them. With this yarn you must weave eleven shirts with long sleeves, and if you then throw them over the eleven swans—the spell will be broken. But remember this; from the moment you commence the work till it is finished, you must not speak a single word, even if it takes years. The first word you utter will pierce the hearts of your brothers like a deadly dagger. Their life depends on your tongue. Remember all this well!'

At the same moment she touched Elise's hand with the nettle. As if burnt by fire, Elise awoke immediately. Already it was daylight, and close to her lay a nettle like the one she had seen in her dream. She fell upon her knees, thanked God and then went out of the cave to begin her task.

With her own delicate fingers she plucked the horrible nettles, which

burnt like fire. On her hands and arms painful blisters appeared, but she gladly bore the pain in the hope of setting her beloved brothers free. She trampled on all the nettles with her bare feet, and spun the green yarn.

At sunset her brothers came and they were frightened by her silence; they thought this must be the result of a new spell of their evil stepmother. But when they saw her blistered hands, they realized that what she was doing was for their sakes, and the youngest brother burst into tears. As his tears fell upon her hands, Elise felt no more pain and the painful blisters disappeared.

During the night she worked too, for she would have no peace until her dear brothers were freed. The whole of the next day, when the swans were away, she carried on with her work in solitude, yet never had time flown so quickly. One shirt was already completed; now she began the second.

Suddenly a hunting-horn rang out in the mountains which frightened Elise. The noise came nearer; she heard the barking of dogs. In terror she ran into the cave, bound up the nettles which she had gathered and combed into a bundle, and sat down on it.

Just then a large hound sprang out of the bushes, followed by another and yet another. They barked loudly, and ran back and then again forward. It did not take long before all the hunters were standing in front of the cave and the handsomest among them was the King of that country. He came over to Elise; never had he seen a maiden so beautiful.

'How came you to be here, you beautiful child?' said he. Elise only shook her head, for she dared not speak, when the life and the freedom of her brothers was at stake. She hid her hands under her apron, so that the King would not see how she was suffering.

'Come with me,' said the King, 'You must not stay here! If you are as good as you are beautiful, I will dress you in velvet and silk; I will place a gold crown upon your head and you will live in my palace!' And he lifted her upon his horse. Elise wept and wrung her hands, but the King said, 'I only want your happiness! You shall thank me for this one day!' And away he rode into the mountains. He held her in front of him on his horse, with the other hunters following.

As the sun was setting, the King's magnificent city appeared before them, with its churches and cupolas. The King led Elise into the palace where, in high marble halls, fountains were humming and on the walls and ceilings the most beautiful paintings were displayed. But Elise cared not for any of this and only wept and worried. She allowed herself to be dressed in royal robes, to have pearls woven in her hair and for soft gloves to be drawn over her blistered hands.

As she stood there in all her splendour, she was so dazzlingly beautiful that all the courtiers bowed low before her and the King chose her for his bride. The archbishop shook his head and whispered that the lovely maiden from the woods must surely be a witch, who had blinded their eyes and charmed the King's heart.

But the King took no notice. He ordered music to be played and the most selected foods to be brought and he told the loveliest maidens to dance around her. He led her through fragrant gardens into magnificent halls, yet not a sign of a smile was to be seen on her lips or in her eyes, only worry was mirrored there as her eternal heritage. Now the King opened the door of a little chamber next to her bedroom; it was adorned with precious green tapestries and exactly resembled the cave in which

she had lived. Upon the floor lay the bundle of yarn which she had spun from the nettles and high on the wall hung the shirt she had completed. All this had been brought by one of the hunters, as a special memory.

'Here you can give yourself to your dreams of your former home,' said the King. 'Here you have the work which occupied you there. In your present splendour it may please you to be able to fancy yourself there again.'

When Elise saw the objects so dear to her heart, a smile formed on her lips and the blood returned to her cheeks. She thought of her brothers' release and kissed the King's hand. He pressed Elise to his heart and ordered the bells of all the churches to be rung to announce their wedding. The lovely dumb maiden from the woods was to become the Queen.

The archbishop whispered evil words in the King's ear, but they reached not his heart. The wedding would take place and the archbishop himself had to place the crown upon Elise's head. With anger and unwillingness he pressed the narrow rim so hard on her forehead that it hurt her. But a far heavier weight lay in her heart, sorrow for her brothers, so that she did not feel this bodily pain. Her mouth remained speechless, for a single word would rob her brothers of life but her eyes expressed her deep love for the kind handsome King, who did all he could to please her. With each day her love for him grew. Oh, if only she could confide in him and tell him of her sorrows! But she had to remain silent and in silence complete her task. So each night she stole away from him to the tiny room fitted up like the cave in the woods; there she worked at the shirts, but when she began the seventh, she found she had no more yarn left.

She knew that the nettles she needed grew in the churchyard, and that she had to gather them herself. But how was she to get to them?

'What is the pain I feel in my hands in comparison to the anguish in my heart,' thought she. 'I must find courage to go. The good Lord shall not forsake me!' Fearfully, as though she was committing a crime, she crept into the garden one moonlit night, and walked through the long alleys and deserted streets to the churchyard. Suddenly she saw sitting on one of the broadest tombstones a group of witches, ugly and wild. They threw aside their ragged clothes as if about to bathe, then dug with their long skinny fingers into fresh tombs, digging up the dead bodies and eating their flesh. Elise was forced to pass close by them and the old witches fixed their evil eyes upon her, but Elise kept on praying, picked the stinging-nettles and carried them back to the palace.

One person only had seen her — the archbishop, who remained awake when the others were asleep. So he felt sure he was right when he thought that all was not as it should be with the Queen. She must be a witch, who through her charm had tricked the King and all the people.

In the Confessional he told the King what he had seen and what he feared. As the harsh words escaped from his lips, the sculptured images of the saints shook their heads, as if to say that this was not true, that Elise was innocent. But the archbishop explained this quite differently; he believed they were testifying against her and were shaking their heads at hearing of her sin. Two large tears rolled down the King's cheeks and he returned home with doubt in his heart. At night he pretended to sleep, but sleep he did not. He saw Elise rise from her bed, night after night. The King followed her secretly each time and saw her disappear in her little room.

With each day the King's face darkened. Elise saw this, but knew not the cause. Nevertheless it pained her, and how she also suffered because of her brothers! Her salty tears ran down on the royal velvet and purple, where they glittered like fiery diamonds, and all the women who saw this rich magnificence, yearned to be in her place. She had now almost finished her work, only one shirt was missing. But she had no more yarn, or a single nettle. Once again, for the very last time, she must go to the churchyard to pick a few handfuls of nettles.

She went, but the King and the archbishop followed behind and they saw her disappear at the churchyard gate. As they came near, they saw the witches sitting on the tombstones, as Elise had seen them, and the King turned away, for he believed the one whose head had rested that very evening on his chest, was among them.

'Let the people judge her!' said the King, and the people condemned her to be burnt.

She was now taken from the magnificent royal apartments to a dark, damp prison, where the wind whistled through the grated window. Instead of velvet and silk she was given the bundle of nettles she had gathered as a pillow for her head. The hard shirts she had woven were to be her cover. But they could not have given her a more valuable gift. So she continued her work, praying to God at the same time. Outside the street boys sang dreadful songs about her. There was no one to console her with a single kind word.

But one evening she heard the rustling of a swan's wing at the grating. It was the youngest of the brothers, who found his sister at last. Elise sobbed aloud for joy, though she knew that the coming night would probably be her last night on earth. But now her work was almost completed, and the brothers were here.

The archbishop came to spend the last hour with her. He promised the King he would do this. But she only shook her head and entreated him with looks and gestures to go away. That night she had to finish her work, otherwise all her suffering would have been in vain; the pain, the anxiety, the tears, the sleepless nights. The archbishop left her with angry words, but poor Elise knew she was innocent, and carried on with her work.

Little mice darted about the floor, dragging the nettles to her feet, trying to help her. A thrush perched on the iron bar of the window, and sang as merrily as he could right through the night, that Elise might not lose courage.

When it was twilight, a short hour before sunrise, the eleven brothers were standing by the palace gate, demanding to be taken to the King. But they were told that this could not be, for it was still night, the King was asleep and he gave orders for no one to wake him. They begged, they threatened, the guards appeared and then the King himself stepped out to see what was going on. But all at once the sun rose and the brothers were nowhere to be seen, only eleven swans flying above the palace.

People swarmed from the gates of the city, eager to see the witch being burnt. A skinny old horse pulled the cart in which she sat. They had dressed her in a coarse frock of sackcloth, her beautiful long hair hung loose, framing her lovely face, her cheeks were deathly pale, her lips moved wordlessly, her fingers worked the green yarn. Even on the way to her death she did not forsake her task. The ten shirts lay at her feet as she was making the eleventh. The rabble mocked her.

'Look at the witch, how she mutters! There is no hymn-book in her hand, but there she sits with her accursed work! Tear it, tear it into a thousand pieces!'

And they all crowded round and would have torn the shirts apart, but all at once the eleven white swans appeared. They settled round her on the cart, flapping their wings and the crowd stepped back in terror.

'It is a sign from Heaven! She must be innocent!' many whispered, but they dared not say so aloud.

The executioner now seized her by the hand but by then Elise had swiftly thrown the shirts over the swans and eleven handsome Princes appeared in their place. The youngest one, though, had only one arm and a wing instead of the other, for one sleeve was missing on his shirt, which his sister had no time to finish.

'Now I can speak,' said she. 'I am innocent!'

And the people who had witnessed what had happened, bowed before her as before a saint. Elise, however, collapsed lifeless in her brothers' arms. She was so exhausted with suspense, fear and grief.

'Yes, she is innocent!' said the eldest brother, and told all that had happened. Whilst he was speaking, a fragrance of millions of roses spread around, for every piece of wood in the funeral pile had taken root and sent forth shoots, till an enormous rose tree with scarlet blooms appeared. Higher than the others blossomed a rose dazzlingly white, shining as brightly as a star. The King picked it and placed it on Elise's bosom, and she awoke from her swoon and her heart filled with peace and joy.

And all the church bells started to ring of their own accord, and birds swarmed to the spot. The return to the palace was a festive procession, such as no King has ever seen.

The Snow Queen

FIRST STORY
The Mirror and its Fragments

Now then, let us start. When we get to the end of the story, we shall know more than we know now. It is about a wicked magician. He was one of the wickedest of all, a real demon!

One day he made a mirror which had the magic power of making everything good and beautiful that looked into it, shrink almost to nothing; but all the things which were useless and ugly were thoroughly magnified and grew even worse. The loveliest landscapes reflected in this mirror would look like boiled spinach and the very nicest people would turn ugly or would stand on their heads without any stomachs, and their faces would be so distorted that no one could recognise them. Moreover, if one of them had a freckle, he could be sure that in the mirror it would spread all over his nose and mouth. This was most entertaining, thought the demon. If a kindly, pious thought passed through someone's head, the mirror showed such a grimace, that the demon couldn't help but roar at his magnificent invention.

All those who went to the School of Magic—for he had his own School of Magic—said to everyone that a miracle had happened. For the first time, they said, one could see what the world and the people really looked like. They ran with the mirror from place to place throughout the world, and in the end there wasn't a country, or a man left who had not been distorted in it. Then they decided to fly up to Heaven, to make fun of the angels and God himself. The higher they flew with the mirror, the more the mirror grimaced, till they could hardly hold on to it. Then all at once the mirror, grinning devilishly, started to shake so much, that it shot out of their hands and crashed to the ground, where it broke into hundreds of millions, billions, and even more little pieces. And this is why it caused even more unhappiness than before, for some of the fragments were hardly larger than a grain of sand and they flew about in the world. When they got into people's eyes, they stuck fast there, and the people saw everything the wrong way, or they had eyes only for what was bad. For each tiny fragment of the mirror had retained the same power that the whole mirror had had. Some people even got a tiny splinter of the mirror wedged in their hearts, and this was indeed dreadful. Such a heart would then be like a lump of ice. Some pieces were large enough to be used as window-panes, but it was a mistake to look through them at your friends. Other pieces found their way into the glass of spectacles, and then everything went wrong when the people put their glasses on in order to see properly and fairly.

The wicked demon laughed and laughed, till his sides ached — it was most enjoyable the way it tickled.

There are still some little splinters of the glass flying about in the air. And now, listen to this!

SECOND STORY
A Little Boy and a Little Girl

In a large town, where there are so many houses and people that there is not enough room for everyone to have their own little garden, and where most people therefore have to be content with flowers in pots, there in that town lived two poor children, whose garden was somewhat larger than a flower-pot. They were not brother and sister, but they loved each other just as much. Their parents were neighbours, and lived opposite in two attics; and where the roof of one house touched the other and where the gutter ran along between, there was a tiny window jutting out of each house. You only had to step across the gutter to get from one window to the other.

The parents of these children each had a large wooden box standing outside their window, in which they grew the herbs they needed, and also a little rose-tree. There was one in each box and it grew beautifully. The parents then had the idea of placing their boxes across the gutter in such a way, that they almost reached from window to window and looked exactly like two flower-beds. Pea vines hung down over the boxes, and the little rose-trees were shooting out, entwining their long shoots round the windows, bending over to each other. It looked like a festive arch of greenery and flowers. As the wooden boxes were rather high, and the children knew they must not climb on them, they were now and then allowed to step out through the window to each other and to sit on the little stools under the rose-trees. It was so pleasant for them to play there together.

The winter, of course, put an end to such pleasures. The windows were quite often frozen up and then the children would heat coins on the stove, and, pressing them against the frozen pane, would make little peepholes, clear and round. And behind each of them a bright little eye would sparkle.

The boy was called Kay and the little girl's name was Gerda. In summer they could get to each other in a single leap from the window but in winter they first had to run down so many stairs, and then climb all the way up again, while outside a snowstorm raged.

'White bees are swarming out there!' said the old grandmother.

'Have they a queen bee?' asked the little boy, for he knew that real bees have one.

'Indeed they have!' the grandmother replied. 'She flies in the thickest of the swarm. She is the biggest of them all, and never stays quietly on the ground, but flies up into the black cloud again. Many a wintry night she flies through the streets of the town and peers through the windows, and then the windows freeze in a strange, wondrous way, as if they were flowers.'

'Yes, I have seen them!' both the children cried, knowing now that this was true.

'And can the Snow Queen come in to us?' asked the little girl.

'Do let her come!' said the little boy. 'Then I'll put her on the hot stove, and she will melt.'

But the grandmother stroked his head and told them other stories.

That evening, when little Kay was back home and half undressed, he climbed on to the stool by the window and peeped out through the little hole. A few snowflakes fell outside just then and one of these—the largest one—came to rest on the edge of one of the wooden flower-boxes. The snowflake grew and grew, and in the end it took the form of a woman dressed in the finest white veils, which seemed to be made of millions of

shining starry flakes. She was extremely beautiful and grand, but she was made of ice, glittering, dazzling ice — yet she was alive. Her eyes shone like two bright stars, but there was no rest nor repose in them. She nodded towards the window and beckoned with her hand. The little boy grew frightened and jumped off the stool and, at that moment, it seemed that some big bird flew past the window.

The next day the frost bit hard, but soon afterwards it thawed, and then came spring — the sun shone, green shoots sprang from the ground, the swallows built their nests, the windows were opened and the children sat down again in their little garden in the gutter high up in the roofs.

The roses blossomed beautifully that summer. The little girl had learnt a hymn in which there was something about roses; it reminded her of her own. And she sang this hymn to the little boy and he sang with her:

'We'll hear little Jesus down below
In the valley, where sweet roses grow!'

And both the children held each other by the hand, kissed the roses, and gazed into God's bright sunshine, talking to it, as if little Jesus himself was there. What lovely summer days these were and how delightful it was to sit together by the rose-trees, which seemed as though they would never stop blooming!

One day Kay and Gerda were sitting outside, examining a picture-book of animals and birds, when, just as the clock in the high church tower was striking five, Kay said: 'Oh dear! What's this sharp pain in my heart! And now I've got something in my eye!'

The little girl put her arms round his neck. Kay blinked his eyes. No, there was nothing to be seen.

'I think it's gone!' he said. But gone it had not. It was one of the glass-splinters from the magic mirror; you remember, that horrid glass which made everything big and good that was reflected in it become small and nasty, while everything mean and ugly became magnified and every fault became plain to seen at once. Poor Kay! A little splinter also got right into his heart. Shortly it would turn into a lump of ice. It hurt no more now, but the glass was there.

'Why are you crying?' asked Kay. 'It makes you so ugly! There's nothing wrong with me! Ugh!' he cried suddenly, 'this rose is all worm-eaten! And look, that one is all lop-sided. How ugly these roses really are! They're like the boxes they're growing in!' Then he kicked the box hard and tore off both roses.

'Kay, what are you doing!' cried the little girl. When he saw how it grieved her, he pulled off another rose and ran in through his window, away from kind little Gerda.

After this, whenever Gerda came to him with the picture-book he said it was for babies, and whenever the grandmother told stories, he interrupted her with some 'but' or another. And whenever he had the chance, he would hide behind her, put on her spectacles and speak just as she did. He imitated her perfectly, and this made people laugh at him. Very soon he could mimic all the people in the street. He would imitate anything that was odd or not very nice about them, and so people said, 'That lad has a remarkable head on his shoulders!' But it was the work of the glass in his eye, and the glass that was wedged in his heart. This was why he tormented even little Gerda, who loved him with all her heart.

One winter's day, when the snowflakes were tumbling down, he came out with a large magnifying glass in his hand, and holding out his blue coat-tail, he let the snowflakes fall on to it.

'Look in the glass, Gerda!' he said. Each flake now was much larger and looked like an exquisite flower, or a ten-pointed star. It was indeed a beautiful sight.

'Isn't it extraordinary!' said Kay. 'These are far more interesting than real flowers! And there isn't a single blemish in them, they are absolutely perfect — so long as they don't melt!'

Soon after this Kay came back wearing thick mittens and carrying a sledge on his back. He shouted right into Gerda's ear, 'I've been allowed to sledge in the big square where the others are playing!' and he was gone.

The boldest boys in the square often tied their sledges to the farmer's cart, and thus rode a good way along with him. This was great fun. When they were at the height of their enjoyment, along came a big sleigh. It was painted white and the person sitting in it was wrapped in a rough white fur coat and wore a rough white fur cap. The sledge drove twice round the square, and by then Kay managed to tie his little sledge to it—and now he was being pulled along. Faster and faster they rode, making straight for the nearest street. The person who drove the large sleigh kept turning round, nodding kindly to Kay, as if they had known each other of old. Whenever Kay tried to untie his sledge, the driver would nod again, and so Kay stayed put. They drove right out of the city gates. And then the snow started to fall so thickly and so fast, that the boy could not see his own hand, as they tore along. So he let go of the rope, trying to free himself from the large sleigh. But it was no use; his sledge held on fast, and flew like the wind. So he started to shout, shout loudly, but no one heard him and the sleigh went racing on through the snow-storm. From time to time his little sledge gave a jump, as though passing over ditches and hedges. He was really terrified, and he so wanted to say the prayer 'Our Father', but all he could remember was the multiplication table.

The snowflakes grew bigger and bigger, till in the end they looked like big white hens. All at once they flew to one side, the sleigh stopped and the driver stood up. The fur coat and cap were entirely of snow, and the person who wore them was a lady, tall and slender, and dazzlingly white—it was the Snow Queen!

'We have driven far,' she said. 'But how freezing it is! Wrap yourself in my bearskin coat!' And she sat him in the sleigh by her side, and wrapped her coat around him; he felt as if he were sinking into a snowdrift.

'Are you still cold?' she asked, and then kissed his forehead. Ugh! That kiss was colder than ice and went straight to his heart, which was already half ice. He thought he should die, but only for a moment, then he felt better for it, and no longer felt the cold.

'My sledge! Don't forget my sledge!' he remembered it first. And his sledge was tied to one of the white hens which flew behind with the sledge on her back. The Snow Queen kissed Kay once more, and he forgot little Gerda, her grandmother, and everyone at home.

'Now you will not have any more kisses!' said the Snow Queen, 'or I'll kiss you to death!'

Kay looked at her. She was so beautiful! He could not imagine a wiser and lovelier face. She no longer appeared to him to be of ice, as when she had sat outside the window, beckoning him. In his eyes she was perfect, and he felt no fear. He told her how well he could count in his head and that he could do fractions, and that he knew how many square miles each country had and how many inhabitants. And all the time she smiled. It occurred to him then that all he knew was not, after all, enough, and he gazed up into the great wide space above. And the Queen flew with him, rising high above the black cloud, while the storm raged and roared, as if it were singing some old, old songs. They flew over forests and lakes, over seas and lands. Beneath them the cold wind whistled, the wolves howled, the snow glittered and over the plain flew black, screeching crows. High above shone the moon, so big and bright and Kay watched it through the long, long winter's night. During the day he slept at the feet of the Snow Queen.

THIRD STORY
The Flower Garden of the Woman who Knew Magic

But what happened to little Gerda, when Kay did not return? Where could he be? No one knew, no one could explain. The boys could only say that they had seen him fasten his sledge to a beautiful large sleigh, which had driven off into the street and then through the city gates. No one knew where he could be and many tears were shed; little Gerda cried so much and for so long. Then they said that he must be dead, that he must have been drowned in the river which flowed past the town. Oh, what long, gloomy winter days these were!

At last came the spring with its warm sunshine.

'Kay is dead and gone!' said little Gerda.

'This I do not believe!' said the sunshine.

'He is dead and gone!' said she to the swallows.

'This we do not believe!' replied the swallows, and in the end little Gerda herself did not believe it.

'I will put on my new red shoes,' she said one morning; 'the ones which Kay has never seen. Then I'll go down to the river and ask after him.'

It was early morning. She kissed her old grandmother, who was asleep, put on the red shoes and went out alone through the gates of the town to the river.

'Is it true that you have taken my little playmate from me?' said she. 'I will give you my red shoes, if you return him to me!'

And the waves seemed to be beckoning to her strangely. So she took off her red shoes, the dearest things she had, and threw them both into the river. But they fell close to the shore and the ripples brought them straight back to her on the bank. It seemed the river did not want to accept the dearest things she had, now that she no longer had little Kay. But Gerda thought she had not thrown the little shoes far enough, so she stepped into a little boat which lay among the rushes and, standing at the farthest end of it, she threw the shoes into the water. But the boat was not tied up, and her jerky movement made it float away from the bank. Gerda swiftly tried to get back on shore, but before she was able to do so the boat was more than a yard out and was floating away faster and faster.

Little Gerda was terribly frightened and she started to cry, but no one heard her but the sparrows. And they could not carry her ashore, but they flew along the bank, twittering as if to comfort her: 'Here we are, here we are!' The boat raced with the current. Little Gerda sat in it perfectly still in her stockinged feet. Her little red shoes floated behind the boat, but they could not reach it, for the boat glided on faster than they did.

Beautiful were the banks of that river, with exquisite flowers, old trees, and hillsides dotted with sheep and cows; but there was not a single person to be seen.

'Perhaps the river will take me to little Kay,' thought Gerda and she became more cheerful, stood up and gazed for many a long hour at the beautiful green shores. In time she came to a big cherry orchard, in which stood a little house with curious red and blue windows and a thatched roof. Two wooden soldiers stood in front of the house, their guns pointing at anyone who happened to sail by.

Gerda called to them, thinking that they were alive, but of course they did not answer. She came quite near to them, for the current carried the little boat to the land.

Gerda called louder still, whereupon an old woman came out of the house, leaning on a stick. On her head she wore a large sun-hat, with most beautiful flowers painted on it.

'My poor little child,' said the old woman, 'however did you get on that great, strong stream, which has carried you far into the wide, wide world?' And the old woman stepped right into the water, hooked her stick on to the boat, pulled it ashore, and lifted little Gerda out.

And Gerda was happy to be on dry land, though she was a little afraid of the strange old woman.

'Come and tell me who you are, and how you came to be here!' said she.

And Gerda told her everything. The old woman shook her head and said, 'Hm, hm!' And when Gerda had finished and asked whether she had seen little Kay, the old woman said that he had not passed by, but that he would surely come; and Gerda should stop being so unhappy, and should taste her cherries and look at her flowers, which were more beautiful than in any picture-book—and each could tell her a story. Then she took little Gerda by the hand and they went together into the little house, the old woman locking the door behind them.

The windows were very high and their panes were red, blue and yellow.

In them daylight shone in all colours—it was something truly beautiful. And on the table some lovely cherries were placed, and Gerda could eat as many as she liked. And while she was eating, the old woman combed her hair with a golden comb, and the hair curled and shone so beautifully golden round her gentle little face, which was so round and as fresh as a rose.

'I have longed for a lovely little girl like you!' said the old woman. 'Now you will see how well we two are going to get on!' And as she combed Gerda's hair, Gerda thought less and less of her playmate Kay, for the old lady was well versed in magic, though she was not a wicked sorceress; she practised magic only for her own amusement and now she wished very much to keep little Gerda. She therefore went into the garden, pointed her stick at all the rose-trees and all the roses; no matter how beautifully they were blooming, they all instantly sank down into the black earth and no one would have guessed that they had ever grown there. The old lady was afraid that if Gerda looked at roses, she would remember her own, and little Kay, and would run away.

Then she led Gerda into the flower garden. Oh, how fragrantly it smelt, how beautiful it was! Every imaginable flower from all the four seasons grew there with the most exquisite blooms. No picture-book could have been more colourful or beautiful. Gerda skipped for joy and played among the flowers, till the sun set behind the tall cherry-trees. And then she was given a lovely little bed with crimson silk eiderdowns, stuffed with blue violets. Gerda fell asleep and had such beautiful dreams as a queen might have on her wedding day.

The next day she was again allowed to play with the flowers in the warm sunshine and so many a day passed. Gerda knew every little flower in the garden, but no matter how many there were, she felt there was one missing—though she could not tell which one. Then one day she was sitting, looking against the sun at the old woman's wide hat with the flowers painted on it, and the most beautiful among them was a rose! The old woman had forgotten to take off the rose from her hat, when she made all the others disappear into the ground. This often happens when things are done in haste.

'How is it,' said Gerda, 'that there are no roses here?' And she ran among the beds and searched and searched, but she did not find a single rose. And she sat down and cried. Her hot tears happened to fall on the very spot where a rose tree had disappered into the ground. As the tears moistened the soil, the tree suddenly sprang up, as fresh and blooming as before. Gerda threw her arms around it, kissing the roses, and thought of the lovely blooms at home, and with them of little Kay.

'Oh, how could I have forgotten for so long!' cried the little girl. 'I set out to find Kay! Don't you know where he is?' she asked the roses. 'Do you think he is dead and that he will never return to me?'

'He is not dead!' said the roses. 'We have been in the ground, and that is where all the dead are, but Kay is not among them!'

'Thank you!' said little Gerda. Then she went over to the other flowers, looked deep into their cups and asked, 'Don't you know where little Kay is?'

But every flower was sunning itself, dreaming its own story or fairy-tale. Little Gerda could hear as many of these as she wished, but not one of them knew anything about Kay.

What did the tiger-lily say?

'Can you hear the drum? Bum-bum! It has only two notes, always: bum, bum! Listen to the women's lament! Listen to the chorus, of the priests! The Hindu woman stands in her long scarlet robe on the funeral fire, the flames leaping around her and around her dead husband. But the Hindu woman thinks only of the living person who stands there in the crowd, the man whose eyes burn more fiercely than the flames, the man whose eyes set her heart on fire more than the flames which shortly will turn her body to ashes. Can the flame of the heart die in the flames of the funeral fire?'

'I do not understand that at all!' said little Gerda.

'That is my fairy-tale!' said the tiger-lily.

'What says the convolvulus?'

'High above a narrow mountain path towers an ancient castle. Thick evergreens cover its old red walls, twining leaf by leaf all the way to the balcony; and there stands a lovely maiden. She leans over the balustrades, her eyes fixed on the path. No rose hangs more freshly on its spray than she, no apple-blossom carried far from the tree by the wind trembles more than she. How her magnificent silky robe rustles! 'Will my dearest one never come?' says she.

'Is it Kay you mean?' asked little Gerda.

'I speak only of my fairy-story, of my dream,' replied the convolvulus. 'What says the little snowdrop?'

'Between two trees on strong ropes hangs a long board, a swing. Two pretty little girls are swinging on it, their dresses as white as snow and with long green silk ribbons fluttering from their hats. Their brother, who is bigger than they, is standing on the swing, his arm round the rope to keep himself steady, for in one hand he has a little cup and in the other a straw—he is blowing soap bubbles. The swing swings and the bubbles fly away. The last still hangs to the edge of the straw, bending in the wind. The swing swings on. A little black dog, as light as the bubbles, stands up on its hind legs, and wants to get on to the swing, too. Away flies the swing, the dog flops down and barks angrily. The bubbles burst; a swinging board, a fleeting picture of a bubble—that is my song!'

'Maybe that what you tell is beautiful, but you tell it so sadly and you don't mention Kay at all. What say the hyacinths?'

'There were three lovely sisters, transparent and delicate they were. One had a red dress, the second blue, and the third pure white. Hand in hand they danced by the silent lake in the clear moonlight. They were not fairies, but daughters of men. There was such a sweet fragrance there, and the girls disappeared into the wood; the fragrance grew stronger still. Three coffins, with the three lovely maidens inside, glided from the wood's thicket on to the lake. Fireflies flew around like little glittering, hovering lamps. Sleep the dancing maidens, or are they dead? The scent of the flowers says that they are dead. The evening bells peal out for them!'

'You're making me quite sad!' said little Gerda. 'You have such a strong smell! I have to keep thinking of the dead maidens. Can little Kay really be dead? The roses have been under the earth, and they say 'No!'

'Ding, dong!' rang out the hyacinth bells. 'We are not ringing for little Kay, we don't know him! We are only singing our song, the only song we know!'

And Gerda went over to the buttercup, which shone brightly from among its glistening green leaves.

'You are like a little bright sun!' said Gerda. 'Tell me, if you can, where to find my little playmate.'

And the buttercup glittered so beautifully and looked at Gerda again. What song would the buttercup sing? But that too had nothing to do with Kay.

'On the first day of spring, God's sun shone warmly upon a little court-yard. The beams were sliding down the white walls of a neighbour's house; growing close to it were the first yellow blossoms, glittering like gold in the warm sunshine. An old grandmother sat outside in her rocking chair, her granddaughter, a pretty but poor servant girl, had just come home from a short visit. She kissed her grandmother; there was gold, heart's gold in that loving kiss, gold on the lips, gold in the heart, gold in the bright first morning light! These three golds make me strong and bold! There, that is my little story!' said the buttercup.

'My poor old grandmother!' sighed Gerda. 'Yes, she must be missing me and wishing for me, just as she wished for and missed little Kay. But I shall soon return home, and bring Kay with me. It is no use asking the flowers, they only know their own little songs, they can't give me a proper answer!' And so she tucked up her little skirt so as to be able to run faster.

But as she jumped over a narcissus, it caught her leg. So she stopped, looked at the tall yellow flower and said, 'Have you, perhaps, anything to tell me?' and she stooped down to the narcissus. And what did it say?

'I can see myself, I can see myself! Oh, oh, how sweetly I smell! Upstairs, in a tiny attic room, stands a little dancing-girl, half dressed. First she stands on one leg, then on both, kicking out at the whole world. She herself is nothing but an illusion. She pours water from the teapot on to a piece of material she is holding in her hand—it is her bodice. Cleanliness is a worthwhile thing! Her white dress hangs on a hook, it too has been washed and dried on the roof. The girl puts the dress on and ties a saffron-yellow scarf round her neck; this makes the whiteness of the dress stand out even more. Leg up! See how she stands on one stalk! I can see myself! I can see myself!'

'I don't really care if you do!' said Gerda. 'Such talk is not for me!' And with that she ran to the edge of the garden.

The gate was shut, but Gerda worked at the rusty lock till it loosened and the gate sprang open and then little Gerda ran out barefoot into the wide world. Three times she looked round, but there was no one following her. In the end she could run no more, and she sat down on a large stone. And when she glanced round, she found that the summer was gone and it was already late autumn. This was not apparent in the lovely garden, where there was always sunshine and where flowers bloomed all the year round.

'Oh dear, how I've been delayed!' said little Gerda. 'Why, it's autumn already! Now I mustn't rest!' And she rose and went on her way.

Oh, how sore and tired her little feet were, how cold and raw were her surroundings! The long willow-leaves had already turned yellow, and the dew ran down them in large drops; the leaves were falling off the trees, one by one; only the sloe still bore fruit, but the berries were so sharp it set one's teeth on edge.

Oh, how grey and gloomy was the big wide world to her that day!

FOURTH STORY
The Prince and the Princess

Gerda was forced to rest again. Suddenly a large raven hopped along the snow to where she sat. For a long time he just gazed at her intently, wagging his head. Then he said, 'Caw! Caw! 'ello! ello!' He couldn't say it better, but he meant the little girl well and asked where she was going to all alone in the big wide world. How well Gerda understood the word 'alone', how well she knew its sad meaning! She told the raven her whole story and asked if he had seen Kay.

And the raven nodded his head and said, 'Perhaps yes, perhaps yes!'

'What are you saying?' cried the little girl, nearly squeezing the raven to death, so hard did she kiss him.

'Now be sensible, sensible!' said the raven. 'I think it could be little Kay! But I certainly believe he has forgotten you for the Princess!'

'Does Kay live with a Princess?' asked Gerda.

'Why, yes!' said the raven. 'But it is so hard for me to talk in your language. Do you understand raven speech? If so, I can talk much better!'

'No, that I have never learnt,' said Gerda. 'But my grandmother knew it. She also knew the secret language. How I wish I'd learnt!'

'It doesn't matter!' said the raven, 'I will talk as best as I can, though it's bound to be frightful!' And he told her all he knew.

'In the kingdom where we are now lives a Princess, who is truly clever; but then she reads all the newspapers in the world, and then forgets them again, that is how clever she is. The other day she was sitting on the throne — and they say it is not much fun at all — and she began to hum a song, which goes like this: 'Why shouldn't I get married! There's some sense in that!' said she, and so she decided she would get married. But she wanted a husband who would know how to answer when spoken to; one who wouldn't just stand, looking high and mighty, for that sort of thing is such a bore. So she asked the drummers to bring all the court ladies together, and when they heard what the Princess wanted, they were really delighted. 'I really like that,' and 'I was thinking the same only the other day,' they said. 'Believe me, that every word I say now is true!' said the raven. 'I have a tame sweetheart, who walks about the palace freely and she told me all this!'

His sweetheart, of course, was another raven, for birds of a feather flock together, and so it had to be a raven for a raven.

'The newspapers came out at once, edged with a border of hearts and with the Princess's monogram. They said that any young man who was good-looking was free to go to the palace and talk to the Princess. The one who would show himself most at home in the palace, and who could speak the best with her, would be chosen by the Princess for her husband.'

'Oh yes!' said the raven, 'It is as true as I am standing here.'

'People poured to the palace, there was so much pushing and shoving, but nobody had any luck the first nor the second day. They all could speak well enough outside in the streets, but the moment they went through the palace gates and saw the royal guard all in silver and then the lackeys on the staircase in gold, and the huge brightly lit halls, they were dumbfounded. An when they stood before the throne where the Princess sat, they couldn't even mutter a single word, except to repeat the last word she had uttered. The Princess, of course, wasn't in the least interested to hear it again. It was as though the men had snuff stuffed into their tummies, and were in a trance. But once they were back in the street again, they talked then alright! There was a long queue stretching from the city gates to the palace. I went myself to have a look! They were hungry and thirsty, but nobody from the palace gave them as much as a glass of water. A few, the cleverest ones, did bring some bread and butter, but they didn't share it with their neighbours, but thought to themselves, 'Let him look hungry, then the Princess won't want him!'

'But Kay, what about little Kay?' asked Gerda. 'When did he come? Was he in the crowd?'

'Patience, patience! We are just coming to him! It was on the third day that a little man arrived without a horse or carriage, and he marched bravely straight to the palace. His eyes shone like yours and he had lovely long hair, but otherwise he was poorly dressed.'

'That was Kay!' cried the delighted Gerda. 'Oh, so I have found him at last!' And she clapped her hands with happiness.

'He carried a bundle on his back,' said the raven.

'No, that would be his sledge,' said Gerda. 'You see he left home with a sledge!'

'It is possible it was a sledge!' said the raven. 'I didn't look too thoroughly. But I do know from my tame, beloved raven, that when he walked through the palace gates and saw the royal guards in silver, and on the staircase the lackeys in gold, he wasn't in the least put off, but nodded to them in a friendly manner and said, 'It must be boring to stand on the stairs. I'm going inside!' The halls were flooded with lights. Cabinet councillors and their excellencies were walking about barefooted, carrying golden trays. It was just the place to make anyone feel solemn. The boy's shoes creaked horribly, yet he wasn't frightened, not in the least!'

'That most certainly was Kay!' said Gerda. 'I know he had new shoes, I have heard them creaking in my grandmother's parlour!'

'Yes, they creaked alright!' said the raven. 'And the boy went up cheerfully to the Princess, who was sitting upon a pearl as large as a spinning-wheel. All the court ladies with their maids and the maids' maids, and all the gentlemen with their servants and the servants' servants, who also had their pages, were standing all around. The nearer they were to the door, the more self-conscious they looked. One would hardly dare look at a servants' servants' page, who always walks about in slippers, so proudly he stands in the door!'

'That must be frightful!' said little Gerda. 'And did Kay win the Princess?'

'If I hadn't been a raven, I should have won her myself, though I am engaged. They say he talked as well as I talk when I converse in raven speech. This I know from my beloved. He was plucky and bright. He had not come to woo the Princess, only to hear how clever she was; and he found she truly was clever, while the Princess in turn found him clever too!'

'To be sure, that was Kay!' said Gerda. 'He was so clever, he could do mental arithmetic, even fractions! Oh, please be kind and take me to the palace!'

'That's easily said!' said the raven, 'but not so easily done. I'll speak about it with my beloved, perhaps she will advise us. For I may as well tell you that a little girl such as you must never show herself there officially!'

'But I want to go there!' said Gerda. 'When Kay hears that I am here, he will come out straightaway and take me inside!'

'Wait for me by those steps!' said the raven, and he flew off, wagging his head.

The raven did not return till the evening, when it was dark. 'Caw, caw!' he cried. 'My beloved sends you her love! And here is a piece of bread for you, she took it from the kitchen; they have plenty of bread, and you must be hungry! There is no chance of you getting into the palace. You have bare feet. The guards in silver and the lackeys in gold wouldn't allow it. But don't cry; you will get there. My sweetheart knows a little back staircase which leads to the bedroom, and she also knows where to get the key!'

And together they went into the garden, down the grand avenue where leaf after leaf fell off the trees. And when the palace lights went out, one by one, the raven led little Gerda to a back door, which was ajar.

Oh, how Gerda's heart hammered with fear and longing! It was as though she was about to do something wrong and yet all she wanted was to be sure whether little Kay was really there. Surely it would be him! She remembered so clearly his wise eyes, his long hair. She could see him smile as he used to when they sat together at home under the roses. He would surely be happy to see her and to hear what a long journey she had undertaken for his sake, and to learn how broken-hearted everyone was at home when he failed to return. Oh, this was fear and joy all in one.

They came to the staircase. A little lamp burnt on a cupboard. In the middle of the floor stood the tame raven, turning her head in all directions and looking at Gerda.

'My fiancé has told me so much about you, my little lady,' said the tame raven. 'Your life's adventures, as one can say, are so touching! Do please take the lamp, and I'll lead the way. We'll go the straight way, there we shan't meet anyone!'

'It seems as if someone were following us!' said Gerda, as something swished near. It was like shadows along the wall, horses with flowing manes and slender legs, huntsmen, ladies and gentlemen on horseback.

'Those are only dreams!' said the tame raven. 'They come to fetch the noble people's thoughts. That is a good thing, for then you will be able to observe them better in bed. I do hope that when you find such honour and favour, you will show a thankful heart!'

'There's no need to talk like that,' said the raven from the wood.

Now they entered the first hall. The walls were covered in rose-coloured satin, embroidered with beautiful flowers. Here the dreams rushed past them so swiftly that Gerda did not catch even a glimpse of the noble people. Each hall was more magnificent than the last and filled Gerda with awe. At last they reached the bedchamber. The ceiling looked like a big palm with leaves of precious glass; in the centre of the room were two beds on a pillar of gold, and these were in the form of lilies. One was white, and in this lay the Princess. The other was red, and in this Gerda hoped to find little Kay. She pushed aside one of the red leaves, and saw a brown neck. Oh, it was Kay! Aloud she called out his name, holding the lamp close to his head and all at once the dreams swept back into the room on their horses. He awoke, turned his head . . . but it was not little Kay.

The Prince resembled him only about the neck, though he was young and handsome. And from the white lily-bed the Princess looked out and asked what was the matter. Then little Gerda wept and told her the whole story and all the two ravens had done for her.

'You poor child!' said the Prince and the Princess; they praised the ravens, saying that they were not in the least cross with them, as long as they did not make a habit of doing that sort of thing. But this time they must be rewarded.

'Would you like your freedom?' asked the Princess. 'Or would you like to become the Court ravens, and live on the abundance of the kitchen scraps?'

And both the ravens curtsied and chose to stay at Court. They were thinking of their old age, and said it would be nice to be comfortable in 'the twilight of their lives,' as they put it.

Then the Prince got out of his bed and made Gerda sleep in it. Gerda clasped her little hands together and thought, 'How kind men and animals are to me!' Then she closed her eyes and slept happily. All the dreams came flying back, and now they looked like angels of God, pulling a sledge with Kay on it, nodding to her. But it was only a dream and the moment she awoke, it vanished.

The next day she was dressed from head to toe in silk and velvet. She was invited to stay at the palace, where she would surely enjoy herself. But Gerda only begged for a little carriage with a horse, and a pair of little boots, so she could drive off again into the wide world in her search for her dearest Kay.

She was given both boots and a muff. When she was ready to leave, a new carriage of pure gold drove up to the door with the coat of arms of the Prince and Princess glittering upon it like a star. The coachman, footmen, and postilions—for postilions were there too—all wore gold crowns. The Prince and Princess helped her into the carriage and wished her good luck. The raven from the wood, who was now married to his beloved, accompanied her for the first three miles. He sat next to her, for he couldn't bear to travel with his back to the horses. The other raven stood at the gate flapping her wings; she did not go with them, for her head hurt from living so well and eating so well! In the coach was a pile of sugar biscuits and under the seat were fruit and ginger-nuts.

'Farewell! Farewell!' cried the Prince and the Princess, and little Gerda cried, and the raven cried too. So they passed the first few miles. Then the raven, too, bade her goodbye, and this was the hardest parting of all. The raven flew up into a tree and flapped his black wings for as long as the coach, which gleamed like the bright sun, was still in sight.

FIFTH STORY
The Little Robber-Girl

They drove through the dark forest, and the carriage shone like a flame. Its brilliance attracted the notice of some robbers and the fierce glow burnt into the robbers' eyes, so that they could not bear it.

'That is gold! Gold!' they cried, and rushing forward from the forest, they stopped the horses, killed the postilions, the coachman and the footmen, and then pulled little Gerda out of the carriage.

'She's beautifully plump, she's been fattened on nut kernels!' said the old robber-woman, who had a long bristly beard and eyebrows hanging down over her eyes. 'She'll be as delicious as a little fat lamb! What a feast she'll make!' And she drew out her polished knife and the knife glittered most menacingly.

'Ooh!' the old hag suddenly cried out. She had been bitten in the ear by her own little daughter, who was clinging to her back and who was as wild and naughty as anything. 'You horrid child!' shouted the mother, missing the chance of cutting Gerda's throat. 'Let her play with me!' said the little robber-girl. 'Let her give me her muff and her nice dress, let her sleep in my bed with me!' And she bit hard again, making the old robber-woman leap into the air and twist round and round. All the robbers laughed and cried, 'Look how she dances with her youngster!'

'I want to go in the coach!' said the robber-girl, stamping her feet. And she got her own way, for she was terribly spoilt and stubborn. She climbed in with Gerda, and off they drove over bramble and stubble deeper into the forest. The little robber-girl was about as tall as Gerda, but stronger, broader, and with a darker skin. Her eyes were quite black, and almost sad. She put her arm round little Gerda's waist and said, 'They won't kill you as long as I don't get angry with you! I expect you're a Princess?'

'No, I am not,' Gerda replied, and she told her about everything that had happened and how very much she loved little Kay.

The robber-girl looked quite seriously at her, lightly nodding her head, and said, 'They mustn't kill you! And if I get angry with you, I'll do it myself!' Then she dried Gerda's eyes and put both her hands into the pretty muff that was so soft and warm.

At last the carriage came to a halt. They were in the courtyard of the robbers' castle. Much of it was in ruins. Crows and ravens were flying out of the holes in it and enormous bulldogs, each looking as if he could eat a man, were leaping into the air, though they did not bark, for that was forbidden.

In a large, smoky hall a huge fire was blazing on the stone floor. Soup was boiling in a big copper pot, and hares and rabbits were turning on the spit.

'Tonight you shall sleep with me and all my little pets!' said the little robber-girl. They had food and drink, and then went to a corner, where there were blankets and straw. Above this bed nearly a hundred pigeons were sitting on sticks and perches. They seemed to be asleep, but they moved slightly when the little girls arrived.

'They are all mine,' boasted the robber-girl, seizing one of the nearest and holding it by the legs and shaking it, till it flapped its wings. 'Give him a kiss!' she cried, slapping Gerda with the bird's wing. 'The wood rabble sits over there!' she continued, pointing to a number of laths nailed across a high hole in the wall. 'Those two are real rascals! If you don't lock them in properly, they fly off at once. And this is my dear old favourite!' And she tugged at the horns of a reindeer, who had a bright copper ring round his neck and was tied to a large stone. 'He's another one we have to keep on a tight rope, or he'd be off. Every evening I tickle him under his neck with a sharp knife. He's scared to death of that!' And the little girl drew a long knife out of a crack in the wall, running it over the reindeer's neck. The poor animal struggled and kicked with his legs and the robber-girl laughed and pulled Gerda into bed with her.

'Are you taking the knife to bed with you?' asked Gerda, eyeing the knife with fear.

'I always sleep with my knife!' said the little robber-girl. 'One never knows what may happen. But now tell me again what you told me earlier about Kay, and why you came into the big wide world.'

So Gerda began all over again, and up above the wood-pigeons cooed in their cage, while the other pigeons slept. The little robber-girl put her arm round Gerda's neck, and holding the knife in the other, she snored loudly in her sleep. But Gerda could not close her eyes throughout that night, not knowing whether she was going to live or die. The robbers sat by the fire, singing and drinking, and the old robber-woman turned somersaults. Oh, what an awful sight it all was for the little girl.

Then all at once the wood-pigeons said, 'Coo, coo! We have seen little Kay. A white hen was carrying his sledge, he was sitting in the Snow Queen's carriage, which sped silently through the wood, while we lay in our nest. The Snow Queen breathed upon us young ones, and all but the two of us died. Coo, coo!'

'What are you saying up there?' Gerda cried. 'Where was the Snow Queen going? Do you know anything about it?'

'She was most likely going to Lapland, where there is always snow and ice! Ask the reindeer who is tied over there.'

'That's the place for ice and snow, a grand place to know!' said the reindeer. 'There you can run about freely in the wide, glistening valleys! There the Snow Queen has her summer tent, but her real home is a castle up near the North Pole, on the island called Spitzbergen.'

'Oh, Kay, my little Kay!' sighed Gerda.

'Lie still,' said the robber-girl sharply, 'or my knife will end up in your tummy!'

In the morning Gerda told her everything the wood-pigeons had said and the little robber-girl looked very serious, nodded her head and said, 'Very well, very well! Do you know where Lapland is?' she asked the reindeer.

'Who should know better than I?' said the reindeer, his eyes sparkling. 'That is where I was born and bred, that is where I have romped in the snowy plains!'

'Now listen,' said the robber-girl to Gerda. 'As you see, all our menfolk are away, but mother is still here and here she'll remain. But, during the morning, she will drink from that big bottle and after that she usually naps. Then I will do something for you!' With that she jumped out of bed, flung her arms round her mother's neck, tugged at her beard and said, 'My dearest nanny-goat, good morning!' And her mother pinched her nose, till it turned purple and blue, but it was all in fun.

When later her mother had drunk from the bottle and was having a nap, the robber-girl went up to the reindeer and said, 'I'd love to tickle you many more times with this sharp knife of mine, for you are always so very funny, but never mind. I am going to untie you and let you out, so you can run to Lapland. But you've got to go like the wind and take this little girl for me to the Snow Queen's castle, where her playmate is. You must have heard what she said, for she spoke loud enough and you have big ears!'

The reindeer leapt for joy. The robber-girl lifted little Gerda up, and was careful enough to tie her on firmly. She even gave her a little cushion to sit on. 'And here,' she said, 'are your fur boots, for it is going to be cold, but I am going to keep the muff, it is too pretty to part with. But I won't let you freeze. Here are my mother's mittens, they are enormously large, they'll reach right up to your elbows. Now hands in! Your hands now look as ugly as my mother's!'

And Gerda wept for joy.

'Stop snivelling!' said the robber-girl. 'Now you should look happy! Here are two loaves and a ham, so you won't go hungry.' She tied both on to the reindeer's back. Then she opened the door, called all the big dogs inside and, cutting the rope with her knife, said to the reindeer, 'Now run! But take great care of this little girl!'

And Gerda stretched out her hands in the enormous mittens to the

robber-girl, and bade her goodbye. And the reindeer flew off as fast as he could, over bushes and briars, through the big forest, over swamps and deserts. The wolves howled and the ravens shrieked 'Ish, ish!' from the sky. One might have fancied the sky was sneezing red.

'Those are my dear Northern Lights!' cried the reindeer. 'See how beautifully they shine!' And he ran on, faster and faster still, night and day he ran. The loaves were eaten and so was the ham, when at last they came to Lapland.

SIXTH STORY
The Lapland Woman
and the Finnish Woman

They stopped at a little house. A miserable little house it was. The roof was almost touching the ground, and the door was so low, that whoever wished to go in or out had to crawl on their stomachs. Nobody lived there except an old Lapland woman, who was cooking fish over an oil-lamp. And the reindeer told her Gerda's whole story but first he told her his own, which he thought far more important. Gerda was so freezing cold, she could not speak.

'Oh, you poor things!' cried the Lapland woman. 'You have still a long way to go! You have a hundred miles journey into Finland, where the Snow Queen dwells in the summer and burns blue lights every night. I will write a few words for you on a piece of dried cod, for I have no paper, but you can take it with you to a Finnish woman, who will advise you better than I can.'

So when Gerda was warm and had eaten, the Lapland woman wrote a few words on a piece of dried cod, asked Gerda to look after it well and tied her to the reindeer again. Onwards they sped. 'Ish, ish!' sounded from the sky, and the wondrous Northern Lights shone right through the night. And so they rode into Finland, and knocked at the Finnish woman's chimney, for she did not even have a door.

It was so very hot within, that the Finnish woman walked about almost naked. She was little, and very grubby. She immediately took off Gerda's clothes and her mittens and boots, for otherwise she would have been much too hot. Then she laid a slab of ice on the reindeer's head, and read the message written on the dried cod. She read it three times, and by then she knew it off by heart, so she threw the fish into the pan. After all, the cod was quite good to eat, and the Finnish woman was not one to waste anything.

Then the reindeer told her his own story and next little Gerda's tale. The Finnish woman blinked her wise eyes, but said nothing.

'You are so wise,' said the reindeer. 'I know you can tie with a single thread all the winds of the world together. When a sailor loosens one knot, he gets a favourable wind; if he undoes the second, it blows sharp, and if he unties the third and the fourth, so great a storm will rage that whole forests will be flattened. Could you not mix this little girl a drink which would give her the strength of twelve men, and so enable her to overpower the Snow Queen?'

'The strength of twelve men,' mumbled the Finnish woman, 'yes, that should do it!' She walked over to a drawer, took out a large roll of skin and opened it out. Strange letters were inscribed on it, and the Finnish woman read till the sweat ran down her forehead.

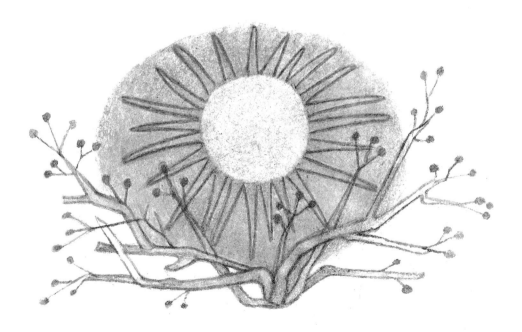

But the reindeer pleaded so earnestly for little Gerda, and Gerda looked so entreatingly at the Finnish woman with eyes full of tears, that the Finnish woman began blinking her eyes again and drew the reindeer into a corner, where she whispered to him, placing at the same time fresh ice on his head.

'Little Kay is indeed with the Snow Queen, where he may have anything he desires or thinks of. He is therefore quite convinced that it must be the best place in the world. But that is because he has a glass-splinter in his heart, and a glass-splinter in his eye. These splinters must come out, or he will never feel like a human again, and the Snow Queen will go on holding him in her power!'

'But can't you give little Gerda something to give her power over things?'

'I cannot give her greater power than that she has already! Can't you see how great is that power? Can't you see how human beings and animals must serve her, how without mishap she has got far in the world, in her bare feet? She must not think she needs such power from us; it is in her heart and comes from the heart of a lovely, innocent child. If she cannot find her own way to the Snow Queen, if she cannot herself take out the splinters from Kay's heart and eye, then we cannot help her. The Snow Queen's gardens begin two miles from here. You can carry the little girl there. Put her down by the big bush which bears red berries in the snow. Do not dawdle there, but hurry back here!' Then the Finnish woman lifted little Gerda onto the reindeer's back, and he ran off as fast as he could.

'Oh, I have forgotten my boots, I have left my mittens!' cried little Gerda, remembering quickly in the bitter cold. But the reindeer did not dare to stop and he ran on and on, till he came to the big bush with the red berries. There he put Gerda down, kissed her on the lips, the tears rolling down his cheeks, and ran quickly back again. And there stood poor Gerda, without shoes, without mittens, in the middle of that dreadful, ice-cold Finland.

She ran on as fast as she could, only to be met with a whole regiment of snowflakes. But they were not falling from the sky, the sky was perfectly clear and brightly lit by the Northern Lights. The snowflakes were running along the ground, and the nearer they came, the bigger they grew. Gerda well remembered how big and mysterious they had looked that time she saw them through the magnifying glass. But here they were big and terrifying in quite a different way—they were alive—they were the Snow Queen's front guards. They had the strangest of shapes. Some looked like great ugly hedgehogs, others like a whole mass of writhing snakes with their heads sticking out, and others like little fat bears with bristling hair, dazzlingly white—all living snowflakes.

Little Gerda now prayed 'Our Father'. And the cold was so fierce that she could see her own breath rising from her mouth like smoke. The smoke became denser and denser, turning into little transparent angels, that grew bigger and bigger the moment they touched the ground. Each one of them wore a helmet and carried a spear and a shield in his hand. More and more of them appeared, and by the time Gerda had finished her prayer, there was a whole legion round her. They stabbed the hideous snowflakes with their spears, till they broke into hundreds of pieces, and little Gerda walked quite safely and happily on. The little angels stroked her feet and her hands, so Gerda did not feel the cold as much, but walked swiftly on towards the Snow Queen's palace.

But first, let's take a look at how Kay is getting on. He of course was not thinking of little Gerda, least of all that she now stood at the palace gate.

SEVENTH STORY
*What Happened in the Snow Queen's Palace,
and Afterwards*

The palace walls were made of drifting snow, the windows and doors of sharp winds. There were more than a hundred halls, depending on how the snow drifted. The biggest hall stretched into the distance for many a mile. They were all illuminated by the strong Northern Lights and were incredibly large, fearfully empty, icy cold and dazzlingly white. Cheerfulness here never entered. Never was a party held here, with games like blind-man's buff and tap-a-paw. Never was there a small coffee-morning for select white young lady-foxes. Vast, empty and cold were the halls of the Snow Queen; the Northern Lights flashed so regularly, that one could work out when it would be at its highest point and when at its lowest. In the centre of the empty, endless hall was a frozen lake. The ice on it was broken into thousands of pieces, but each piece was so exactly like the next, that it was a true work of art. And in the middle of the lake sat the Snow Queen; she would say then that she was sitting on the mirror of reason, and that hers was the best, in fact the only such mirror in the world.

Little Kay was quite blue with cold, indeed almost black. But he did not feel it, for he had been kissed by the Snow Queen, which sent away the shivers and turned his heart into a lump of ice. He was playing about with some sharp, flat pieces of ice, pulling them and building them on top of each other in different ways, trying to form a pattern, just as people do with Chinese puzzles. Kay could make pictures too, the most curious of patterns — in his eyes these patterns were something quite exceptional and of the greatest importance. That was because of the glass-splinter in his eye! He made patterns which formed whole words, but he never managed to find the right patterns to make the one word he really wanted: eternity.

The Snow Queen said to him: 'If you can put that word together, you shall be your own master and I will give you the whole world and a pair of new skates.' But Kay could not do it.

'Now I am off to the warm countries!' said the Snow Queen. 'I want to peep into the black pots! By that she meant the mountains which spit fire, Etna and Vesuvius, as we call them. 'I'll whiten them up a little! They need it. It will be good for the lemons and grapes!' With that the Snow Queen flew away and Kay was left all alone in the empty hall of ice many miles long.

He gazed at the pieces of ice and thought and thought till his head ached and throbbed. So still and so stiff he sat, that one would have believed he had frozen to death.

It was then that little Gerda walked into the palace through the big gates of sharp winds. But she had said an evening prayer, and the winds immediately died down, as though they had gone to sleep, and Gerda entered the empty, vast, cold halls—and saw Kay. She knew him at once, her arms flew round his neck, she held him tight and cried, 'Kay, dear little Kay! At last I have found you!'

But Kay remained perfectly still, stiff and cold. Little Gerda shed hot tears and they fell upon his chest and penetrated his heart, where they

melted the piece of ice and swallowed up the glass-splinter. Kay looked at Gerda, and Gerda sang the hymn:

'We'll hear little Jesus down below
In the valley, where sweet roses grow!'

Then Kay burst into tears. He wept till the glass-splinter fell out of his eye, and then he recognized Gerda and joyfully cried, 'Gerda! Dear little Gerda! Where have you been all this time? And where was I?' And he looked all around him. 'How cold it is here, how bare, how oppressive is this vast empty space!' And he held Gerda tight and she laughed and cried for joy.

It was so wonderful to see that even the bits of ice started dancing round them, and when they got tired and laid down to rest, they formed the very letters of the word the Snow Queen had said if Kay ever put them together, he would become his own master, and she would give him the whole world and a new pair of skates besides.

Then Gerda kissed his cheeks, and they became rosy and glowing. She kissed his eyes, and they started to sparkle like hers. She kissed his hands and feet and he was once again completely healthy. Let the Snow Queen come home whenever she likes! Kay's charter of release was written there in letters of sparkling ice!

Holding each other by the hand, they walked out of the big palace. They talked about grandmother and about the roses high on the roof. And wherever they walked, the winds dropped and the sun shone through. And when they came to the bush with the red berries, they found the reindeer waiting for them. With him was another, young reindeer, whose udder was full. She gave the children her warm milk and kissed them both on the lips. Then they carried Kay and Gerda first to the Finnish woman, where they warmed themselves in the hot room and were told how to get back home, and then to the Lapland woman, who made them new clothes, and mended Kay's sledge.

And the old reindeer and the young hind ran alongside, accompanying them all the way to the border of that country. And there, where the first sign of green was showing from the soil, Kay and Gerda bade the pair of reindeer and the Lapland woman goodbye.

The first little birds began to twitter, the wood was in green bud and suddenly a horse came galloping out of it. Gerda recognised it for it had been harnessed to the gold coach. A young girl sat astride the magnificent horse, a bright scarlet cap on her head, and pistols in front of her. It was the little robber-girl, who had grown tired of staying at home, and had decided to travel first north and then to other parts of the world if she did not like it. She recognized Gerda straightaway, and Gerda recognized her. How happy was their meeting!

'A fine roamer you are!' she said to little Kay. 'I wonder if you deserve to have people running after you to the ends of the earth!'

But Gerda stroked her cheeks and asked after the Prince and the Princess.

'They've gone away to foreign lands!' replied the robber-girl.

'And the raven?' asked little Gerda.

'The raven? Why, the raven is dead!' she replied. 'The tame sweetheart is a widow now, and wears a piece of black wool round her leg. She moans awfully though it is all put on, I say. And now tell me all that has happened and how you found him!'

And Gerda and Kay both told her.

'And so rang the bell, there's no more to tell!' said the robber-girl and taking them both by the hands, she promised to come and see them if she ever passed through their town. With that she rode away into the big wide world.

Kay and Gerda walked on hand in hand, and wherever they walked it was spring, beautiful spring, with bright flowers and lots of green leaves.

By and by they came to a town where church bells were ringing. They recognized the tall towers and the big town; it was the one where they lived. So they walked into it and went to grandmother's door and then up along the stairs into the room where everything was exactly as it had been before. The clock said 'Tick, tick!' and the hands moved round. But as they went in through the door, they found that they had become grown-up people. The roses in the gutter were blooming by the open windows and over there stood the tiny stools. And Kay and Gerda sat down, each on their own, holding each other by the hand. Like a bad dream, they forgot the cold, hollow splendour of the Snow Queen's palace. The grandmother was sitting in God's bright sunshine, reading aloud from the Bible: 'Unless ye become as little children, ye shall not enter into the Kingdom of Heaven!'

And Kay and Gerda gazed into each other's eyes, understanding now the words of the old hymn:

'We'll hear little Jesus down below
In the valley, where sweet roses grow!'

So there they both sat, grown up and yet children, children at heart.

The Shepherdess
and the Chimney-Sweep

Have you ever seen an old cupboard, black with age, with scrolls and leaves carved on it? Just such a piece was standing in the drawing-room; it had been inherited from great-grandmother and from top to bottom was covered with carved roses and tulips. The carving-work was indeed most curious, with little stags' heads with many antlers peeping out and in the centre of the cupboard a complete man was carved, wearing the most ridiculous grin. He really was grinning — you could not call it laughing. He had legs like a goat, and little horns on his forehead and a long beard. The children of the house called him Goat-legged Field-Marshal-Major-General-Commander-Sergeant, because such a name was quite a mouthful and there are not many who boast such a title; and carving him on that cupboard must have been quite some task! But there he was. His eyes were for ever glued to the table under the mirror, for there stood a pretty little porcelain shepherdess. Her shoes were gilded, her frock was charmingly gathered and fastened with a rose, and she had a gold hat and a shepherd's crook. Oh, she was lovely! Right next to her stood a little chimney-sweep, black as coal, but also of porcelain. He was as clean and neat as anybody. And, after all, he was only representing a chimney-sweep. The porcelain-maker could have just as easily made a prince of him — it was all the same to him.

He stood there so charmingly with his ladder, and his little face was as fresh and rosy as a little girl's; this, actually, was a mistake, he should have been at least slightly black. He was standing quite close to the shepherdess; they both stayed put where they had been placed, and being thus placed they became engaged. They were, after all, well suited; they were both young, of the same porcelain and equally fragile.

Next to them stood a figure three times their size; this was an old

Chinaman, who could nod his head. He too was of porcelain, and he said he was the little shepherdess's grandfather; but he couldn't prove it. He insisted he had great authority over her, and so he nodded to the Goat-legged Field-Marshal-Major-General-Commander-Sergeant, who wanted to marry the little shepherdess.

'There you'll have a man,' said the old Chinaman, 'a man who, I do believe, is of mahogany wood. You will be the wife of Goat-legged Field-Marshal-Major-General-Commander-Sergeant. He has a whole cupboard full of silver—not to mention all he has in his secret drawers!'

'I don't want to go into that dark cupboard!' said the little shepherdess. 'I've heard it said that he has eleven porcelain wives there already!'

'Then you can be the twelfth!' said the Chinaman. 'Tonight, as soon as the old cupboard begins to creak, you will be married—as surely as I am a Chinaman!' And with a nod of his head he nodded off to sleep.

But the little shepherdess cried and turned to her dearest beloved porcelain chimney-sweep.

'I think I shall have to ask you,' said she, 'to come with me out into the wide world, for here we cannot remain!'

'I'll do anything you want!' said the chimney-sweep. 'Let's go right now! I think I can support you by my trade!'

'I wish we were safely off this table!' said the shepherdess. 'I shan't be happy till we are out in the wide world!'

And the chimney-sweep comforted her, and showed her how to place her little foot on the carved ledges and gilded leaves of the table-leg; his ladder was a help, and so they managed to reach the floor. But when they glanced at the old cupboard, there was such a commotion! All the carved stags were straining their heads, raising their antlers and turning their necks. Goat-legged Field-Marshal-Major-General-Commander-Sergeant was leaping into the air and shouting at the old Chinaman, 'They're running away! They're running away!'

This made them rather frightened and they quickly jumped into a drawer. In there were several incomplete packs of cards, and also a little puppet-theatre that had been set up in a haphazard way. A play was being performed, and all the queens—the queens of hearts, diamonds, clubs and spades—sat in the front row, fanning themselves with their tulips; behind them stood all the jacks, showing they had two heads—one above and one

below—as is normal with playing-cards. The play was about two sweet-hearts who were not permitted to marry and it made the shepherdess burst into tears, for it was so similar to her own story.

'I can't bear it!' she cried. 'I simply can't remain in this drawer!' But when they got down to the floor and looked up at the table, they saw that the Chinaman had woken up and his whole body was shaking with rage.

'The old Chinaman is coming!' screamed the little shepherdess, falling to her porcelain knees in the greatest distress.

'I have an idea!' said the chimney-sweep. 'What if we crawl into the big pot-pourri jar over there in the corner? There we can rest on a bed of roses and lavender and throw salt into his eyes, if he comes near.'

'That won't do at all!' said the shepherdess. 'Besides, I happen to know that the old Chinaman and the pot-pourri jar are old sweethearts; and when two people have been so close, they always keep a soft spot for each other. No, there is nothing else for it, but to get out into the big wide world!'

'Have you really enough courage to go with me into the big wide world?' asked the chimney-sweep. 'Have you considered how big it is, and that we should never again be able to return here?'

'Yes, I have!' she said.

And the chimney-sweep looked at her intently and said, 'My path leads through the chimney! Have you really the courage to crawl with me through the stove, the flues and the tunnel? That is how we'll get into the chimney and there I know my way so well! We'll climb so high that they will never reach us, and right at the very top there is an opening into the big wide world!'

And he led her to the door of the stove.

'How black it is in there!' said the shepherdess, but nevertheless she went on with him, through the flues and through the tunnel, where it was pitch dark.

'Now we are in the chimney!' said the chimney-sweep. 'And look! Can you see? The loveliest star is shining up above!'

And indeed, it was a star in the sky, and it shone straight down on them, as if to show them the way. So they climbed and slithered, all that awful way, high, ever so high. And the chimney-sweep guided her and supported her, holding her and showing her the best places to put her little porcelain feet; and at last they came to the edge of the chimney, where they sat down to rest, for they were tired—and no wonder too!

The sky with all its stars was up above, and all the city roofs lay beneath them. They could see far, so far into the big wide world. The poor little shepherdess had never imagined it to be like this; she laid her little head on the chimney-sweep's shoulder and cried so much the gilt washed off her bodice.

'It's all too much!' she sighed. 'I simply can't bear it! The whole world is much too big! If only I were back on the table under the mirror! I shan't be happy till I am there again! I've come with you into the big wide world, and now I beg you to come back with me home again, if you love me at all!'

The chimney-sweep talked sensibly to her, trying to change her mind, reminding her of the old Chinaman and the Goat-legged Field-Marshal-Major-General-Commander-Sergeant, but she sobbed so pitifully and

kissed her little chimney-sweep so fondly, that he could not but give in.

And so back they went, crawling and slithering with great difficulty down the chimney, and creeping through the flues and the tunnel—it wasn't a bit nice—but at last, they stood once more in the black stove. First they waited behind the door, listening to hear what was going on in the room. But there was absolute silence. They peeped out, and oh, there in the middle of the floor lay the old Chinaman! He had fallen off the table trying to follow them, and had broken into three pieces. His back was one of the pieces, and his head had rolled into a corner. The Goat-legged Field-Marshal-Major-General-Commander-Sergeant stood where he had always stood, and was thinking hard.

'This is terrible!' cried the little shepherdess. 'Poor old grandfather is all in bits and we're to blame! I'll never get over this!'

'He can be put together again!' said the chimney-sweep encouragingly. 'He can be mended quite easily. You mustn't get upset so quickly! If they glue his back on, and put a strong rivet in his neck, he'll be as good as new, and will be just as unpleasant to us as ever!'

'Do you really think so?' asked the shepherdess. And they climbed back to their old place on the table.

'See how far we've got!' said the chimney-sweep. 'We could have saved ourselves all that trouble!'

'If only we could have old grandfather put together again!' sighed the shepherdess. 'Will it be terribly expensive?'

And he was mended. The family had his back glued back on and his neck riveted, and he was as good as new, but he could no longer nod his head.

'You have certainly turned very proud since you broke into pieces!' remarked old Goat-legged Field-Marshal-Major-General-Commander-Sergeant. 'I don't honestly see what there is to be proud of! Now then, is she to be mine, or isn't she?'

And the chimney-sweep and the little shepherdess looked so imploringly at the old Chinaman; they were so afraid he would nod. But this he could not do, and he would have found it embarassing to tell a stranger that he had a rivet in his neck for always. And so the two porcelain figures stayed together, and they blessed grandfather's rivet and loved each other until they broke in pieces.

The Snail and the Briar

Round the garden there was a hazel hedge and behind it fields and mead-ows with cows and sheep. In the middle of the garden a rose-tree was in bloom and under it sat a snail. There was something in that snail; he himself.

'Just you wait till my time comes!' said he. 'Then I shall do much more than shoot out buds, yield hazel nuts, or give milk like cows and sheep.'

'I am expecting great things of you,' said the rose-tree. 'May I be permit-ted to enquire when it is to be?'

'I'll take my time,' said the snail. 'All of a sudden you are in such a hurry. Fancy all that eagerness!'

A year later the snail was still almost on the very same spot, in the sunshine under the rose-tree, where buds appeared and opened into roses, always fresh, always new. And the snail crawled half out, threw out his feelers, then drew them in again.

'Everything looks exactly the same as a year ago, there has been no development. The rose-tree still only has its roses, it has not got any farther!'

The summer passed, the autumn sped by and on the rose-tree new buds appeared and its roses bloomed, until the snow fell and the weather turned dismal and damp. Then the rose-tree stooped towards the ground and the snail crawled into the earth.

And then again a new year began and once more the roses and the snail appeared.

'You're turning into an old broom,' said he. 'It is about time you were gone. You've given your all to the world. Was it of any importance? That is a question about which I've had no time to meditate. But one thing is obvious, you've done nothing at all for your own inner development, otherwise you would have probably been able to yield something else. Can you justify that? Soon there'll be nothing left of you but thorns!'

'You terrify me,' said the rose-tree. 'I have never given the matter any thought.'

'Naturally, for you've never been one for deep thought! But have you ever tried to justify to your own self, why you keep on blossoming and how this comes about? Why that and not something else?'

'No,' replied the rose-tree. 'I blossomed with joy—I just could not help myself. The sun shone so warmly, the air blew so freshly, I drank clear dew and heavy rain, I breathed and I lived! Strength seeped into me from the soil and also filled me from above. I felt happiness, for ever new and for ever greater, and that is why I kept on blossoming. That was my life, I could not do otherwise!'

'You led a very pleasant life!' said the snail.

'Most certainly! I had everything!' agreed the rose-tree. 'Yet you have been blessed with even greater gifts! You are of a thinking, enquiring nature, you have great talent, which will astound the world.'

'I am not thinking of that in the least,' said the snail. 'I don't care about the world! What is the world to me? I am entirely self-sufficient in every way.'

'But shouldn't we on earth give to others the best we can? To give what we are capable of? I know, of course, that I only gave roses, but what about you? You were blessed with so many gifts, so what have you given the world and what are you giving it now?'

'What have I given? What am I giving the world? I spit on it! It is worthless and to me uninteresting. Give it your flowers, that is, after all, the only thing you can give! And let the hazel bush give it nuts, and cows and sheep milk — somebody will use them. But I have use only for myself. I'll crawl into myself, into my shell, and there I'll remain. I am not interested in the world!'

With that the snail crawled into his house and sealed it up.

'How sad!' said the rose-tree. 'With all the best will in the world I can't crawl away like that; I have to keep on budding, I have to keep on growing roses. The petals fall and the wind blows them away! Yet I have seen a woman place a rose in her hymn-book, and how another rose of mine found itself on the bosom of a beautiful maiden, and how the lips of a child kissed another bloom with sheer joy. This truly pleased me, this was a real blessing. This is my memory, my life!'

And the rose-tree, in its innocence, blossomed on, while the snail lazed about in his house, for he cared not about the world.

And so the years passed.

The earth buried the snail, the earth buried the rose-tree; the rose in the hymn-book turned to dust, but in the garden new rose-trees bloomed, and in the garden new snails grew; they crawled into their little houses, they spat—they cared not in the least about the world.

Shall we start at the beginning again? The tale would be exactly the same.

The Old Street Lamp

Have you ever heard the tale of the old street lamp? Not that it is particularly entertaining, but it is nice to hear, just for once. She was such a respectable, old lamp, who for many, many years had given good service, and now she was to be taken away. On her very last evening she sat on the lamp-post, lighting up the street; she felt somewhat like an old ballerina dancing for the very last time, knowing full well that tomorrow she would be turned into old iron.

The old lamp was terrified by the thought of the approaching day, for she knew she would then be taken first to the town hall, to be examined by the thirty-six 'wise men' of the town council, who would decide whether or not she was still fit for service. There it would be determined whether she should be sent to light up one of the bridges, or perhaps to one of the factories right out in the country; or perhaps she would go direct to an iron-foundry, to be melted down and made into something different. This thought worried her the most, for she feared whether in that case she would retain her memory of ever having been a street lamp.

Whatever the outcome, she knew she would have to bid goodbye to the lamp-lighter and his wife, whom she considered as her own family. She was made a street lamp at the very same time he had been made a lamp-lighter. In those days his wife considered herself rather noble; only when she passed the lamp at night did she throw her a glance, never by day. But now, in the latter years, when all three had grown old, the lamp-lighter, his wife and the street lamp too, the wife tended her well, cleaned her and filled her with fresh oil. The lamp-lighter and his wife were indeed most honest people; they had never cheated her of a single drop of oil.

Now it was her last night in the street, and tomorrow she would go to the town hall — two gloomy thoughts for the old street lamp to think about. You can well imagine, how she burned! But other thoughts passed through her head. Why, she had seen so much in her life, she had shone for so many people, guiding them on their way — perhaps as many as the thirty-six 'wise men' of the town did; but she thought none of this out loud, for she was an old, modest lantern, who did not wish to hurt any-one's feelings, least of all her superiors. She remembered so much and now and again she flamed and blazed at her thoughts.

'Oh yes, they too remember me! That handsome young man, for in-stance—though it is many years ago now! He came with a letter in his hand, it was written on rose-coloured paper, so fine, so very fine, with gilt edges—it was beautifully written in a lady's handwriting. The young man read the letter twice over, kissed it and looked up at me with eyes which seemed to say: 'I am the happiest man in the world!' Oh yes, only he and I knew what was written in that first letter from his beloved! And I recall another pair of eyes, how strange it is that one can jump so from one thought to another! There was a splendid funeral passing down our street. In the coffin inside the carriage lay a young, beautiful woman; there were such a lot of flowers and wreaths and so many bright torches that I was

almost lost among them. The pavement was packed with people who had followed the procession, but when the torches had disappeared from sight and I glanced around, I saw someone standing by my post, weeping. Never will I forget those sorrowful eyes, staring into me!'

Thus many memories passed through the old street lamp, who shone for the last time that night. The sentinel on guard, when he is relieved, sees his successor and can exchange a few words with him, but the lamp would not see who was to replace her. Yet she could have given so many useful hints, about rain and sleet, about moonlight spreading over the pavement and from which side the wind blew.

On the board across the gutter stood a trio, who had come to present themselves to the lamp, thinking that she herself would appoint her successor. The first of the trio was a herring's head, which, as you know, shines in the dark. He was of the opinion, that if he were placed on the lamp-post, a great saving would be made on oil. The second was a piece of tinder, which also shone in the dark. It did indeed declare that it shone more brightly than a stock-fish, not to mention it was the last stem of a tree, which had once been the pride of the forest. The third was a glow-worm. How she got there, the street lamp could not imagine, but there she was and there she shone. But the herring's head and the piece of tinder swore that the glow-worm could only shine at certain times, and could not, therefore, be considered for the job as a street lamp.

The old lamp explained that none of them shone strongly enough for a street lamp, but this none of the three would believe. And when they heard that it was not the lamp herself who could choose her successor, they said that they were glad of that, for she was far too old to be able to make such an important decision.

At that moment the wind came rushing round the corner of the street and blew through the top of the old lamp and said; 'What is this I hear? That you want to leave us tomorrow? Are we seeing each other for the last time tonight? In that case I must give you something to remember me by! I will blow right through your head, so that you shall not only remember plainly and clearly all you will hear and see, but when in your presence anything is read or said, you will be able to actually see it!'

'Oh, that is a valuable gift indeed!' said the old street lamp. 'I thank you most sincerely! I only hope I shall not be melted down!'

'That won't happen yet!' said the wind. 'And now I shall blow into you your memory! If you get a few more gifts like this, you will truly have an enjoyable old age!'

'If only I am not melted down!' sighed the old lamp again. 'Or could you secure me my memory, even in that case?'

'Now, old street lamp, please be reasonable!' said the wind, and then it blew. Just then the moon came out. 'What will you give?' asked the wind.

'I shan't give anything at all!' the moon exclaimed. 'I am on the wane and besides, lanterns have never shone for me, but I shine for the lanterns.' And the moon retired again behind the clouds, so that she would not be bothered. Just then a drop of water fell right on to the cover of the lamp, as if from a roof's gutter; but it declared that it came from the grey clouds and that it too was a gift, perhaps the most valuable one of them all. 'I will penetrate you and will give you the ability to turn rusty, in a single night, if you so wish, and so fall to pieces and return to dust.' But the lamp thought this a horrid gift, and the wind thought so too. 'Have you nothing

better? Have you nothing better to give?' it swished as loud as it could. Just then a glittering shooting star flew past, a long bright trail.

'What was that?' cried the herring's head. 'Did a star fall down here? I truly believe it flew right into the lamp! Well, to be sure, if such highly placed individuals are seeking that office, we may as well pack up and go home!' And he did just that, and the other two candidates did the same.

But the old lamp suddenly flared up most brightly. 'What a wonderful gift!' said she. 'Those bright stars, which had always given me such pleasure and which shine so beautifully, as I have never been able to shine, though I have tried, heart and soul—those brilliant stars have noticed me, a miserable old lantern, and have sent a messenger down to me with a rare gift—that everything, that I myself remember and see vividly and clearly, can be seen also by those whom I love. Now indeed this is a precious gift, for if you cannot share your joy with others, it is only half a joy!'

'What honourable thoughts!' said the wind. 'But it appears you are not aware, that a wax-candle is necessary. Unless a candle is lit inside you,

nobody else will be able to share your pleasure, to see anything. The stars did not think of that. They imagine that everything that shines, must have at least a candle inside. But now I am truly tired,' announced the wind. 'I am going to rest!' And he died.

The next day—well it would be better to pass over the next day! The next evening the old lamp lay in an arm-chair—and where? In the old lamp-lighter's room! He had begged the 'wise men' of the town, in consideration of his long and faithful service, to be allowed to keep the old street lamp. They laughed at him when he asked for it, and gave it to him. And so now the lamp lay in the arm-chair by the warm stove. It seemed as if this had made her grow bigger, till she almost filled the arm-chair. The old people were sitting at supper, gazing fondly at the old lamp, as though they would have liked it best to have her sit at the table. Actually they lived in a cellar, slightly underground. It was necessary to pass through a paved hall before coming into their room, but it was pleasantly warm, for the door was bound with strips. The whole room looked comfortable and clean. There were curtains round the bed and in the little windows, and on the window-ledges there were two very strange flower-pots; they had been brought home by their neighbour Christian, a sailor, from the East or the West Indies. They were two earthenware elephants, without backs, and hollow inside, and out of the soil with which they were filled grew in one of them the most beautiful leeks—that was the old folk's kitchen-garden — and in the other was a large flowering geranium—that was their flower-garden. On the wall hung a big coloured picture of the Viennese Congress—all the Kings and Emperors were there nicely together! A Bornholm clock, with heavy leaden weights, went 'tick! tack!'—it always went too fast, but the old folk would say, that this was better than going too slow.

And now they were eating their supper and the old lantern lay, as we have already mentioned, in the arm-chair right by the stove. And she felt as if now the whole world was upside down. But when the old lamp-lighter looked at her, and talked about all the two had gone through together, in rain and sleet, in bright brief summer nights and in wintry snow-storms, when it was good to get back to his cellar-home—then the old lamp felt happy again. For she saw all he spoke of, as if it were happening right then, and she knew the wind had indeed not deceived her.

The old couple were so hard-working and agile; they did not let a single hour pass by in idleness. On Sunday afternoons some book or other always appeared on the table, usually a travel book, and the old man would read aloud about Africa, about the great forests and the wild elephants which roamed there freely. The old woman would listen, and eye the earthenware elephants that served her as flower-pots!

'Yes, I can almost see it all!' she would say. And the lamp would wish so fervently that someone would light a candle and put it inside her—for then the old woman would see the whole scene as clearly as she did, the tall trees, their thickly-leaved, intertwined branches, the naked black men on horseback, and whole herds of elephants, crushing reeds and bushes with their broad feet.

'What use are all my abilities, when there is no candle here!' sighed the lamp. 'They only have oil and tallow-candles, and neither of those will do.'

But one day a whole pile of wax-candle ends were brought into the cellar-room; they used the larger pieces for burning, and the smaller ones

the old woman used to wax her thread with, when she was sewing. They were real wax-candles indeed, yet no one thought of placing the tiniest little bit into the lamp.

'So here I stand with my rare abilities,' grumbled the lamp. 'There is so much within me, yet I cannot share with anyone my joy! They do not know that I could turn their bare white walls into the richest tapestry, to fresh green woods, to anything they might desire! They do not know!'

One day, on the old lamp-lighter's birthday, the old woman came up to the lamp and said with a smile, 'I will make him some illumination!' And the lamp's iron hat creaked, for she thought, 'Now at last I will get my candle!' But they gave her oil, not wax. She burned all the evening, but now she knew that the gift the stars had given her—the most wonderful gift of all—would in this life remain an undiscovered gift.

And so she dreamt—for surely, someone so very gifted must be able to dream—she dreamt that the old couple were dead and that she herself was taken to the iron-foundry to be melted down and made into something else. She felt just as frightened as when she was to go to the town hall to face the council of thirty-six 'wise men'. But though she knew she had the power of turning rusty and changing to dust, she chose not to do so. And so she ended up in the furnace, and became a most exquisite iron candle-stick made for holding wax-tapers. It was in the form of an angel carrying a bouquet of flowers, and in the centre of the bouquet the wax-candle was placed. The candlestick was put upon a green writing-table, and the room in which it stood was such a pleasant room. There were many books all over the place, and lovely pictures hung on the walls.

It was a poet's room, and everything he thought about and wrote about was pictured all around—deep, dark forests, meadows flooded in sun, with a stork striding about proudly, or a stately ship, riding high on the seas.

'Oh, what rare abilities I have!' thought the old lamp, as she awoke from her dream. 'I could almost long to be melted down! But no, that must not happen whilst the old folk are alive! They love me for my own sake. To them I am like their own child. They have scrubbed me so nicely and they have given me oil! I am as well off here as the 'Viennese Congress' over there, and that is an honour indeed!'

And from that time she was inwardly more at peace, and surely this the honest, respectable old street lamp truly deserved.

The Flying Trunk

Once upon a time there was a merchant who was so rich that he could have paved the whole street and also almost a whole alley with silver. But this he did not do, for he had better uses for his money. For every meagre coin he laid out, he got a sovereign in return. Such a fine merchant was he! But then one day he died.

All his money now went to his son, and he lived merrily, going to carnivals night after night, making paper kites out of bank notes, and playing ducks and drakes on the pond with gold pieces instead of stones. This was an easy way to go through his money, and go through his money he did. In the end he only had a few coins left and all he had to wear were a pair of slippers and an old dressing-gown. His friends lost interest in him, now that they couldn't show off in the streets with him, but one of them, a kindly soul, sent him an old trunk with this advice: 'Pack up and go!' Now this was good advice, but the young merchant had nothing left to pack. So he got into the trunk himself.

It was a most unusual trunk. The moment the lock was pressed, the trunk would fly. And that is what it did now: swish! and up it flew with the young merchant through the chimney, high above the clouds, farther and farther away. It creaked at the base and the merchant was terrified that the trunk would fall to pieces and he'd fall out!

However, he flew safely to the land of the Turks. He hid the trunk under a heap of dry leaves in the wood and went into the town. He could do this quite well, for all the Turks went about dressed as he was, in dressing-gowns and slippers. He met a nursemaid with a baby. 'Tell me, Turkish nurse,' he asked, 'what palace is that close by the town with the very high windows?'

'That is where the King's daughter lives,' replied the nursemaid. 'It has been prophesied that a lover will make her very unhappy, and so nobody is allowed in to see her except when the King and the Queen are there.'

'Thanks!' said the young merchant and went back into the wood, sat in the trunk, flew on to the roof of the palace and climbed through the window to the Princess.

She was lying on the sofa, fast asleep. She was so beautiful, that the young merchant couldn't help but kiss her. She woke up and was awfully frightened, but he said that he was the Turkish God and that he had flown to her through the air. She liked that.

So they sat down side by side, and the young merchant talked to her about her eyes describing them as the loveliest dark pools, in which her thoughts swam like mermaids. And he talked about her brow as a snowy mountain with magnificent halls and paintings.

They were truly lovely stories! And then he asked the Princess for her hand, and she agreed at once.

'But you must come again on Saturday,' she said. 'On Saturdays the King and the Queen always come to have tea with me. I am sure they will be most proud that I am to marry the Turkish God. But mind that you have a very nice fairy-tale to tell them, for my parents are terribly fond of them. Mother always likes them to be moral and noble, and father likes a merry tale, to make him laugh.'

'Very well, the only wedding present I shall bring then will be a fairy-tale!' the young merchant announced. With that they parted and the Princess gave him a sword studded with gold coins. He certainly needed them. Then he flew off. He bought a brand-new dressing-gown and then sat down in the wood and made up the fairy-tale. It had to be ready by Saturday, and that wasn't easy!

At last it was finished and at last it was Saturday.

The King, the Queen and the whole court were waiting tea for him at the Princess's palace. The young merchant was wonderfully received.

'Tell us a story!' asked the Queen. 'One with a deep meaning and a moral!'

'But let it make us laugh too!' said the King.

'With pleasure!' he said, and began his tale. Listen carefully now!

'Once upon a time there was a bundle of matches. They were extremely proud of their high descent. They came from the main branch of a tall old fir-tree, each of them was its splinter. The matches now lay on the shelf between a tinder-box and an old iron pot, and they were talking to them about their youth. 'While we were still on that tree,' they said, 'it was like living in paradise. Each morning and each evening we had diamond tea—that was the dew—and sunshine all day long, if there happened to be sunshine, while all the little birds told us stories. And it was easy to see we were rich, for the other trees were dressed only in the summer, while our family could afford green clothes both summer and winter. But then came the woodcutters—that was the Great Revolution!—and our family was broken up. The paternal trunk—the forefather of our clan—became the mainmast of a splendid ship, that sailed all around the world; other branches went to other places, and it became our task to bring light to low, common people. That is why we, who are of noble birth, have come into this kitchen.'

'Mine is a very different story,' announced the iron pot, which was next to the matches. 'From the very moment I came into this world, I have been constantly scrubbed and boiled. I'm solidly reliable and am really of the first importance in this house. My only pleasure is to stand after meals clean and bright upon the shelf and to talk sensibly with my friends. Though, with the exception of the bucket, which now and then goes into the yard, we live here cut off from the world. Our only link with it is the peat basket, but all he talks about is the government and the people in a most disturbing way; only the other day an old pan, scared by all that talk, fell down from the shelf and broke. He's a proper free-thinker!'

'You talk too much!' the tinder-box shouted him down, and the steel struck the flint, till sparks flew out. 'Why don't we make this a pleasant evening?'

'Yes, let's talk about which of us comes from the noblest family!' proposed the matches.

'Oh no, I hate talking about myself!' objected the earthenware pot. 'Let's make our own evening entertainment. I'll begin. I'll tell you something from everyday life. You will all easily identify yourselves with it and I think you'll enjoy it: On the shores of the Baltic, where the Danish beech groves grow . . .'

'A lovely beginning,' cried all the plates. 'This is going to be just the sort of story for us!'

'I spent my youth in a quiet family. They polished the furniture, scrubbed the floors and put clean curtains up once a fortnight.'

'How interestingly you tell a story!' said the broom. 'It's easy to tell you're a lady. It's such a clean tale.'

'Yes, you can feel it!' announced the watering-can and it gave a little jump of delight, till water splashed on the floor.

And the pot continued with its story, the end of which was every bit as good as the beginning.

The plates clattered for joy and the broom pulled a sprig of parsley from the sand and crowned the pot with it, knowing full well this would make the others cross, but it thought: 'If I crown her today, she will crown me tomorrow.'

'We're going to dance!' said the fire-tongs, and they did just that. Gracious me, how well they kicked their legs high into the air. The old chair-cover in the corner of the kitchen burst at the sight of it. 'Perhaps you could crown us too,' asked the fire-tongs. And so they were.

'They are only the common rabble,' thought the matches.

The tea-urn was now called upon to sing, but he insisted he **had**

a cold—that he simply couldn't sing unless he was on the boil. However, he refused out of sheer conceit. He didn't want to sing unless he was on the table in front of his mistress!

An old quill-pen lay on the window sill, which the maid used for writing. There was nothing remarkable about it, except that it had been dipped too far into the ink-well. But the pen was proud of that very fact.

'If the tea-urn doesn't wish to sing, we can do without!' the pen now announced. 'Hanging outside is a cage with a nightingale and he will sing for us! He hasn't had any singing lessons, but we'll be kind and understanding this evening!'

'According to my opinion it would be highly improper to listen to such a foreign bird!' observed the tea-kettle, who was kitchen singer and half-sister to the tea-urn. 'Would it be patriotic? Let the shopping basket be the judge!'

'I'm really cross!' announced the shopping-basket. 'I'm more cross than anybody can imagine! Is this a proper way to spend an evening? Wouldn't

it be better to set the house in order? Everyone then would take up their proper place and I'd be in charge of the lot. You'd see a change then!'

'Oh yes, let's start!' they all cried.

Just then the door opened. The housemaid was coming in. They all remained silently in their place, without breathing a word: yet there wasn't a single pot in the kitchen who did not know all the things it could do and how superior it was. 'Yes, if it had been my wish,' they all thought, 'this could have indeed been a merry evening!'

The maid picked up the matches and struck them. How they sparkled, how they flared up!

'Everybody can see now that we are the noblest of you all!' they boasted. 'How we glitter! How we shine!' Then they were burnt out.

'What a lovely story!' cried the Queen. 'I felt as if I were there in the kitchen with those matches! You shall have our daughter!'

'Yes, indeed!' agreed the King. 'You'll get our daughter on Monday!' And they called him by his Christian name, now that he was almost a member of the family.

The wedding date was fixed and on the preceding evening the whole town was ceremoniously illuminated. Buns and cakes were scattered among the people in the streets; the street-boys, standing on tiptoe, cheered 'Hurrah!' and whistled through their fingers; it was really a splendid sight.

'Well, I suppose I ought to play my part too!' the young merchant said to himself. So he bought rockets, sparklers and all the fireworks imaginable. He put the lot into his trunk and flew off high above the town.

Wow! How he whizzed through the air, how the fireworks crackled and flashed!

The sight made the Turks jump into the air with delight, their slippers flying over their heads. Such a heavenly apparition they had never seen. Now they knew for sure it was the Turkish God himself whom the Princess was about to marry.

When the young merchant returned into the wood with the trunk, he thought, 'I'll pop into the town so I can hear what an impression I made!' It was quite natural for him to be inquisitive.

Oh, the stories that were going around! Every single person with whom he talked had seen it in his own way, but one and all agreed it was grand.

'I saw the Turkish God himself,' one of them swore. 'He had eyes like shining stars and a beard like frothy waves.'

'He flew in a fiery cloak,' said another. 'The sweetest little cherubs were peeping out from under its folds.'

The young merchant was hearing the most wonderful things—and the next day was to be his wedding day!

Then he returned to the wood, for it was time to get into the trunk—but where had it gone?

It was burnt up. A spark from a firework had been left in it, and set it on fire. The trunk now was turned to ashes. The young merchant could fly no more, no more could he go to his bride.

She stood waiting on the palace roof all day. She's waiting still, while he goes round the world telling fairy-stories. But they are no longer as merry as the one he told about the matches.

The Elf and the Grocer

Once there was a true student—he lived in the attic and owned nothing. And there was a true grocer—he lived in comfort on the ground floor and owned the whole house. And the elf kept well in with him, for every Christmas Eve he would be given a dish of porridge, with a lump of butter on top. The grocer could afford it. So the elf stayed in the shop and found it most instructive.

One evening the student came into the shop by the back entrance, to buy some candles and cheese. He had no one else to send, so he had come himself. He got what he asked for, paid for it, and the grocer and his wife nodded to wish him good night. But her ladyship was a woman who could do more than nod, she had the gift of the gab! The student returned their greeting, whilst he busied himself reading the sheet of paper that had been wrapped round the cheese. It was a page torn from an old book, which should never have been torn up. It was an old book full of poetry!

'There's a bit of it still left over there!' said the grocer. 'I gave an old woman a handful of coffee for it. If you give me eight shillings for it, you can have the rest!'

'Thank you,' replied the student. 'I'll take it instead of the cheese. I'll eat plain bread without cheese. It would be a crime to tear it all up! You're a fine businessman, a clever businessman, but you understand poetry as much as that bin!'

It was rather a rude thing to say, particularly about the bin, but the grocer laughed and the student also laughed, for after all, it was said jokingly! The elf, however, was most upset that anyone would dare to say such things to the grocer, who was the landlord and who sold the very best butter!

When night fell and the shop was closed and everybody, except the student, was in bed, the elf crept into the room and took the grocer's wife's gift of the gab; she did not use it when she was asleep. And whatever object the elf put it on in that room found its tongue at once and proceeded to express its thoughts and feelings just like the grocer's wife. But only one could have it on at a time, which was a real blessing, for otherwise they would have all talked at once without being able to hear one another speak.

The elf placed the gab on the bin, where the old newspapers were kept. 'Is it really true,' asked he, 'that you have no idea what poetry is?'

'Of course I have!' said the bin. 'It is something that usually appears in the papers right down the page, and gets cut off. I think I can truly say I carry more of it in my interior than some students! Yet I am only a miserable bin in comparison to the grocer!'

Next the elf placed the gab on the coffee-mill. How it chattered on! Then he put it on the butter cask and on the till. Both were of the same opinion as the bin, and one should respect whatever the majority agrees upon!

'Now it is the student's turn!' said the elf, and he crept silently up the backstairs to the attic where the student lived. The light was on inside. The elf peeped in through the keyhole. He saw the student reading that tattered book. But how bright it was in there! From the book came out a strong ray of light, which grew into a trunk and then into a huge tree that towered high above, spreading its branches over the student's head. Every leaf was wonderfully fresh and every flower was the head of a beautiful girl—some with eyes dark and sparkling, others with eyes blue and crystal clear; and every fruit was a glittering star. And what wondrous music and beautiful singing filled the air!

The little elf had never dreamt of such splendour, let alone seen or heard it. So there he stood on tiptoe like a statue, looking and looking till the light went out. The student had blown out the lamp and obviously had gone to bed, yet the elf stayed on by the door, for the soft, sweet singing carried on, as a lovely lullaby for the student to drift into sleep.

'How lovely it is here!' thought the elf. 'This I never expected! So I think I'll stay with the student!' And he thought it over—very sensibly too—but then he sighed. 'The student hasn't any porridge!' And he went—yes, he went downstairs again to the grocer. And just as well it was that he did, for the bin had used up nearly all of the grocer's wife's gab. It had told all that it ever had in it, from one end, and was just preparing to turn round and start its telling from the other end when the elf came in, took away the gab and returned it to the woman.

The whole shop, however, from the till to the firewood by the stove, allowed its opinions to be guided from then on by the bin. Their respect for it was so great and they expected great things of it, so whenever the grocer read aloud from his newspaper, the one which comes out in the evenings, the art and theatre reviews, they truly thought it was all being told by the bin.

But the little elf no longer could bear to sit listening to all the shop's wisdom and common sense. The minute the light went on in the little attic room, he seemed to be pulled by the beams as if they were strong anchor cables, pulling him upwards. He simply had to go up and peep in through the keyhole. There he felt the surge of grandeur such as a man feels when facing the stormy seas, as God passes over it in the storm. The little elf burst into tears; he did not know why he cried, but in his tears was a touch of happiness! How beautiful it would be to sit with the

student under that shining tree, but this was not possible—the elf had to be content with the keyhole. He went on standing there in the cold passage, even when the autumn wind whistled through the trap-door and it was cold, bitterly cold. Yet the little chap never felt it, not until the light went out in the attic room and the wondrous music died out in the wind. Ugh! how frozen he felt then! He would crawl downstairs again to his warm little corner, it was snug and cosy there! And then, when Christmas Eve came with porridge and the big lump of butter on top—why, then the grocer was again his favourite!

Then one night, the little elf was woken up by a terrible clanging at the window, and banging from outside. The night-watchman was blowing his trumpet—there was a fire! The whole street was lit up by the flames. Was this house on fire, or was it next door's? Where was it? How terrifying it all was! The grocer's wife was in such a state that she took her gold ear-rings off and put them into her pocket, so she would at least save something. The grocer rushed for his valuable papers and the servant girl

for her silk mantilla; she had earned enough to buy one! Everybody wanted to save their best things.

The same applied to the elf. In a couple of leaps he was upstairs and in the student's chamber. The student was standing quite calmly by the open window, gazing at the fire—it was in the house opposite. The little elf seized the wondrous book on the table, pushed it into his little red cap and held on to it with both his hands; the greatest treasure in the house was saved! Then he dashed away, outside on to the roof and right up to the chimney. There he sat, lit up by the glow of the burning house opposite, clutching with both hands the little red cap with the treasure inside. Now he knew where his heart lay and where he himself belonged. But when the fire had been put out and reason again returned to the little elf—well, then he said, 'I'll split my time between them! I can't turn my back on the grocer altogether, if only for the porridge!'

And that was perfectly human! We also go to the grocer for the porridge.

Five Peas in a Pod

There were five peas in a pod. They were green and the pod was green, so they thought the whole world must be green, and quite rightly too! The pod grew and the peas grew, arranging themselves according to their dwelling; they sat all in a row.

Outside the sun shone and warmed the pod, and the rain made it transparent. Inside it was damp and cosy, light in daytime and dark at night, just as it should be, and the peas kept on growing bigger, and as they sat there, they kept on thinking more and more, for after all, they had to do something.

'Are we going to stay here for ever?' each one of them said. 'I'd hate to harden from so much sitting about. I almost believe that outside there is something, too.'

The weeks went by. The peas were turning yellow and the pod was turning yellow.

'The whole world is turning yellow!' they said.

Suddenly they felt the pod jerk; it had been picked and then put into a coat pocket with many other full pods.

'Now they will surely open us!' said the peas, and waited.

'I'd like to know which one of us will get the farthest,' said the smallest pea. 'We'll soon find out.'

'What must happen, will happen,' said the biggest.

Snap! the pod burst open and all the five peas rolled into the bright sunshine. They found themselves in a child's hand; a little boy held them and said they were exactly right for his gun. And straightaway one pea was placed in the gun and was fired.

'Now I am flying into the big world! Catch me if you can!'

And it was gone.

'And I,' said the second pea, 'I will fly straight to the sun, for that is quite a pea and will suit me fine!'

And it was gone.

'We'll sleep wherever we get to,' the others said. 'But we'll end up somewhere!'

First they rolled to the ground, before ending up in the gun, but they got there in the end.

'We'll get the farthest of all!'

'What must happen, will happen!' said the last pea, and then it was fired into the air and found itself flying towards an old board under a little garret room, straight into a crevice where there was moss and soft earth; and the moss closed round it. There it stayed hidden, but not forgotten by God.

'What must happen, will happen!' said he.

In the little garret room lived a poor woman, who spent her days cleaning stoves, sawing logs and doing other heavy work, for she was very strong and diligent, but she remained poor all the same. In a tiny chamber of the house lay her half-grown, only daughter. She was very delicate and

frail, for she had spent the whole year in bed and it seemed that she could not live nor die.

'She will join her sister!' the woman said. 'I had two children, but it was hard for me to look after them both, so God decided to share them and took one to Himself. I should like to keep the other one, the one I have left, but He doesn't want them to be separated, so she too will go above to her sister!'

But the sick maiden lived on. She lay patiently and quietly in her bed all day, whilst her mother went out to earn a little money.

It was spring and early one morning, just when the mother wanted to leave for her work, the sick maiden looked at the bottom window pane through the little window on to the floor.

'What is that bit of green peeping out by the window pane? It is moving in the wind!'

The mother went over to the window and opened it slightly.

'Oh!' she said. 'Why, it is a little pea, with its green petals shooting out. How did it get into this crevice? Now you have a little garden and can watch it!'

And she pulled the bed of the poorly child nearer to the window, so the girl could see the growing pea more clearly. Then the mother went to work.

'Mother, it seems to me I am getting better!' the maiden said that evening. 'The sun has shone on me so warmly today. The pea is growing so very nicely, I too want to grow and improve and get well in the sunshine!'

'If only this could happen!' said the mother, but she never thought it could be so. Nevertheless she made a little trellis for the small green herb, which had brought happiness to her child, so it would not break in the wind. She fastened the twine to the board and to the upper window frame, so the pea shoots would have something to cling to and to twist around, as they grew. And grow they did.

'Well I never! It is in bud!' the woman cried out one morning and now she, too, was filled with hope and faith that her sick daughter would get well. Her mind recalled how much livelier the little girl's speech was of late and how only the previous morning she had sat up in bed without any help, and gazed with shining eyes upon her very own little pea garden.

A week later the little patient got up for the very first time for more than an hour. Happily she sat in the warm sunshine; the window was open and outside she could see the fully developed pale pink pea flower. The little girl bent her head and gently kissed its fragile leaves. It was a very special day.

'God himself must have planted this little herb and made it grow, so it would give you hope and joy, my darling child, and me too!' the mother said happily, smiling at the bloom as at God's angel.

But now to the other peas! Yes, the one who was shot into the big world, crying 'catch me if you can!' fell in a gutter and then ended in a pigeon's claw, where it lay like Jonah in the whale's stomach. The two lazy peas fared the same and got no farther, they were gobbled up by pigeons, which made them very solidly useful indeed. And the fourth, the one that wished to fly to the sun, it fell in a drain and remained for days and weeks in the foul-smelling water, swelling to quite a size.

'I am growing so wonderfully fat!' said the pea. 'I may even go pop! I don't think any other pea could get any farther, or have got any farther. I am the most remarkable of all the five peas from our pod.'

And the drain showed its agreement with this.

But under the garret window stood a young girl with shining eyes, the glow of good health on her cheeks; clasping her hands over the pea flower, she thanked God for it.

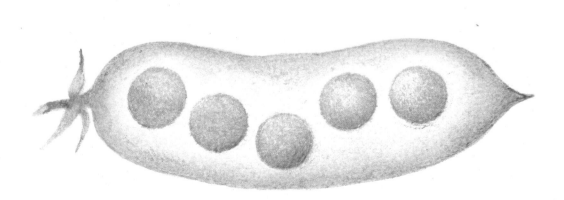

What Father Does is Always Right

I will tell you a story I heard when I was a boy. Since then, whenever I think of it, it seems to grow nicer and nicer. With stories it is the same as with people, their beauty tends to improve with age, and that is the very nicest thing about them!

I am sure you have been in the country. You must have seen some old, old cottage with a thatched roof, overgrown with moss and weeds, with a stork's nest on its ridge, not to mention the stork! The walls are crooked, the windows low, and only one will open. The stove juts out like a fat little tummy and the lilac hangs over the fence and, behind the fence, there is a large puddle with a duck or some ducklings, right under the knotted willow-tree. And, of course, there is a dog on a chain, who barks at all the passers-by.

Such a cottage was right out in the country where we lived, and in this cottage there lived a married couple, a farmer and his wife. Though they had very little, there was still one thing they could do without — that was a horse, who used to graze at the edge of the ditch by the roadside. The farmer rode him into the town, the neighbours borrowed him, repaying the farmer in kind. But it would have been more useful for the farmer and his wife to sell the horse, or to exchange it for something more to their advantage. But what was that to be?

'You, Father, understand such matters best!' said the wife. 'There's a market in town right now. Ride there and sell the horse, or make a good exchange! Whatever you do, is always right. Off with you to market!'

With that she tied his scarf round his neck, for she was better at that than he, tying it in a double knot, so he looked really smart. Then she wiped his hat with the palm of her hand and kissed him on his warm lips. And the farmer rode away on the horse that was to be sold or exchanged. Oh yes, Father would know what to do!

The sun was scorching, there was not a cloud in the sky. The road was dusty, filled with too many people, all going to the market, in carts, on horseback, or by foot. It was baking hot, without a bit of shade on the way.

Along the road came a man driving a cow, she was as sweet as only a cow can be. 'I bet she gives lovely milk!' thought the farmer. 'To get her would be an excellent exchange!'

'My good man, you with the cow! I want a word with you! Look here, a horse, as far as I know, is more valuable than a cow, but I don't mind that! The cow would be more useful to me. Wouldn't you like to exchange it?'

'Why not?' said the man with the cow. And so they did.

The farmer could have turned round, for he had done what he had set out to do. But having once made up his mind that he would go to market, to market he meant to go, if only just to see it. So he walked on with his cow. He hurried along, and the cow hurried too, and soon they caught up with a man driving a sheep. It was a very handsome sheep, beautifully plump and beautifully woolly.

'My word, I'd like to get her!' thought the farmer. 'There's plenty of grazing by that ditch of ours, and in the winter she could come indoors with us. In fact it would be more proper for us to have a sheep than a cow.'

'Shall we exchange, my good man?' said he.

The man with the sheep was quite happy about that, and so they swopped, and the farmer walked on along the road with his sheep. By a stile he saw a man with a large goose under his arm.

'That's quite something!' said the farmer. 'Plenty of feathers and flesh there! How splendid she'd look in our pen by the pond! She'd be the very thing for Mother, she'd have someone to gather peelings for! So often she had said, "If only we had a goose!" Now she can have one—and she will have one! Wouldn't you like to exchange? I'll give you the sheep for the goose, and I'll add my thanks too!'

And of course, the other man was more than willing, and so they swopped. The farmer got the goose. He was near the town now, and the road was packed more than ever. It was some crowd of people and beasts!

They pushed along the road right up to the gate-keeper's potato patch. That was where his hen was tied up, so that she wouldn't get frightened and run off. It was a lovely hen, she had a short tail and blinked with one eye. 'Cluck, cluck!' she clacked; I can't really say what she meant, but the farmer, when he saw her, said to himself, 'This is the most beautiful hen I have ever seen; more beautiful even than the parson's brooding hen. If only I could get her! Such a hen will never be short of a grain or two, she'd look after herself. I think I'd make an excellent bargain if I got her for the goose.' 'Shall we exchange, my good man?' he asked the gate-keeper. 'Exchange?' said the other. 'That's not a bad idea at all!' And so they did.

What a lot of business he had managed to do on his way to town! And it was hot and he was tired. He badly needed a drink and a bite to eat. He came to an inn and was just about to enter, when he bumped into a stable-boy coming out of the inn; on his back he had a sack.

'What's inside that sack?' asked the farmer.

'Rotten apples!' replied the stable-boy. 'A whole sackful for the pigs!'

'Gracious me, what a lot! How I wish Mother could see it! Last year we only had one apple on that old tree of ours by the hay-stack. We wanted to keep that apple, and so it stayed on top of the cupboard, till it turned rotten. To have a row of apples on top of the cupboard is a mark of prosperity, that is what our Mother used to say. And here she could see real prosperity! Oh yes, I will let her see it!'

'What will you give?' asked the stable-boy.

'What will I give? I'll swop my hen for those apples.'

And so he gave him the hen in exchange for the apples, and walked into the inn, right up to the counter. He left the sack of apples by the stove. The stove was lit, but he never gave this a thought. There were many customers in the room, horse-dealers, cattle-dealers, and also two Englishmen. These Englishmen were so rich that their pockets bulged with gold sovereigns. And how they liked to bet—but we are just coming to that!

Hiss! Hiss! Whatever was that sound near the stove? The apples were beginning to bake.

'What is that?' they asked, and they soon found out! The whole tale about the horse who had been swopped for the cow, and all the rest of it, right down to the rotten apples.

'You'll be in for it, when you get home!' laughed the Englishmen. 'What a beating you'll get!'

'It will be a kiss I'll get, not a beating,' said the farmer. 'My wife will say, "What Father does is always right!"'

'Lets bet on that!' cried the Englishmen. 'A barrelful of gold sovereigns we'll give! One such sovereign is worth a hundred ordinary ones!'

'I'll be content with a bushel!' said the farmer. 'All I can offer is a bushelful of apples with me and Mother thrown in. But that wouldn't only be a full measure, but a measure filled to overflowing!'

'Done! Done!' cried the Englishmen, and so the wager was sealed.

The inn-keeper's cart was brought to the front of the inn. The Englishmen got in, the farmer got in, and the rotten apples were put in too. And so they drove off to the farmer's cottage.

'Good evening, Mother!'

'Good evening, Father!'

'I've certainly done some exchanging!'

'And who's better at it than you!' said the wife, embracing him, and forgetting all about the sack and the strangers.

'I swopped the horse for a cow!'

'Lord be thanked for the milk!' said the wife. 'Now we can have milk puddings, butter and cheese. What a splendid exchange that was!'

'Yes, but then I exchanged the cow for a sheep!'

'That was even better!' said the wife. 'You always think of everything. We have plenty of grazing for a sheep. So now we shall have sheep's milk and sheep's cheese, and woollen stockings, yes, even woollen night caps! A cow wouldn't have given us that! A cow sheds her coat! You truly are a thoughtful man!'

'But I exchanged the sheep for a goose!'

'Oh Father, do you mean we'll have a Christmas goose this year? How hard you always try to please me! How sweet of you! We can put the goose in the pen, she'll grow even fatter there by Christmas!'

'But I exchanged the goose for a hen!' said the man.

'For a hen! What a good swop that was!' said the wife. 'The hen will lay eggs, she'll sit on them and hatch them and we'll have little chicks. We'll build a hen-house! It's the very thing I've always wanted!'

'But I exchanged the hen for a sackful of rotten apples!'

'For that I must give you a kiss!' said the wife. 'Thank you so much, my dear husband! Now I'll tell you something. Whilst you were away, I thought I'd cook you a really good supper, an omelette with chives. I had the eggs, but no chives. So I went across the road to the schoolmaster's house. I know full well they have chives, but the wife is such a mean, false creature! I begged her to lend me some. 'Lend?' said she. 'Nothing grows in our garden, not even a rotten apple! I couldn't lend you even that!' And now I shall be able to lend her ten, maybe even a whole sackful! Oh Father, what fun!' And she kissed him smack on the lips.

'What a scene!' cried the Englishmen. 'Nothing throws her off balance, though he went down and down! It's worth every penny of our money!' And so they paid out the bushel of sovereigns to the farmer, who got a kiss instead of a thrashing.

Yes, it always pays for a wife to be wise and to declare that Father is the wisest, and that what he does is always right.

And this is the story! I heard it when I was a small boy and now you've heard it as well, and so you know that what Father does is always right.

The Old House

In the street opposite stood an old, old house. It was, indeed, standing there for almost three hundred years, as anyone could read by looking at the beam, for the year it had been built was carved here amid tulips and hop-tendrils. Verses too were written here in the by-gone manner, and over each window a grotesque face was carved in the wooden frame. The first floor of the house projected quite a way beyond the ground floor, and right under the roof ran a gutter with a dragon's head on it; rain-water was meant to gush out from its mouth, but it ran out of the stomach instead, for the gutter was full of holes.

All the other houses in the street were new and neat, with big windows and smooth walls. It was quite plain to see that they would have nothing to do with the old house. It was obvious they were saying to themselves, 'How much longer is that ugly old hag going to disgrace our street! The upper storey is so far out in the road, that one cannot see from our windows what is happening in that direction! And those steps leading to the front door, they are as broad as if they belonged to a castle and as high as if they led up to a church-steeple. And that iron balustrade looks just like the entrance to an ancient tomb, and has in fact brass knobs too!'

On the opposite side of the street all the houses were also new and neat and pretty, and they were of the same opinion as the other houses. But at one of the windows used to sit a little boy with fresh, red cheeks and bright sparkling eyes; he liked the old house better than all the others, in sunshine, or by moonlight. And when he gazed at the wall opposite, from which the mortar had worn away, he imagined the strangest of scenes—how the street probably looked centuries ago, when all the houses had steps leading to their front doors, projecting upper storeys, and pointing gables. He could see soldiers marching about with halberds in their hands, and ornamented gutters running round in the shapes of dragons and griffins. Oh yes, that old house indeed was worth looking at!

An old gentleman lived in it, and he wore velvet trousers, a coat with large brass buttons on it and such a wig! You could see straightaway it was a real wig. Every morning an old servant came to him, to clean his rooms and run his errands, otherwise the old gentleman in the velvet trousers lived quite alone in the old house. Now and again he walked to his window and looked out. Then the little boy from opposite nodded to him, and he nodded back in return, and thus they became friends, though they had never spoken to each other; but that did not seem to matter.

The little boy heard his parents say, 'That old gentleman opposite is very well off, but it must be dreadful to be so much alone.'

The next Sunday the little boy wrapped something up in a piece of paper, then he ran down to the door and waited till the old servant from opposite passed by. Then he said to him, 'Would you please give this to the old gentleman opposite from me? I have two tin soldiers, this is one of them. I want him to have it, for I know he is so terribly lonely.'

The old man seemed quite pleased; he nodded and took the tin soldier

into the old house. A little later he returned with a message; would the little boy like to pay the old gentleman opposite a visit? His parents gave their permission, and the little boy went across to the old house.

The brass knobs on the balustrade by the steps were shining even more brightly than usual; one would almost think they had been polished specially in honour of his visit. And the carved trumpeters—for on the front door were carved trumpeters standing in tulips—they blew with all their might; their cheeks seemed to be more puffed out than ever before. And they blew on their trumpets: 'Trarara! The little boy comes! Trarara!'

The front door opened. The whole passage was full of hanging portraits of knights in armour and ladies in silk robes; the armour rattled and the silk dresses swished and rustled. Then there was a staircase; first it led up high, and then a little way down—and next, it opened on to a balcony, which was very decayed, with chinks and crevices in it, and grass and weeds sprouted through every hole. There was so much greenery round the entire balcony that it looked just like a garden. Ancient flower-pots

were standing on it, each with a face and asses' ears. Inside them, plants were growing exactly as they liked. In one pot carnations were growing over the edge, or rather the green leaves and shoots, and they were saying quite plainly, 'The breeze has caressed me, the sun has kissed me, and promised me a little flower on Sunday, a Sunday little flower!'

Then the old man and the little boy entered a chamber and its walls were lined with pigskin, which had gold flowers stamped upon it. And it called:

'Time dims and destroys the gilding,
But pigskin's life is never ending.'

Here stood armchairs with high, richly carved backs and arm-rests on either sides. 'Sit down! Sit down!' they cried in invitation. 'Ugh! How I am cracking inside! I am sure to get dry rot in my back like that old cabinet! Dry rot in my back, ugh!'

And then the little boy walked into the room with the bay window, where the old gentleman sat.

'Thanks for the tin soldier, little friend!' said the old gentleman. 'And thanks also for coming to see me.'

'Thanks! Thanks!' and 'Crack! Crack!' said all the furniture in the room. There were so many pieces of furniture there, that they got in each other's way when they wanted to see the little boy.

In the middle of the wall hung the picture of a lovely lady; she looked so young and so happy, but was dressed in a very old-fashioned way with powder in her hair and in a stiff, starched gown. She said neither 'crack', nor 'thanks', like the furniture, but gazed upon the little boy with kindly eyes. And he immediately asked the old gentleman, 'Where did you get her from?'

'From the pawnbroker opposite,' replied the old gentleman. 'There are many pictures there. Nobody knows the people in them, or cares about them, for they have all been buried long ago. But this lady I happened to know many, many years ago. She has been dead too, for fifty years.'

Under the portrait hung a bouquet of faded flowers behind glass; they must have been at least fifty years old too, and looked so. And the pendulum of the big clock swung from side to side, and the clock's hand went round and round, and everything in the room grew older and older.

'They say at home,' said the little boy, 'that you are so awfully lonely.'

'Oh no!' the old man cried. 'So many old memories come to visit me, bringing so much to my mind. And now you have come too! I am truly happy here.'

Then the old gentleman took a picture-book from the bookcase. What wonderful pictures were here—the strangest carriages, such as are never seen today. Soldiers resembling knaves of clubs, and citizens with flying banners of different types: the tailors held a banner with a pair of scissors gripped by two lions; the shoemakers did not have a pair of boots on their flag, but an eagle with two heads, for with shoemakers everything, of course, goes in pairs. Oh, what a wonderful book that was!

The old gentleman went to the next room for some sweetmeats, apples and nuts. It was really nice in this old house.

'I can't stand it here!' cried the tin soldier, who was standing on the chest of drawers. 'It is so sad and lonely here! No one who has lived in a family can ever grow used to such a life! I can't stand it here! The days are so terribly long and the evenings are longer still. It is nothing like being at home with you. There, your father and mother talk together pleasantly and you and all the other dear children play happy, noisy games. But this old gentleman is such a hermit! Do you think there is anyone to look at him fondly? Do you think he is ever kissed, or that there is someone to dress a Christmas-tree for him? He will never have anything — except his own funeral! No, I can't stand it here!'

'Don't take it so tragically!' said the little boy. 'I like it here very much, and old memories visit here, bringing much with them!'

'But I can't see them and I don't know them at all!' cried the tin soldier. 'I can't stand it here!'

'But you have to stand it!' announced the little boy.

The old gentleman returned, his face alight with contentment and with delicious sweetmeats, apples and nuts in his hands. The little boy thought about the tin soldier no more.

He returned home happy and pleased. Days and weeks passed by with mutual nodding towards the old house and from the old house, until the little boy went to call there again.

The carved trumpeters blew 'Trararara! The little boy comes! Trarara!' and the swords and the armour in the old portraits rattled and the silk robes rustled, and the pigskin on the wall chanted its opinion, while the old armchairs with dry rot in their backs sighed 'ah!' Everything was exactly as the first time, for every day in the old house was the same as the last and the next.

'I can't stand it here!' cried the tin soldier. 'It is so terribly sad, I keep shedding tin tears. Let me go to the wars instead, and lose my arms and legs! That at least will be a change. I can't stand it here! — Now I know what it means to be visited by old memories which bring all sorts of things to one's mind! They visit me, too, but believe me, there is no pleasure in it at all when it goes on for some time. They made me want to run away from this chest of drawers! I saw you all in the house opposite as plainly as if you had been standing here. It was Sunday morning again — do you remember? You children stood by the table and sang your hymns, as you always do. You looked so pious with your hands clasped, and your father and mother looked grave and important.

'Then the door opened and your little sister Maria ran into the
room—the one who is not yet two years old and who always starts to
dance whenever she hears music or singing. It wasn't the proper thing to
do just then, but Maria began to dance. But she could not keep time, for
the tune of the hymn was so slow. So she stood first on one foot, her head
bent forward, then on the other foot, her head bent down towards the
opposite side; but still she wasn't in time. You all looked so serious,
though this couldn't have been easy at all, but I laughed inwardly so much
that I fell off the table and hurt myself. In fact, I still carry the mark of that
fall to this day!

'All this is going through my mind, and everything else I have lived
through. This must be what the old gentleman means by 'old memories,

and all the things they bring to mind!' Tell me, do you still sing on Sundays? Tell me about Maria, and how my comrade, the other tin soldier, is getting on—that lucky fellow! Oh, I can't stand it here!'

'I gave you as a present!' said the little boy. 'You have to stay here. Can't you understand that?'

The old gentleman brought out a drawer, in which were many wonderful things; an ancient money-box, a balm-box, and packs of old cards—very large gilt cards, such as one never sees now. Then the old gentleman opened the piano; there was a landscape painted on the inside of the lid, and when he played the instrument, it sounded very tinny. Then he hummed an old tune.

'Ah, how beautifully she used to sing that!' said he, nodding to the portrait he had bought at the pawnbroker's; his eyes sparkled brightly at the thought.

'I want to go to the wars! I want to go to the wars!' cried the tin soldier as loud as he could, and he threw himself off the chest to the floor.

Where had he gone? The old gentleman searched for him, the little boy searched for him, but the tin soldier had disappeared and he did not reappear. 'Don't worry, I will find him!' the old gentleman said reassuringly, but he never did find him. The floor was too worn and full of cracks and crevices. The tin soldier had fallen through a crack and now he lay in an open tomb.

The day sped by and the little boy returned home. Weeks, many weeks passed. The windows were now frozen over. The little boy had to breathe hard upon them to make a little peep-hole, through which he could see the old house opposite. The snow hid all its wooden carvings and inscriptions, it lay thickly upon the steps all the way to the front door, as though no one were at home. And no one was at home—the old gentleman had died.

That evening a carriage drove up to the old house and a coffin was carried down the steps; the old gentleman was to be buried somewhere in the country. They were taking him there now, but no one accompanied him, for all his friends were dead. As they passed by, the little boy blew the old gentleman in the coffin a kiss.

A few days later an auction was held at the old house. The little boy watched from the window as the knights and the old ladies, the flower-pots with the long asses' ears, the armchairs and cabinets were all taken away. The portrait of the young lady bought at the pawnbroker's returned again to the pawnbroker, and there it remained, for no living soul knew the sweet face, or cared for such an old picture.

The following spring the house was pulled down, for it was, as people said, such a sight. Now it was possible to look from the street right into the room with the pigskin hangings, which had been torn and gashed. The green weeds round the balcony clung wildly to the decaying planks. Slowly all of it was taken away.

'About time too!' declared the neighbouring houses.

They built a beautiful house in its place, with large windows and smooth white walls. But in front of it, where the old house had actually stood, they made a little garden. Clusters of vines grew from it over the neighbour's walls and it was fenced in by iron grating with a trellis-gate; it really looked grand. People stopped to peep inside. And on the branches of the vines dozens and dozens of sparrows clustered, and chirped away nineteen to the dozen.

Many, many years went by. The little boy grew up to be a man, a really fine man, who made his parents pleased and proud. In time he married, and moved into the new house with the little garden. One day, his young bride was planting a field-flower in the little garden and the young man was standing by her side. She planted it with her own pretty hand and smoothed the earth round it with her fingers. Oh! What was that? She had pricked herself. Something sharp and pointed was sticking out of the soft ground.

It was the tin soldier, the very same one that disappeared from the old gentleman's room! He had tumbled under the joist and for many years had lain in the earth.

The young woman wiped the tin soldier clean, first with a green leaf, and then with her own fine handkerchief, which was deliciously perfumed and the tin soldier felt as though he were awakening from a trance.

'Show him to me!' said the young man. He smiled and shook his head. 'No, it cannot be the same tin soldier! But it reminds me of something which happened to me when I was a little boy.' And he told his wife about the old house, and the old gentleman, and the tin soldier that he had given him, because he was so terribly lonely. He told it all so sincerely, exactly as it had been, and his young wife's eyes brimmed with tears thinking of the life and fate of the old house and the old gentleman.

'This can be the very same tin soldier!' she said. 'I will keep him just to remind myself of all you have told me. But you must show me the old gentleman's grave!'

'I wish I knew where it was,' replied her husband. 'I believe no one knows where it is. All his friends were dead, nobody really cared, and then I was only a small boy!'

'How terribly lonely he must have been!' she said.

'Yes, terribly lonely!' repeated the tin soldier. 'But how wonderful it is not to be forgotten!'

'Yes, wonderful!' cried something close by—but no one except the tin soldier knew that it was a shred from the old pigskin hangings that had spoken. The gilding was all gone, and it merged completely with the moist earth, but it still had a high opinion of itself and still declared:

> *'Time dims and destroys the gilding,*
> *But pigskin's life is never ending.'*

The tin soldier, however, did not believe this.

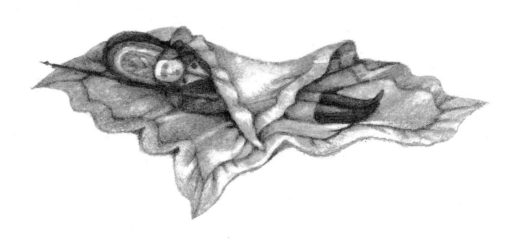

The Snowman

'I am all a-crackle, it's so beautifully cold!' said the snowman. 'And that biting wind, when it nips, most certainly blows life into one! But how that glare up there glares at me!' By that he meant the sun, which was just about to set. 'I shan't give her the pleasure of even batting an eyelid, and will stand firm on my ground.'

His eyes were two triangular pieces of tile, his mouth a part of a broken old rake, which gave him teeth too.

He had been born to the cheering of boys and to the greeting of ringing sleigh-bells and the cracks of whips.

The sun went down and the full moon rose, round and large, shining brightly in the blue air.

'There she is again, but this time she is turned the other way round!' cried the snowman, for he thought the sun had reappeared. 'But I've stopped her from glaring! Let her hang and shine up there, so I can see myself clearly. If only I knew what one should do to be able to move! How I wish I could move! Then I would slide on the ice, the way I've seen the boys doing. But I don't know how to run.'

'Go away! Go away!' barked the old watch-dog. He was a bit croaky, and had been right from the day he had stopped being a house-dog, lolling about under the stove. 'That sun will teach you how to run! I saw it happen last year to your predecessor, and before that to his predecessor. Go away! Go away. Away they all go!'

'I don't understand you, my friend,' said the snowman. 'Do you mean to say that the creature up there will teach me to run? When I looked her straight in the eye the first time, she ran well, sure enough. But now she's sneaked back again from the other side.'

'You don't know anything!' said the watch-dog. 'But then you've only just been thrown together today! What you see up there now is the moon; what went down was the sun. She will be back again tomorrow, and will be sure to teach you how to run to the ditch. We're in for a change of weather, I can feel it in my left hind leg. The weather is on the change, to be sure.'

'I don't understand him,' said the snowman. 'But I have a feeling that it is something unpleasant. That glare which glared at me, and then went down, the one he calls the sun, is no friend of mine.'

'Go away! Go away!' barked the watch-dog again. He turned round his tail three times, then crawled into his kennel to sleep.

There was, indeed a change in the weather. In the morning thick, damp fog settled over the whole district. An icy wind was blowing, and a sharp frost was in the air. What a wonderful sight it was when the sun rose! Trees and bushes were covered with hoarfrost and looked like a forest of white coral, with the branches studded with glittering, silvery blossom. Countless twigs and sprigs, which in summer one cannot see for the leaves, now stood out clearly, each and every one. It was like delicate lace,

so dazzling white it was, as though a brilliant light streamed from every spray. The silver birch stirred in the wind and seemed to be as full of life as trees are in summer-time. How indescribable was all the splendour! When the sun came out, oh, how everything sparkled, as if sprinkled with diamond dust. And on the snow-covered plain, large diamonds sparkled, you would think they were countless, tiny candles burning, whiter than the white snow itself.

'How very beautiful!' exclaimed the young woman, who came into the garden with a young man. They stopped right by the snowman and gazed at the glistening trees. 'It is never so beautiful in the summer!' said she.

'And we never see such a grand fellow as this in the summer,' added the young man, pointing to the snowman.

The young woman laughed, gave a friendly nod to the snowman and danced away with her friend across the snow, which crunched under their feet as if it were starched.

'Who were those two?' said the snowman to the watch-dog. 'You've been in this garden longer than I have. Do you know them?'

'Of course I do,' said the watch-dog. 'She strokes me and he gives me bones with bits of meat. I never bite them.'

'But who are they?' asked the snowman.

'Sweethearts!' said the watch-dog. 'They are going to move into the same kennel and gnaw on the same bone. Go away! Go away!'

'Are those two as important as you and I?' asked the snowman.

'Why, of course, they belong to our owners!' said the watch-dog. 'It's pathetically little a fellow knows who was born only yesterday. I can see this with you! I, on the other hand, am old and experienced, and I know everybody in this place. And there was a time when I didn't stand here chained up in the freezing cold. Go away! Go away!'

'The frost is lovely!' argued the snowman. 'Tell me more, tell more! Only stop rattling that chain, it makes my inside all a-crackle.'

'Go away! Go away!' barked the watch-dog. 'In those days I was still only

a puppy, a tiny, pretty puppy, so they say. I used to lie on a soft velvet stool, sometimes even in the lap of my noble master or mistress. And I was kissed on my nose and my paws were wiped on an embroidered handkerchief. They called me 'Poppet' and 'Cuddles'. But then I grew too big for them, so they gave me to the housekeeper. What a comedown that was, right into the basement! You can see into the room from where you stand. But in that room I was the master. Yes, at the housekeeper's I was the master. It may have been a poorer place than the one above, but it was far more comfortable. There were no children to squeeze me and drag me around as they did upstairs. My food was just as good, and there was much more of it! I had my very own cushion and then there was the stove. Such a stove; at this time of the year it is the most wonderful thing in this world! I always crawled right under it, out of everyone's sight. Oh, I dream of that stove even now! Go away! Go away!'

'Is a stove really so beautiful?' asked the snowman. 'Does it look like me?'

'It is the exact opposite of you! It is as black as soot! And it has a long neck with a brass ring. It devours wood, till flames shoot out of its mouth. You have to stay right near it, then you'd see how very cosy it is! If you look through the window from where you stand, you must be able to see it!'

And the snowman looked in and saw a truly black, polished object with a brass ring. The fire shone from underneath it. The snowman felt most peculiar, he felt something he could not even explain to himself. He was overcome by something he did not recognize.

'And why did you leave her?' asked the snowman, thinking that the stove must be a she. 'How could you leave such a place?'

'I was forced to, of course,' said the watch-dog. 'They threw me out and tied me to this chain. I bit the young master in the leg, for he kicked away the bone I was gnawing. I said to myself, a bone for a bone! But they didn't understand that at all, and so I've been chained ever since and I've lost my clear voice; just listen how hoarse I am, Go away! Go away! And that was the end of my wonderful life!'

The snowman was no longer listening. He was still staring into the housekeeper's basement flat, into her room where the stove was standing on its four iron legs, looking as big as the snowman himself.

'I've got such a funny, crunching feeling inside,' said he. 'Will I never get inside? It is such a modest wish, and surely our modest wishes must come true. It is my greatest wish, my only wish; it would be rather unjust if it didn't come true. I must get in there, I must cuddle up to her, even if it means breaking the window.'

'You will never get in there!' said the watch-dog. 'And if you did get to the stove, you would be gone straightaway!'

'I am as good as gone now,' said the snowman. 'It seems to me I am falling to bits.'

All day long the snowman stared through the window. At dusk the room was even more inviting. A pleasant glow came from the stove, such as the moon and the sun cannot give, a glow such as only a stove can give when it is well fed. Whenever its door was opened, the flames shot out as was their custom, making the snowman's white face glow bright red and flooding his chest with scarlet light.

'I can't bear it,' he said. 'She's so beautiful when she puts her tongue out at me!'

The night was very long, but not for the snowman. He stood engrossed with his beautiful thoughts, which straightaway froze solid.

In the morning the basement windows were frozen up; they were covered in the most lovely frosty flowers any snowman could wish to see, but they hid the stove. The flowers did not want to melt, and so the snowman could not see her. Everything crunched and crackled; it was the sort of frosty weather to make any snowman truly happy, but our snowman was not happy at all. He could have been happy and he should have been happy, but he was unhappy, for he was suffering with stove-sickness.

'That is a dangerous illness for a snowman,' said the watch-dog. 'I suffered with it too, but I got over it. Go away! Go away! We're in for a change in the weather!'

And the weather did change. It started to thaw.

As the thaw increased, the snowman decreased. He said nothing, he complained not, and that is a good sign.

One morning he collapsed. Where he had stood, something that looked like a broomstick was left sticking in the air. He had been built by the boys round that broomstick.

'Now I understand why he was paining,' said the watch-dog. 'The snowman had a poker in his body, and the poker moved him. But now it's all over. Go away! Go away! Gone!'

And soon the winter was gone too.

'Go away! Go away!' barked the watch-dog. But in the yard little girls sang:

> *'Flower, sweet primrose, show us your face;*
> *Now willow, t'is time to bud, make haste!*
> *You, cuckoo and lark, come and sing,*
> *February's end brings us spring!*
> *I shall sing too, tweet-tweet! Cuckoo!*
> *Beautiful sun, shine for us, do!'*

Then, no one gave a thought to the snowman.

The Little Match Girl

It was dreadfully cold. The snow was falling fast and it was almost dark. This was the last evening of the old year, New Year's Eve. And in this cruel cold and darkness a poor little girl was still wandering about the streets, with bare head and feet. When she had left her home she had slippers on, but they were much too large — indeed, they were last worn by her mother, that is how large they were. And whilst the little girl was running across the street, to get out of the way of two fast carriages, they had dropped off her feet. One of the slippers was lost for good; a boy ran off with the other, he thought it might come in useful one day as a cradle.

The little girl walked along the street, her bare feet quite red and blue with the cold. She carried a little bundle of matches in her hand, and a whole pile of them in her tattered old apron. No one had bought anything from her the whole day; no one had given her a single penny. She wandered through the streets starving and frozen, a pitiful little thing.

Snowflakes fell on her long, golden hair, which curled charmingly round her shoulders, but the little girl did not think about her beauty at all. Lights were glimmering behind every window and the wonderful smell of roast goose came to her from several houses; it was, after all, New Year's Eve! It was of this the little girl thought.

She found a corner made by two houses, one of which jutted out into the street slightly further than the other, and there she crouched. She drew her little feet right under her, but could not warm them — she was even colder than before. Yet she dared not go home, for she had sold no matches and had earned not a single penny. Her father would only beat her and besides, her home was almost as cold as the street, they hardly had a roof over their heads and the wind always whistled through their attic room, though they filled the worst chinks with straw and rags.

Her little hands were stiff with cold. Oh, how nice it would be to warm them over the flame of a match! If only she dared take one from the bundle, strike it against the wall, and warm her fingers ... she drew one out, and with a strike—how it sparkled, how it burned! It was a bright, warm flame, like the flame of a candle, and she held her hands over it.

What a wondrous light it was! It seemed to the little girl that she was sitting by a large iron stove with brass ornaments and a brass chimney; how beautifully blazed the fire within! The little girl stretched out her feet to warm them too—but alas, at that moment the flame died. The stove vanished and the little girl sat on the cold pavement with the burnt match in her hand.

She struck a second match against the wall; it kindled and flamed, and as its glow fell on the wall, the wall became as transparent as a veil and through it the little girl could see right into the room. A table stood inside, spread with a sparkling white damask cloth and the most delicate china; the deliciously smelling roast goose stood at one end, stuffed with apples and plums! And, nicest of all, the goose, with knife and fork in her breast, jumped down from the dish, and waddled along the floor right up

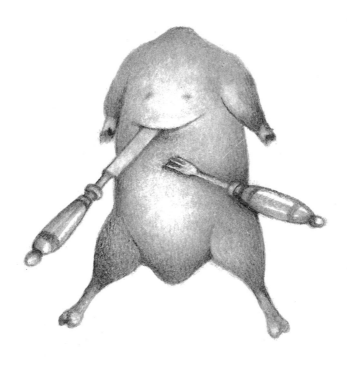

to the poor little girl. But then the match went out and all the little girl could see was the cold, grey wall.

She lit yet another match. As it flared up, she found herself before the most beautiful Christmas-tree. It was even larger and prettier than the one she had seen last Christmas through the glass doors of a rich merchant's house. Hundreds of candles lit up the green branches, and gay decorations, such as she had seen in shop windows, looked down upon her from the tree. The child stretched out her little hands towards them—then the match burnt out. The Christmas candles, however, burned on, rising higher and higher and the little girl could see that they became bright stars in the sky. One of them fell, drawing a long, fiery tail through the sky.

'Someone is dying!' whispered the little girl, for her old grandmother—the only person who had been kind to her, and who was now dead—used to say, 'Whenever a star falls, an immortal spirit returns to God.'

The child struck yet another match against the wall; it flamed up, and in its glow her dear grandmother appeared, so bright and happy, and as gentle and loving as always.

'Grandmother!' cried the little girl. 'Take me with you! I know you will disappear when the match dies—you will vanish like the warm stove, like the lovely roast goose and the beautiful Christmas-tree!' and she quickly lit the rest of the matches left in the bundle, to keep her grandmother as long as she could. The matches gave out such a splendid glow, that it was brighter than daylight. Never before had grandmother looked so pretty and so tall. She took the little girl in her arms, and together they flew in joy and in glory high, so high, till they came to the place where cold, hunger and pain are never known—they were in Paradise!

But in the freezing morning-hour, a little girl crouched in the corner of the wall, her cheeks glowing, her lips smiling—but she was dead. She had frozen to death on the last night of the old year. The dawn of the New Year lit up the lifeless child, crouched there with the matches in her lap, with the one bundle burnt out.

'She wanted to warm herself,' people said. But none of them knew of the wondrous visions she had seen, or the bright glory in which she left with her grandmother into the joys of the New Year.

The Fir-Tree

Far away, deep in a forest, there grew a pretty little fir-tree. He stood in a nice spot, where the sun shone full upon him and where there was plenty of fresh air. And many bigger fir-trees grew all around, some older and some younger. But the little fir-tree longed to grow as tall as the others. He did not care about the warm sunshine and about the fresh air; he paid no attention to the village children, who passed by picking straw-berries and raspberries. Often they came along and sat down by the little tree, saying, 'What a pretty little fir-tree this is!' The tree hated to hear that!

A year later he was a good deal bigger, and the next year bigger still, for one can always tell how many years a fir-tree has lived from the number of joints in his stem.

'Oh, if only I were as big as the others!' sighed the little tree. 'Then I could spread my branches far out, and through my crown I would see over the wide world! Birds would build nests in my branches, and when the wind blew, I would be able to nod as grandly as the other trees!'

Nothing pleased him, the sun, the birds, not even the crimson clouds which sailed above in the morning and evening.

In the winter-time, when the glistening white snow lay all round, often a hare would come hopping along and leap right over the little tree. That made him truly livid! But two winters passed, and by the third the fir-tree was so big that the hare was obliged to run round him. 'To grow, to grow, to be tall and grown-up—that is the only thing worthwhile in this world!' so thought the tree.

Every autumn the woodcutters came and felled some of the tallest trees. It happened year after year, and the young fir-tree, which by now was quite big, always trembled when he saw the magnificent trees falling to the ground with a deafening crash. Then their branches were cut off, so they looked terribly naked, long and thin. They were almost unrecognisable. And then, they were stacked on wagons and horses pulled them away out of the forest.

Where were they being taken? What was in store for them?

In the spring, the storks and the swallows returned. The tree asked them, 'Do you know where they are taken? Do you ever see them?'

The swallows knew nothing, but the stork looked thoughtful for a moment, then said with a nod of his head, 'Yes, I do believe it is so! When I flew from Egypt, I met lots of new ships which had splendid masts. I have little doubt they were the ones—they smelt of fir. How high they reached to the sky! They really looked grand!'

'Oh, if only I were big enough to sail upon the sea! And tell me, what is it, this sea, and what does it look like?'

'That would take too long to explain!' declared the stork, and off he went.

'Be glad that you are young!' chided the sunbeams. 'Rejoice in your healthy growth, in the fresh life that is in you!'

And the wind kissed him and the dew wept tears over him, but the fir-tree did not understand them at all.

As Christmas approached, many very young trees were felled—often trees which were not even as tall or as old as the young restless fir-tree who knew no peace and who was always longing to be away from the forest. The young trees, which were felled shortly before Christmas—and they were the prettiest ones of all—were left with their branches on. They were put on wagons and horses drew them away.

'Where are they going?' asked the little fir-tree. 'They are no bigger than I—one of them, in fact, is a lot smaller. And why did they leave all their branches on? Where will they get to?'

'We know! We know!' twittered the sparrows. 'We've been in the town, peeping in through the windows! We know where they are going! The greatest honour and glory is waiting for them! We looked in through the windows and saw them planted in the centre of a warm room and decorated with many beautiful things—golden apples, gingerbread, toys and hundreds of little lights.'

'And then?' asked the fir-tree, trembling in every branch. 'What then? What happens then?'

'Oh, we didn't see any more! But it was marvellous!'

'I wonder if I, too, was born for such a glorious destiny?' thought the tree joyfully. 'That's even better than sailing over the sea! Oh, how this longing hurts! If only Christmas was here! I am just as tall and just as wide-branched as those who were carried away last year! Oh, if only I were on the wagon right now! And in that warm room, with all the honour and glory. And what then? Something greater must surely come—why would they decorate me so otherwise? It must be something grand . . . But what? Oh, what torture this is! How I suffer with longing! I don't myself know what has come over me.'

'Be happy you have us!' said the air and the sunshine. 'Be happy you have the freshness of youth, here in freedom!'

But the fir-tree was not at all happy. He grew and grew. Winter and summer he was always clothed in green, dark green. People who saw him said, 'What a lovely tree!'

Just before Christmas he was the first to be felled. The axe cut deep into his marrow and he fell to the ground with a heavy groan. It hurt so much,

he almost fainted. He was far from being able to think of anything happy, he was so grieved at the thought of parting from home, from the spot where he had grown up. Now he realized full well that he would never see his old companions again, or the little bushes and flowers which grew round him, perhaps not even the birds. Going away was not in the least pleasant.

He did not come to himself until he was unloaded with all the other trees in the yard, and heard a man's voice say, 'This one is splendid, we'll have it, and no other!'

Then came two smartly-dressed servants, and carried the fir-tree into a lovely big room. Portraits hung on all the walls, and by the large stone fire-place stood big Chinese vases with lions on their lids. There were rocking-chairs, silk sofas and enormous tables piled high with picture-books and toys. The fir-tree was planted in a barrel filled with sand, though nobody would guess it was a barrel, as a green cloth was hung all round it. And it was placed on a large gaily coloured carpet. How the tree trembled! What would happen next? Servants and young ladies began to decorate him. On some of the branches they hung little baskets of coloured paper, each one filled with sweets. Golden apples and nuts hung from the tree as though they had grown there; more than a hundred little candles, red, blue and white, were fixed here and there to the boughs and, suspended in all this greenery were little dolls—the tree had never seen anything like it. Right at his very top, they fastened a big, golden star, truly magnificent, magnificent beyond compare.

'This evening the fir-tree will be lit up!' they all said.

'If only it was tonight already!' thought the tree. 'If only the candles were lit soon! But I wonder what will happen then? Will the trees from the forest come to see me? Will the sparrows fly to peep at me through the window? Shall I grow fast here and remain decorated winter and summer?'

The fir-tree certainly knew what to yearn for; but all that yearning had given him barkache, and barkache is for a tree as bad as headache is for us.

At long last the candles were lit. Oh, what a glow, what splendour! The tree was so overcome, he trembled in every branch, so much so, that one of the candles set some of the needles alight.

'Goodness gracious!' cried the young ladies, rushing to put the fire out.

The tree was now too frightened even to tremble. How horrible it was! He was so afraid of losing something of his splendour. He was completely bewildered by all the glitter and glory. All at once the door was flung open and a crowd of children burst in—it is a wonder they did not knock the tree over. Their elders followed in a more orderly manner. The children stood silent for a short moment—but only for a moment—then they burst into joyful cries, till the whole place echoed with their voices. They danced round and round the tree, tearing one present after another from his branches.

'What are they doing?' wondered the tree. 'What will happen next?' The candles were burning down to the very branches, and as they did so, they were put out. Afterwards, the children were allowed to strip the tree. They rushed at him till all his branches creaked and had his top with the star not been fastened to the ceiling, he would have crashed to the ground.

The children danced about with their beautiful toys; no one thought any more about the tree, except the old nurse, who came and peered into his branches, but only to see whether a fig or an apple had been forgotten.

'A story! A story!' cried the children, pulling a plump little man towards the tree. He sat down and said, 'Now we are as in a wood. And it will do the tree good to listen too. But I am only going to tell you one story. Do you want to hear about Moany Groany, or about Dizzy Ninny, who fell down the stairs, yet came to the throne and married a Princess?'

'Dizzy Ninny!' cried some. 'Moany Groany!' cried the others. There was so much shouting and screaming, only the fir-tree was silent, thinking to himself, 'Why don't they let me in among them, why don't they give me something to do!' He did not realize that they had finished with him, that he had played his part.

In the meantime the man under the tree was telling the story of Dizzy Ninny. The children clapped their hands and shouted, 'Go on! Go on!' They wanted to hear about Moany Groany as well, but they had to be content with Dizzy Ninny.

The fir-tree stood perfectly still, deep in thought. The birds in the wood had never told him anything like this. 'Dizzy Ninny fell down the stairs, and yet he got the Princess! Oh well, that is the way of the world!' he said to himself. He thought the tale to be true, as it had been told by such a dignified gentleman! 'Ah, who knows, perhaps I too will fall down the stairs and marry a Princess!' And he looked forward to tomorrow, when he would be again decorated with candles, toys, gold and fruit.

'I won't tremble tomorrow!' he vowed. 'I'll rejoice in my splendour. Tomorrow I will hear the story about Dizzy Ninny again, and perhaps the one about Moany Groany as well.' And all through the night the tree stood still, deep in thought.

In the morning the servants came in.

'Now all the glory begins again!' thought the tree. But they dragged him out of the room and up the stairs to the attic, and there they pushed him into a dark corner, where not a ray of light could penetrate. 'What does this mean?' thought the tree. 'What am I to do here? What will I hear in this place?' He leant against the wall, and thought and thought. He had plenty of time for thought, for day after day, night after night passed away. Nobody came, and when at long last someone did, it was only to put some boxes in a corner. The fir-tree was now completely hidden and, so it seemed, completely forgotten.

'It is now winter,' thought the tree. 'The ground will be hard and covered with snow. They cannot plant me now. So I must wait here in this shelter till spring comes again. How well thought out it is! How kind people are! If only it wasn't so dark and so terribly lonely! There's not even a little hare to be seen! It was really nice in the wood, when the snow lay on the ground and the hares were scampering around. Yes, even when they jumped over me, though I did not like it then. But up here it's so dreadfully lonely!'

'Squeak, squeak!' cried a little mouse, creeping towards the tree. Then out came another mouse from its hole. They sniffed around the fir-tree and chased in and out of his branches.

'It is horribly cold!' said the little mice. 'Apart from that, it is very comfortable here. Don't you agree, you old fir-tree?'

'I am not at all old!' said the fir-tree. 'There are many a lot older than I am!'

'Where are you from?' asked the mice. 'And what do you know?' Sud-

denly they were most inquisitive. 'Tell us about the best and loveliest place in the world! Have you been there? Have you been in the pantry, where there are cheeses on the shelves and hams hanging from the ceiling? Where one can dance over tallow-candles, and where you go in thin and come out fat?'

'I don't know that place,' said the tree. 'But I know the forest where the sun shines and where the birds sing!' And he told them all about his youth. The mice had never heard anything like it. They listened attentively and then cried, 'Oh, what a lot of things you have seen! How happy you must have been!'

'Happy?' said the fir-tree, thinking over all he had just told them. 'Yes, to be sure, those were rather pleasant days!' And he proceeded to tell them about Christmas Eve, when he had been decorated with gingerbread and candles.

'Oh!' cried the mice, 'how happy you have been, you old fir-tree!'

'I am not old at all!' protested the tree. 'I only came out of the forest this winter. I am in the prime of life, but I rather rushed my growth.'

The following night they brought four more little mice, so they too could listen to the tree. And the more he talked, the more clearly he remembered everything and he said to himself, 'Yes, they were indeed pleasant days! But they may return, they may return! Dizzy Ninny fell down the stairs and yet married the Princess—perhaps I may marry a Princess one day!' His thoughts then turned to a birch-tree, a pretty young birch-tree, which grew in his forest. To the fir-tree she was a real and beautiful Princess.

'Who is this Dizzy Ninny?' asked the little mice.

So the fir-tree told them the whole fairy-tale; he could recall every single word. The little mice almost climbed to his very top for sheer joy. The next night many more mice came and on Sunday came also two rats. But they pronounced that the story was not at all amusing, which saddened the little mice, who, after this opinion, thought less of it too.

'Do you know only that story?' asked the rats.

'Only that one!' answered the fir-tree. 'It is a part of the happiest evening of my life, only then I never realized how happy I was!'

'It is such a poor story! Don't you know one about bacon and tallow-candles? No pantry tales?'

'No,' said the tree.

'Well then we've heard enough!' said the rats, and they went home.

In the end the little mice also stopped coming, and the tree sighed more than once, 'It was so nice when those busy little mice used to sit round me, listening to my tales! Now that too is past! But I must remember to enjoy life once I am taken away from this place!'

But when would that be? One morning people came rummaging about in the attic. They took away the boxes and then they pulled out the fir-tree. They threw him rather roughly to the floor, but soon afterwards a man dragged him towards the stairs, where he could see the light of day.

'Now life begins again!' thought the tree. He felt the fresh air, the first sunbeams and now he was outside in the yard. It all happened so fast, that he quite forgot to look at himself, for there was so much to see all around. The yard joined a garden, where everything was in bloom. Over the fence hung fresh, fragrant roses, the lime-trees were in blossom, and the swallows flew about, twittering: 'Tweet, tweet, tweet, my sweet husband has come!' but it was not the fir-tree they were tweeting about.

'Now I shall live again!' the tree cried joyfully, and he spread his branches wide. But, alas! they were all dried up and yellow. He lay in a corner among weeds and nettles. He still carried the gold paper star on his crown, and it now glittered in the bright sunshine.

Several children were playing merrily in the yard, the same who at Christmas-time had danced round the tree and had been so delighted with him. One of the smallest now ran to the tree and tore off the gold star.

'See what was still on that ugly old Christmas-tree!' cried he, trampling on his branches till they broke under his boots.

And the fir-tree gazed upon all the beautiful, fresh flowers in the garden and then he looked at himself, and wished he had been left in the dark corner of the attic. He thought of his happy youth in the forest, of the merry Christmas Eve, and of the little mice that had listened so eagerly to the story of Dizzy Ninny.

'All is over, all is over!' sighed the poor fir-tree. 'Why wasn't I happy, while I could have been! All is over!'

The servant came and chopped the tree into small pieces. There was quite a pile of them. It made a lovely blaze under the large copper pan. And the tree groaned deeply, and every groan sounded like a faint crackle of a gun. The children playing in the yard ran inside and sat down by the fire, gazing into it and crying 'piff, piff!' But with each crackle, which was a deep groan, the tree thought of a summer's day in the forest, or a winter's night, when the stars were shining. He thought of Christmas Eve, and of Dizzy Ninny, the only fairy-tale that he had heard and knew how to tell. At last he was completely burned.

In the yard the boys were playing about, and the smallest wore on his breast the gold star that the tree had worn on the happiest evening of his life. But that is all over; Christmas Eve is long over, it is all over with the tree, and the story is all over as well! For all stories must come to an end at some time or other.

The Nightingale

In China, as you must surely know, the Emperor is a Chinaman, and all around him are Chinese also. Many years have passed since what I am about to relate had taken place, but for that very reason it is important for you to hear the story at once, before it is forgotten.

The Emperor's palace was the most magnificent palace in the whole world; it was made entirely of fine porcelain, terribly expensive, but also terribly fragile and delicate, so that one had to be very careful indeed. In the garden grew the most wonderful, exquisite flowers and to the loveliest of these, little silver bells were fastened, which tinkled so that no one would go by without noticing them. Honestly, everything in the Emperor's garden was most excellently arranged! It was so long, that even the gardener did not know where it ended. If one kept on walking further, one came to a beautiful wood with high trees and deep lakes. The wood stretched right down to the sea, which was blue and deep. Large ships could sail close under the branches. And there in the branches lived a nightingale, who sang so sweetly that even the poor fisherman, who had so much else to do, would stand still and listen to her song when he came out at night to draw in his nets. 'Oh, how beautiful that is!' he would sigh; but he was obliged to get on with his work, and forget the bird. But if on the following night the nightingale sang again, and the fisherman happened to be there again, he would sigh, 'Oh, how beautiful that is!'

Travellers from all over the world came to the Emperor's city; they admired the town, the palace and the garden, but when they heard the nightingale sing, they all said, 'This is best of all!'

After their return home, they talked about it all and scholars wrote many books about the Emperor's city, the palace and the garden; nor did they forget the nightingale, for they placed her above everything else. And those who could write poetry, wrote the loveliest poems, all about the nightingale of the wood by the deep sea.

The books went round the world, and some of them reached the Emperor. He sat in his golden armchair and he read and read, every now and then nodding his head; he was really delighted by the splendid descriptions of his city, palace and garden. 'But the best of all is the nightingale!' was written there.

'What is this?' exclaimed the Emperor. 'The nightingale? I've never heard of it! Is there really such a bird in my empire, in my own garden in fact? I have never heard anyone talk about it! I have to learn of such a thing from books!'

So he called his gentleman-in-waiting, who was so grand a person that if anyone of inferior rank dared to speak to him or ask him a question, he would only answer 'pish!', which has no meaning at all.

'I hear there is a most remarkable bird here, called the nightingale,' said

the Emperor. 'They say it is the most wondrous thing in the whole of my empire! Why have I never been told about this?'

'I have never heard her mentioned!' replied the gentleman-in-waiting. 'She has never been presented at Court.'

'I wish her to come here tonight to sing for me!' the Emperor commanded. 'The whole world knows what I have here, and I do not.'

'I have never ever heard of her!' insisted the gentleman-in-waiting. 'But I will search for her, and I will find her!'

But where was she to be found? The gentleman-in-waiting ran up and down the stairs, and through halls and corridors, but none of the people he met had ever heard of the nightingale. So the gentleman-in-waiting ran back to the Emperor, saying that it surely must be some invention of the people who write books. 'Your Imperial Majesty should not believe all that is written in books! Much of it is pure invention and the so called black magic!'

'But the book in which I have read it,' said the Emperor, 'was sent to me

by the powerful Emperor of Japan, and therefore it cannot be untrue! I want to hear that nightingale! She must be here this evening! She has my highest favour. And if she does not come, I shall have the whole Court thrashed, after they had eaten their supper!'

'Tsing-pe!' said the gentleman-in-waiting, and off he ran again, up and down all the stairs, through all the halls and corridors, and half the Court ran with him, for none relished the idea of being thrashed. What a lot of questioning there was regarding the wondrous nightingale, who was known to all the world, but to nobody at Court.

At last they found a poor little girl in the kitchen, who said, 'Oh yes, the nightingale! I know her well! My word, how she sings! Every evening I am allowed to take a few scraps from the table to my poor sick mother, who lives down by the shore. On my way back when I grow tired and rest in the wood, I hear the nightingale sing. It makes the tears come into my eyes, for I always feel as if my mother were kissing me!'

'Dear little kitchen-maid,' said the gentleman-in-waiting, 'I will secure for you a permanent position in the Emperor's kitchen, even permission to watch the Emperor eat, if you will only lead us to the nightingale; for tonight I am to bring her to Court.'

So they all went together to the wood where the nightingale usually sang; half the Court was there. As they were on their way, a cow began to bellow.

'Ah,' said the Court pages, 'now we have her! What an extraordinary power for such a small animal! I am pretty sure I have heard her before!'

'Oh no, those are cows mooing!' said the little kitchen-maid. 'There is still a long way to go yet.'

The frogs in the pond began to croak.

'How lovely!' cried the Chinese chaplain. 'I hear her now! It sounds just like little church bells.'

'Oh no, those are cows mooing!' said the little kitchen-maid.

And then the nightingale began to sing.

'There she is!' said the little kitchen-maid. 'Listen! Listen! There she sits!' and she pointed to a little grey bird up in the branches.

'Is it possible?' wondered the gentleman-in-waiting. 'I did not dream she would look like this! How common she seems! I think she must have lost her colour at the sight of so many distinguished people!'

'Little nightingale!' cried the little kitchen-maid loudly, 'our gracious Emperor wishes you to sing for him!'

'With the greatest of pleasure!' replied the nightingale, and sang in a manner which would charm anyone's heart.

'It sounds like glass bells!' said the gentleman-in-waiting. 'And just look at her little throat moving! It really is strange that we have never heard her before. She will be a big success at Court!'

'Shall I sing again to the Emperor?' asked the nightingale, thinking that the Emperor was present.

'Most excellent nightingale!' said the gentleman-in-waiting, 'it is my great pleasure to invite you to a Court festival to be held this evening, when you will have the opportunity to charm his Imperial Majesty with your enchanting song.'

'But it sounds best here in the open!' said the nightingale. Nevertheless she followed willingly when she heard that this was the Emperor's wish.

Everything at the palace was sparkling clean. The walls and floors, which were all of porcelain, glittered in the light of thousands of lamps. The loveliest flowers—the ones, with the merriest and loudest tinkle—were arranged along the passages; here too was much hurrying and scurrying and quite a draught, which made the flower-bells ring all the louder, so that one could not hear one's own words.

In the middle of the grand hall, where the Emperor sat, a golden perch was built for the nightingale to sit on. The whole Court was present and the little kitchen-maid was allowed to stand at the back near the door, now she had the title of a true maid of the kitchen. Everybody was dressed in his best clothes and they all gazed at the little grey bird, to whom the Emperor now signalled with a nod.

The nightingale sang so wonderfully, that tears came into the Emperor's eyes and rolled down his cheeks. And the nightingale sang all the more beautifully, and her song touched everyone's heart. The Emperor was so delighted, that he announced that the nightingale should have his golden slipper to wear round her neck. But the nightingale thanked him and said she was already well rewarded.

'I have seen tears in the Emperor's eyes, and that to me is the very greatest reward! The Emperor's tears have strange power. Heaven knows I have been sufficiently rewarded!' And then she sang again.

'This is the prettiest piece of coquetry I have ever known,' said the ladies present. They filled their mouths with water, so they could cluck when anyone spoke to them—they imagined themselves to be nightingales too! And even the footmen and the chambermaids showed they were quite content, and that means a lot, for they are the most difficult people to satisfy. Yes, indeed, one can truly say the nightingale was a great success.

She was to remain at Court, to have her own cage and the right to fly out twice a day and once a night. She was always accompanied by twelve attendants, each holding on to her by a silk ribbon tied round her leg, and they held her tight. Such an outing was no fun at all.

All the city was talking about this wondrous bird. And when two people met, one would say only 'Night—!' and the other would add 'gale!' and they would sigh and understand each other perfectly. Eleven grocers

named their children after the nightingale, but not one of them managed to give out a single melodious note.

One day the Emperor received a large parcel which was marked, 'Nightingale' on the outside.

'This will most probably be another book about our famous little bird!' thought the Emperor. But it was not a book, but a clever little toy—an artificial nightingale, intended to resemble the living one. It was covered with diamonds, rubies and sapphires. When wound up, it could sing one of the songs which the real nightingale sang, wagging its tail of glittering gold and silver at the same time. Round its neck a little band was fastened, and it read, 'The nightingale of the Emperor of Japan is poor compared with the nightingale of the Emperor of China.'

'How fantastic!' everyone cried. And the one who had brought the artificial bird was immediately given the title of Chief Imperial Nightingale Bringer.

'Now let them sing together! What a duet that will be!'

So they had to sing together, but it did not work out very well, for the real nightingale sang in her own way, and the artifical bird according to its wheels.

'It is not his fault,' said the Court music-master, 'his timing is exceptionally good, and he is of a good school!' So the artificial bird was now to sing alone. He was quite as successful as the real nightingale, but so much prettier to look at.

Thirty-three times he sang the very same tune, and yet he was not weary at all. Some would have liked to hear him right from the beginning again, but the Emperor was of the opinion that the real nightingale should now sing a little—but where was she? Nobody had noticed that she had flown through the open window towards her own green woods.

'What is the meaning of this?' said the Emperor. All the courtiers abused the nightingale, saying what an ungrateful creature she was. 'But we still have the best of the pair!' they said, and the artificial bird had to sing once more. They were hearing that same tune for the thirty-fourth time, but still they did not know it well, for it was quite a difficult one. The Court music-master was full of praise for the artificial bird, he insisted, in fact, that he was better than the real nightingale, not only in his dress of beautiful diamonds, but inside as well.

'For you see, my noble lords and ladies and Your Imperial Majesty above all, you must consider this, with the real nightingale you can never know what is coming but with the artificial bird everything is fixed beforehand. That is how it is and that is how it will be! We can take him to pieces, we can open him up and understand with our human mind, how the mechanism works, how his wheels are put together, how they move, and how one thing follows another!'

'That is exactly my opinion too!' said everybody, and the Court music-master was given permission to show the bird to the Chinese people on the following Sunday. 'Let them hear him sing too,' said the Emperor.

So they heard him, and were as merry as if they had been drinking tea, for it is tea that makes the Chinese merry. And they all said 'Oh!' and held up their forefinger which they also call 'nibbler', and nodded their heads. But the poor fisherman, who had heard the real nightingale, would say, 'It sounds quite nice and it is rather like it, but something is missing!'

The real nightingale was banished from the empire.

The artificial bird was given a place on a silken cushion right by the Emperor's bed. All the presents he had received, gold and precious stones, lay round him, and in rank he was now raised to the title of High Imperial Bedside Table Singer; in fact his place was number one on the left, for the Emperor regarded the side where the heart is as the place of highest honour, and the heart is on the left side even in an Emperor. The Court music-master wrote twenty-five volumes about the artificial bird; they were terribly learned and long, and full of the most difficult Chinese words; so everyone preferred to say they had read them and understood them, for otherwise they would have been considered stupid and would have been punished.

And so a whole year went by. The Emperor, the Court, and all the Chinese knew every note of the artificial bird's song by heart, down to the last cluck, and that was exactly why they liked the song so much. They could now sing with him, and sing with him they did. The boys in the street would sing 'zezeze, cluck, cluck, cluck!' and so would the Emperor.

But one evening, when the artificial bird was singing away and the Emperor lay in bed listening, something suddenly went 'rip!' inside the bird. Something had snapped. There was a whirring sound, all the wheels went round, and the music stopped.

The Emperor jumped quickly out of bed and summoned his physician; but what use was he! So a watchmaker was called in, and he, after much talking and much examining, managed to make the bird work again, but he warned that he would have to be treated with care and used only rarely, for the pegs were almost worn out, and it was not possible to guarantee that new ones would make the bird sing. This was such a blow! Now the artificial bird was allowed to sing only once a year, and even then he managed this only with great difficulty. The Court music-master, however, made a short speech full of long words; he pronounced the bird as good as ever, and so it was as good as ever.

Five years went by. Suddenly the whole country was stricken with great grief, for in their hearts the people loved their Emperor; but now he was ill, and it was said that he would not live. A new Emperor had already been chosen, and outside the palace people stood about in the street, asking the gentleman-in-waiting how the Emperor was.

'Pish!' he would say, shaking his head.

Cold and pale the Emperor lay in his enormous, magnificent bed. The whole Court thought him already dead, and so everyone ran to greet the new Emperor. The men-servants ran out to talk about it, and the maids organized a big coffee party. Carpets and covers were laid in all the halls and passages throughout the palace, so not a single step would be heard. It was so still and so quiet everywhere.

But the Emperor was not yet dead. Stiff and pale he lay in his splendid bed with the long velvet curtains and the heavy golden tassels. The top of one window was slightly open, and the moon shone down on the Emperor and on his artificial bird.

The poor Emperor could hardly breathe; there seemed to be something pressing on his chest. He opened his eyes and saw that it was Death, who had put on the Emperor's crown, and held with one hand his gold sword and his magnificent banner with the other. And out of the folds of the big velvet curtains round the bed, the strangest heads were peering in. Some were truly hideous, others looked kind and gentle; they were all the bad and the good deeds of the Emperor. They had come to watch him, now that Death sat on his heart.

'Do you remember?' they whispered one after another. 'Do you remember?' And they told him so much that the sweat broke out on his forehead.

'I never knew that!' moaned the Emperor. 'Music! Music! The great Chinese drum!' he cried. 'I don't want to hear what they say!'

But they kept on in their reproach, whilst Death, like a proper China-man, nodded his head to every word.

'Music! Music!' screamed the Emperor. 'My precious little golden bird, sing, I beg you, sing! I gave you gold and precious stones; with my own hands I hung my gold slipper round your neck — sing, I beg you, sing!'

But the bird was silent; no one was there to wind him up, and he could not sing without. And Death kept on staring at the Emperor with his great hollow eyes. It was so silent there, so dreadfully silent!

All at once the sweetest singing was heard from near the window. It was the little nightingale, who was sitting outside on a branch. She had heard of the Emperor's suffering and had come to sing to him of hope and comfort. And as she sang, the spectral forms round the bed grew fainter and fainter, the blood flowed faster and faster through the Emperor's feeble body, and even Death himself listened and urged the nightingale, 'Sing on, little nightingale, sing on!'

'Yes I will, if you give me the magnificent gold sword! And if you give me the splendid banner and the Emperor's crown!'

And Death gave up each of these treasures for a song, but even afterwards the nightingale continued to sing. She sang of the silent churchyard, where white roses bloom, where the elder-tree spreads sweet fragrance, and where the fresh grass is soaked with the tears of the bereaved. Then Death became homesick for his own garden, and he floated out of the window like a cold, white mist.

'Thank you, thank you, you heavenly little bird!' said the Emperor. 'I know you well! I drove you from my country and empire! Yet you have sung away those evil visions from my bed, and Death from my heart! How shall I reward you?'

'You have rewarded me already!' said the nightingale. 'When I sang to you the first time, you rewarded me with the tears which filled your eyes, and for that I will never forget you. They are the jewels which warm a singer's heart! But now you must sleep, so you will grow well and strong! I will sing for you!'

And she sang and the Emperor fell into a sweet sleep.

When the Emperor awoke, feeling strong and healthy, the sun was shining in to him through the windows. None of his servants had come to him, for they all thought him to be dead. But the nightingale was there still, singing away.

'You must stay with me for ever!' said the Emperor. 'You shall only sing when you wish to do so. And I will smash that artificial bird into a thousand pieces!'

'Don't do that!' said the nightingale. 'He served you well, as best as he could. Keep him as before. I cannot build my nest in the palace and live here; but let me come whenever I feel like coming. I will sit in the evening on a branch close to the window and sing to you to make you happy, but also thoughtful. I will sing to you of good, and of evil, which is kept from you. I will sing to you of those who are happy, and of those who are sad. Such a little singing-bird as I flies far and wide; to the poor fisherman, to the peasant's cottage, to all who live far away from you and your Court. I love your heart more than your crown, and yet your crown has the fragrance of something holy. I will come and sing for you again. But you must promise me one thing.'

'Everything I will promise!' cried the Emperor. He was standing now in his imperial robes which he had put on himself, and he held the heavy gold sword to his heart.

'One thing I ask of you! Let no one know that you have a little bird who tells you everything. Then everything will be alright!'

And then the nightingale flew away.

The servants came in to look at their dead Emperor. There they stood in a daze, and the Emperor said, 'Good morning!'

The Little Mermaid

Far out in the sea, where the water is as blue as the blooms of the loveliest cornflower and as clear as the cleanest crystal; where it is so deep, far too deep for any anchor to reach its bottom, and many church towers would have to be stacked one on top of the other in order to reach from the very bottom to the surface above — there dwell the Mer-people.

Now you must not imagine that there is only bare white sand at the bottom. Far from it! The most wondrous trees and plants grow there, whose stalks and leaves are so flexible that they move at the slightest stir of the water, almost as if they were alive. Many kinds of fish, large and small, dart about their branches, just as birds fly in the air and around our trees.

In the very deepest part stands the palace of the Mer-King. Its walls are of coral, and the high, pointed windows of the clearest amber, while the roof is made of mussel-shells, which open and shut with the flowing water. This indeed is a beautiful sight, for each shell contains a number of sparkling pearls, any one of which would make an imposing ornament on any Queen's crown.

The Mer-King had been a widower for many years. His mother looked after his household. She was a wise woman, though extremely proud of her noble birth; that is why she wore twelve oysters on her tail, whilst other ladies of rank were only allowed six. In every other respect she deserved much praise, particularly for being so very fond of the six little Mer-Princesses, her grand-daughters. They were six lovely girls, the youngest being the most beautiful of them all. Her skin was as clear and as soft as a rose petal, her eyes as blue as the deepest sea but, like all the others, she too had no feet — her body ended in a fish's tail.

The whole day long the children would play in the spacious halls of the palace, where real flowers grew out of the walls. When the high amber windows were opened fishes swam into the rooms, just as swallows fly in to us when we open a window. But the fishes swam right up to the little Princesses, and would eat out of their hands and let themselves be stroked.

In front of the palace was a large garden, full of fiery red and dark blue trees, whose fruit gleamed like gold and their blooms like a blazing fire, for their stalks and leaves were constantly moving. The earth—it was the finest sand—was blue like a sulphur flame and over everything there was a strange blue glow, so you could easily believe you were standing high up in the air, with only sky above and beneath you, instead of being at the bottom of the sea. When the waters were calm, it was possible to see the sun, which resembled a purple flower, with all the light streaming forth from its cup.

Each Princess had her own plot in the garden, where she could dig and plant to her heart's content. One made her little plot in the shape of a whale, another preferred hers to resemble a mermaid, but the youngest made her plot round like the sun, and planted in it flowers which glowed red, like the sun. She was an unusual child, quiet and thoughtful. While

the other sisters were adorning themselves with many wonderful things
that came out of wrecked ships, all she wanted, beside her rose-red flowers, was a marble statue of a handsome boy. It was made of clear, white
stone and had fallen to the sea-bed when a ship had been wrecked. She
put the statue in her garden, and planted a rose-red weeping willow by its
side, which grew splendidly and soon covered the statue on all sides. The
tree's fresh boughs fell right down to the blue sand, where shadows appeared in violet hues and stirred like the boughs. It looked as if the roots
were playing with the boughs of the tree and root and bough were embracing.

Nothing pleased the little Princess more than to hear about the world
of the people above. Her old grandmother had to tell her all she knew
about ships and cities, men and animals and it seemed particularly lovely
to her, that on earth the flowers were scented, for those of the sea carry no
smell; that the forests were green, and the fishes to be seen fluttering
among the branches, could sing so loudly and beautifully, that it was a joy
to hear them. By fishes the grandmother meant birds, for otherwise her
grandchildren would not have understood her, having never seen a bird.

'When you are fifteen years old,' said the grandmother, 'you will be
allowed to rise to the surface, to sit upon rocks in the moonlight and
watch the big ships sailing by. You will see woods and towns too!'

The following year one of the sisters reached her fifteenth birthday, but
the others—alas! Each was a year younger than the other, so that the
youngest had five whole years to wait before being allowed to rise to the
surface and see how the world looked. Each sister promised to tell the
others what she had seen on the first day of her fifteenth birthday; for
their grandmother had not told them enough, and they wanted to find out
many things for themselves.

Not one of the sisters longed for this release as much as the
youngest, the very one who had the longest to wait, and who was so quiet
and thoughtful. Many times at night she stood by the open window,
gazing upwards into the dark blue water, where fishes flicked their tails
and fins. She could just make out the moon and the stars, though their
light was rather pale, but seen through water, it made them appear much
bigger than they do to us. If a shadow resembling a black cloud slithered
underneath them, she knew this to be either a whale swimming above her,

or perhaps a ship with many people on board. They would never dream that a lovely little mermaid was standing below, stretching her white arms towards their ship.

So now the eldest Princess was fifteen years old and could rise to the surface of the sea.

On her return she had much to relate; the loveliest thing of all, said she, was to lie in the moonlight upon the sandy shore by the calm sea and to watch the large town close to the coast, where lights glittered like hundreds of stars; to hear music and the bustle and the noise of carriages and people. She had seen many church towers and spires of the most varied shapes, and had listened to the ringing of bells and, because she could not go ashore among the people, she longed for this the most.

Oh, how attentively did her youngest sister listen, and afterwards, whenever she stood of an evening at the open window, gazing upwards through the dark blue water, she would think of the big town, with all its hustle and bustle, and fancy she could hear the sound of church bells right down there in the deep.

The following year the second sister was allowed to rise to the surface and to swim wherever she wished. She came up from the sea just as the sun was setting, and this was the sight she thought the loveliest. 'The whole sky looked like gold,' said she, 'and as for the clouds . . .' no, she could find no words to describe the beauty of the clouds! They sailed over her, now scarlet, now violet; but far swifter than the clouds was the flight of a flock of white swans, which flew like a white veil above the sea towards the sun. The mermaid swam towards it too but the sun disappeared, and the red glow upon the sea and on the clouds disappeared too.

The year after that the third sister came up from the sea. She was the most daring of the six, and swam up a river which flowed into the sea. She saw beautiful green slopes covered with vines, and palaces and manors peering out of magnificent woods; she heard birds singing, and the sun shone so warmly, that often she had to dive under the water, to cool down her burning face. In a small bay she met a whole crowd of children. They paddled and played in the water, and she wanted to play with them. But they were frightened of her, and ran away. Then a little black animal came. It was a dog, but she had never seen a dog before. It barked at her so nastily, that she grew afraid and turned back towards the sea. But she knew she would never forget the beautiful woods, the green hills and the sweet children, who could swim, though they had no fins.

The fourth sister was not so bold for she remained on the turbulent sea and said that this was loveliest of all. One could see for many miles all around and to her the sky resembled a large glass bell. She had also seen ships, but only from a great distance. They looked like seagulls; and the playful dolphins turned somersaults and the big whales spurted water from their nostrils, like fountains.

Now it was the fifth sister's turn; her birthday happened to be in winter and so she saw things which the others had not seen the first time they were out. The sea was quite green and huge icebergs floated about, each she said like a pearl, and yet much larger than the church towers that humans built. They appeared in the most varied shapes and sparkled like diamonds. She sat down on one of the largest, and let the wind play with her long hair, but then all the sailing ships avoided the iceberg she sat upon, in terror.

That evening the sky grew dark with clouds, there was thunder and lightning and the black sea lifted the great mountainous icebergs, which gleamed brightly in each flash of lightning. The sails of all the ships were taken down, their crews were seized with dread and terror; but she sat calmly on her floating iceberg, watching the blue lightning zigzag through the sky and disappear in the glittering sea.

When one of the sisters rose above the surface for the very first time, she was always enchanted at the sight of all the new and beautiful things. But once they were permitted, as grown up maidens, to go at their will, the novelty soon wore off, and they lost interest. After a month or so, they became homesick, saying that home was the most beautiful place in the world, and there they chose to stay.

Many an evening the sisters would take each other's hand and rise to the surface together. They had sweet voices, sweeter than any human being's, and when a storm was brewing, and they expected some ships to be wrecked, they would swim in front of them, singing so sweetly about

the wonderful life at the bottom of the sea, urging the sailors not to be afraid of going down; but the sailors understood not a word and thought their voices were the voice of the storm; nor could they see the beauty of the sea-bed, for if their ships were wrecked, those on board would drown, and could reach the Mer-King's palace only as dead men.

On the evenings when the sisters thus rose hand in hand to the surface, the youngest would remain behind all by herself, gazing after them, and looked as if she was about to burst into tears. But a mermaid has no tears, and therefore suffers all the more.

'Oh, if only I were fifteen!' sighed she. 'I know I shall love the world above, and the people who live in it!'

And at last she was fifteen.

'So you see, now you too are grown up,' said the grandmother, the old widowed Queen. 'Come, let me make you beautiful like your sisters!' With this she placed a wreath of white lilies upon her head, where every petal was a half of a pearl. And to her tail she attached eight large oysters, as a mark of her high rank.

'It hurts!' sighed the little mermaid.

'If you want to look good, it is worth putting up with a bit of discomfort!' said the grandmother.

Oh, how the little mermaid would have liked to shake off all this splendour and put away the heavy wreath! The scarlet flowers from her garden suited her much better, but she dared not change anything. 'Goodbye!' she cried, rising up through the water as lightly as a bubble.

The sun was already sinking when she raised her head above the sea for the first time, but the clouds were still shimmering like roses and gold, and in the rose-tinted sky the evening star was shining brightly and beautifully; the air was mild and refreshing, the sea smooth and calm. She saw a large ship with three masts, with only one sail unfurled, for not a wind was stirring, and the sailors were sitting in the rigging and on the poles. There was music and singing, and as the evening dusk turned to night, hundreds of coloured lanterns burst into light; it looked as if flags of every nation were fluttering in the air. The little mermaid swam to the very window of the cabin, and each time a wave lifted her, she was able to see inside through the portholes, clear as a mirror. She saw many smartly-dressed people standing there, but the handsomest one was a young

Prince with large black eyes, who could hardly be more than sixteen years old. It was his birthday, and that was why they were all celebrating. Sailors were dancing on the deck, and when the young Prince appeared, hundreds of rockets were fired into the sky, turning the night into broad day-light, and making the little mermaid so terrified that she dived quickly under the water. But her little head soon popped up again, and then it seemed as though all the stars in the sky were falling down to her. Such a display of fireworks she had never seen. Fiery suns spun round and round, magnificent fishes flew in the blue air, and all was reflected on the clear, calm surface of the sea. It was so light on the ship, that you could see every bit of rope, every person quite clearly. Oh, how handsome the young Prince was! He stood there, shaking hands with everyone, laughing and smiling, whilst the music rang out into the night.

It was now very late, but the little mermaid could not take her eyes off the ship and the handsome Prince. The coloured lights were put out, the rockets no longer soared into the sky, and the gun-firing had ceased but deep in the sea the waters frothed and foamed. The little mermaid remained all this time sitting on the waves, rocking up and down, so she could see into the cabin. But now the ship started to move faster. The sails were unfurled one after the other, the waves grew in strength and power, thick heavy clouds gathered in the sky and the distant rumble of thunder was heard.

A terrible storm was brewing, and so the sailors took the sails down again. The great ship tossed to and fro while it raced on the tempestuous sea, with the waves rising like high black mountains. But the ship slipped between them like a swan, allowing itself to be lifted again and again by the towering waves.

To the little mermaid all this seemed great fun, but the sailors thought differently. The ship creaked and cracked, its heavy planks bent under the fierce blows dealt by the sea; then the mast broke in two, as if it were a reed, and the ship keeled over and the water rushed in.

The little mermaid could now see that the crew was in danger, and she herself had to beware of beams and debris from the ship which were floating on the water. One minute it was so pitch-dark that she could not make out anything at all; but with each flash of lightning she could make out everybody on board. Everyone tried to save themselves as best as they

could. The mermaid's eyes sought the young Prince, and when the ship broke in two, she saw him sinking into the sea. At first she was delighted, for now he could come down with her, but then she remembered that man cannot live in the water, and that he would only reach her father's palace as a corpse.

No, he must not die! And so she swam among the beams and the debris strewn in the water, quite forgetting the danger. She dived deep into the water, rising up again in between the waves, till at last she reached the young Prince, who by then had no more strength to swim in the raging sea. His tired arms and legs were growing limp, his beautiful eyes were closing, he would have died, had not the little mermaid appeared. Holding his head above the water, she allowed the waves to carry them both where-so ever they wished.

By morning the storm was gone. Of the ship there was not even a splinter to be seen. The scarlet, fiery sun rose out of the sea, and its beams seemed to bring life into the Prince's cheeks — though his eyes remained closed. The mermaid kissed his high, handsome forehead and brushed his wet hair away from his face. To her he looked like the marble statue in her garden, and she kissed him again and wished that he might come to life.

Now before her she saw dry land, with high blue mountains, the peaks of which glittered with white snow, as though swans were nesting there. Down below by the shore she saw lovely green woods, with a church or a convent in front; she did not exactly know, what it was, but it was a building, to be sure. Lemon and orange trees grew in the garden, and tall palm-trees in front of the gates. Here the sea formed a little bay, which was perfectly calm, but extremely deep, tight up to the cliff, upon which it had strewn fine white sand. To this the mermaid swam with the handsome Prince. She laid him on the sand, taking great care to keep his head high, facing the warm sunshine.

The bells in the large white building began to ring, and many young maidens appeared in the garden. The little mermaid swam a little farther out, hiding herself behind a few high rocks which jutted out of the water and, covering her hair and breast with foam so no one could see her face, she watched to see who would come to rescue the poor Prince.

Before very long one of the young maidens approached him. She seemed quite frightened, but only for a moment. Then she called the others over, and the little mermaid saw the Prince revive and smile at all those standing round him. He did not smile at her, for he did not know that she had saved him. She was filled with a deep sadness, and when the Prince was led into the big white building, she plunged sorrowfully into the sea and made her way home back to her father's palace.

She had always been quiet and thoughtful, but now she was doubly so. Her sisters kept asking what she had seen on her first visit to the upper world but she told them nothing.

Many a morning and many an evening she surfaced to the place where she had left the Prince. She saw the fruits in the garden ripen, she saw the snow melt on the high mountains, but the Prince she never saw, and so she always returned home sadder than ever. Her sole consolation was to sit in her garden and to put her arms round the marble statue which so resembled the Prince. But she stopped tending the flowers and they grew wildly, spreading over the garden paths, and twining their long stems and leaves into the boughs, making it all quite dark and overgrown.

At last she could bear it no longer, and told her secret to one of her sisters. Soon her other sisters heard too, and they told a few of their closest friends. One of them knew who the Prince was, for she too had seen the celebrations on the ship. She knew where he was from, and where his kingdom lay.

'Come, little sister!' said the other Princesses, and with their arms round one another's shoulder, they rose in a long row out of the sea, right in front of the Prince's palace.

The palace was built of shiny bright-yellow stone with large marble steps; one flight of steps led straight down to the sea. Beautiful gilded cupolas crowned the building, and marble statues, which looked alive, stood among the pillars surrounding it. Through the clear glass of the high windows one could see into magnificent apartments hung with splendid silk curtains and drapes, where all the walls were adorned with beautiful paintings, which were a joy to behold. In the centre of the largest hall a fountain was playing, whose waters reached right up to the glass cupola in the ceiling, through which the sun shone down on the water, brightening the pretty plants growing round it.

Now she knew where the Prince lived, she often went there in the evening. She would swim much nearer to the land than her sisters had ever ventured, sometimes even up the narrow channel that flowed under the magnificent marble balcony. Here she would sit, watching the young Prince, who would think himself quite alone in the bright moonlight.

Many an evening she would see him sailing to music in a large boat, with coloured flags waving above. Then she would peep out from among the green reeds and, if the wind caught her long, silvery veil and someone happened to see it, they only thought it was a swan spreading its wings.

Many a night she would hear the fishermen, as they set out with lights to fish, talk well of the young Prince. Then she was glad she had saved his life when he was tossed by the waves, and remembered how firmly his head had rested on her breast and how ardently she had kissed him though he knew nothing about it and could not even dream of such a thing.

Human beings became more and more dear to her, and she wished more and more that she could go on land among them. Their world seemed so much larger than her kingdom; they could fly over the seas in their ships, they could climb high mountains above the clouds; and the land which belonged to them, with forests and fields, stretched further than she could see. There was so much she wished to know, but her sister did not know the answers to all her questions. So she often asked her old grandmother, who knew the upper world so very well, and called it justly the land above the sea.

'If human beings don't drown,' asked the little mermaid, 'do they live for ever? Do they not die as we do down here in the sea?'

'Oh no!' said the grandmother, 'they too have to die, in fact their life is shorter than ours. We can go on living for three hundred years, but when our life comes to an end, we turn to foam on the sea, and we do not even have a grave among our loved ones. We are like the green rushes; once they are cut down, they cannot grow green again! Human beings, on the other hand, have a soul which lives for ever, even when the bodies turn to dust. Their souls rise through the clear air to the glittering stars above! Just as we rise out of the sea to admire land inhabited by man, these souls rise to glorious, unknown places, which we shall never see.'

'Why don't we have immortal souls?' asked the little mermaid sadly. 'I would gladly give up my three hundred years just to be a human being for one day and to be given a place in the heavenly world.'

'You must not think of that!' said the grandmother. 'Our lives are much happier and better than the lives of human beings!'

'Am I then to die and to turn to foam on the sea, never hearing the music of the waves, never seeing the beautiful flowers and the scarlet sun! Is there nothing I can do to obtain an immortal soul?'

'Nothing!' replied the old lady. 'Only if some human being were to fall in love with you to such an extent, that you would be more dear to him than his mother and father; if all his heart and all his thoughts were centred on you, and if he allowed the priest to place his right hand in yours, with a promise to be true to you now and for ever; then his soul would flow into your body and you too would partake in human happiness. He would give you a soul, and yet keep his own. But that can never be! Your tail, which to us in the sea is so beautiful, is considered hideous up there on earth. They know no better; everyone up there has to have two clumsy stubs, which they call legs, in order to be handsome.'

The little mermaid sighed and looked mournfully at her fish's tail.

'Let us be content,' said the old lady, 'let us leap and swim about for the three hundred years we are given to live; it is quite long enough. Afterwards we can rest peacefully in our death. This evening we are going to hold a Court ball!'

What a splendid sight it was too, such as we never see on earth. The walls and ceiling of the great ballroom were of thick, crystal-clear glass. Several hundred enormous cockle-shells, some rose-coloured, some grass-green, stood in rows on either side, each holding a flaming blue torch which lit up the entire hall and shone through the glass walls, to the sea around the palace. One could see countless numbers of fishes, big and small, swimming towards the glass wall, the scales of some glowed purple, others silver and gold.

Through the centre of the hall flowed a wide stream, and on it danced the inhabitants of the sea, mermen and mermaids, to the sound of their own melodious voices. No human beings have such pretty voices. The little mermaid sang most sweetly of all, and they all clapped their hands, and she felt for a moment gladness in her heart, knowing that hers was the most beautiful voice on earth and in the sea.

Soon her thoughts turned again to the world above; she could not forget the handsome Prince and her sorrow that she did not have an immortal soul like him. And so she stole away from her father's palace, and while the evening passed in song and merriment, she sat unhappily in her little garden. Suddenly she heard the sound of a horn through the water, and thought, 'I expect it is he who sails up there! He, whom I love more than my father and mother, he, on whom all my thoughts are centred, and in whose hands I would so gladly place my life's happiness! I will risk everything to win him and an immortal soul! Whilst my sisters are still dancing in my father's palace, I will go to the sea-witch, the one I have always feared so much; perhaps she will help and advise me!'

And so the little mermaid left her garden and set off for the foaming whirlpools, beyond which the sea-witch lived. She had never been that way before; neither flowers nor sea-grass grew there, only the grey bare sand stretched towards the whirlpools, whose waters churned like a mill-wheel, dragging everything they seized down with them into the deep. She had to pass right through these dangerous waters to reach the sea-witch's domain. And then, for a long stretch, there was no other way but over hot bubbling mud, which the sea-witch called her peatbog. Her house stood in a very strange wood beyond this mud. Instead of bushes and trees, all that one could see were polypi, looking like hundred-headed snakes growing out of the ground; their branches were long, slimy arms with fingers like wriggling worms, and all the members of these weird trees were constantly moving, from the root to the uppermost tip. Whatever there was to seize in the sea, these springy arms would catch, twisting themselves round it, never to let it go again.

The little mermaid stopped in horror in front of this wood; her heart was pounding with fear, and she very nearly turned back. But then she thought of the Prince and of the human soul, and plucked up courage. She wound her long flowing hair round her head, so the polypi could not catch hold of it, crossed her hands over her breast, and then she glided, as swiftly as only a fish can glide through the water, passing the hideous polypi, who stretched their waving arms and fingers after her. She saw that each of them held something it had caught, as firmly as in an iron grip. Human beings, who had died at sea and had sunk to the bottom, were grinning from the arms of the polypi, now only white skeletons. They held on to oars, wooden chests, skeletons of animals, even a little mermaid they had caught and strangled; this, to the Princess seemed the most dreadful of all.

Then she arrived at a big, slippery forest clearing, where huge fat snakes were writhing about, showing their ugly yellow-white stomachs. In the middle of this clearing stood a house built with the white bones of people who had perished in the sea; and here sat the sea-witch, with a toad feeding out of her own mouth, the way people will let a canary take a piece of sugar. The repulsive fat sea-snakes she called her 'little chicks', she allowed to slither all over herself.

'I already know what you want,' said she to the mermaid. 'It is a foolish idea, but nevertheless you shall have your way, for this idea will bring you misfortune, my lovely Princess! You want to get rid of your tail, and have a pair of stumps to walk on instead, like people do, so the young Prince will fall in love with you, and so you would get him and an immortal soul too!' With that the witch laughed so loudly and so horridly, that the toad and the snakes fell to the ground and rolled about there. 'You've come just at the right time,' said the witch. 'Had you come after sunrise tomorrow,

I could not have helped you for another year. I will brew you a drink with which you must swim to land before the sun rises; you must sit down on the shore and drink it, and then you will be rid of your tail and will have instead the things which men call legs. But it will hurt, as if a sharp sword passed through you. All who will look at you will say that you are the loveliest maiden they have ever seen! You will keep your graceful, flowing movements, no dancer will be able to move as gracefully as you; but every step you take will cause you pain — it will be like treading on a sharp knife which cuts deep into your feet. If you are prepared to suffer all this, I will help you.'

'Yes!' said the little mermaid in a trembling voice, remembering the Prince and the immortal soul she might win.

'But do not forget,' continued the witch, 'that once you have gained human form, you can never again become a mermaid. Never again will you be able to descend to the bottom of the sea to your sisters and to your father's palace; and, unless you shall win the Prince's love, so that for you he will forget his mother and father, so that all his thoughts shall be centred on you, and unless he will get the priest to join your hands so that you become man and wife, you will never win the immortal soul! The morning after he weds another, your heart will break, and you will turn to foam on the sea.'

'I want it!' said the little mermaid, and she was as white as death.

'But you still have to pay me!' said the witch, 'and my charges are not small. You have the loveliest voice of all the dwellers in the sea, and I am sure you intend to charm the Prince with it. That voice you must give to me. In exchange for the magic drink I demand the best you possess! I must, after all, put my own blood into the drink, to make it as sharp as a two-edged sword!'

'But if you take my voice from me,' said the little mermaid, 'what shall I have left?'

'Your graceful figure,' replied the witch, 'your flowing movements, and your expressive eyes. With these you can surely charm a human heart. Well now! Have you lost courage? Show me your tongue, I will cut it off in payment and then you shall get the magic drink!'

'Be it so!' said the little mermaid and the witch put the cauldron on the fire, in order to mix the magic drink. 'Cleanliness is next to godliness!'

remarked she, rubbing the cauldron with a tight bundle of snakes. Then she scratched her chest, and let the black blood trickle into the cauldron. At the same time the steam took on the weirdest of forms, which would fill anyone with terror; the witch kept on throwing different things into the cauldron and, when the potion was truly on the boil, it sounded like a crocodile shedding tears. At last the drink was ready, and then it looked like the purest water.

'Here it is!' said the witch and she cut out the little mermaid's tongue, so that she was now dumb and could neither sing nor speak.

'If the polypi should seize you when you pass through my wood,' said the witch, 'sprinkle a single drop of this potion on them, and their arms and fingers will disintegrate into a thousand pieces!'

But there was, however, no need for the little mermaid to do such a thing, for the polypi shrank back from her in terror as soon as they saw the bright potion in her hand, which glittered like a star. And so she soon passed safely through the wood, the bog, and the foaming whirlpools.

She could now see her father's palace. The lights in the large ballroom were out, and all the family were asleep, but the little mermaid dared not go in to them now that she was dumb and about to leave them for ever. She thought her heart would break with grief. She stole into the garden, plucked a flower from the bed of each of her sisters, threw a thousand kisses in the direction of the palace, and then rose upwards through the dark-blue sea.

The sun had not yet risen when she saw the Prince's palace and found herself on the marble steps. A bright moon was still shining as the little mermaid drank the burning liquid; she felt it running through her body like a two-edged sword, till she fainted with the pain and lay there as though dead. When the sun rose over the sea, she woke up and felt a sharp pain, but standing right in front of her was the handsome young Prince, his coal-black eyes fixed intently upon her. She cast down her own eyes and saw that her fish's tail was gone and that she now had two slender white legs, the nicest little white legs that any girl could have. But she was quite naked, and so she wrapped herself in her long thick hair. The Prince asked who she was and where she had come from, but she could only look at him softly, though sadly with her dark blue eyes, for, alas! she could not speak. Then the Prince took her by the hand and led her into the palace.

As the witch had predicted, every step caused much pain, it was like walking on pointed needles and sharp knives, but she bore the pain gladly and walked at the Prince's side as lightly as an air bubble and he, and everyone who saw her marvelled at her graceful, flowing movements.

They dressed her in rich garments of silk and muslin and even in the palace she was the loveliest of all who lived there, but she was dumb, she could neither speak, nor sing. Beautiful female slaves, dressed in silk and gold, came out and sang before the Prince and his royal parents; one of them sang more beautifully than the rest and the Prince clapped his hands and smiled at her. This made the little mermaid very sad, for she knew that she used to sing far more beautifully. And she thought, 'Oh, if only he knew that for his sake I have given my voice away for ever!'

The slave-girls began to dance with graceful, flowing movements to the most wonderful music; and then the little mermaid raised her pretty white arms, stood on tiptoe, and glided about the hall, dancing as no one had ever danced before; with every movement her beauty became even more striking, and her eyes touched the heart of everyone who saw her, far more than the songs of the slaves.

Everyone was enchanted with her dance, particularly the Prince, who called her his little foundling. She danced again and again, though every step was like treading on sharp knives. The Prince said that she must always be with him and allowed her to sleep outside his door on a velvet cushion.

He had a man's riding-habit made for her, so she could accompany him on horseback. They rode together through the fragrant woods, where green branches brushed against her shoulders and where among the fresh leaves little birds sang. With the Prince she climbed high mountains, and though her tender feet bled for all to see, she only laughed and followed him till they could see the clouds floating beneath them, like a flock of birds migrating to foreign lands.

At night in the Prince's palace, when everyone else was asleep, she would come out onto the marble stairs, and, when she walked into the cool sea-water, the pain in her burning feet eased. Then she would also think of those who dwelt deep down in the sea.

One night her sisters appeared, arm in arm, singing so sadly as they swam by. The little mermaid beckoned to them and her sisters recognised

her and told her how unhappy she had made them all. After that her sisters visited her night after night. Once in the distance she even saw her old grandmother, who had not risen to the surface for many, many years. The Mer-King was there, too, with his crown on his head; they stretched their hands towards her, but they did not dare to swim near enough to land to speak to her.

With each day she grew dearer and dearer to the Prince. He was fond of her, as one is fond of a good, sweet child, but the thought of making her his Queen never entered his head. Yet she had to become his wife, otherwise she could not gain an immortal soul, but would turn to sea foam on his wedding morning.

'Do you not love me more than all others?' her eyes seemed to ask when he embraced her and kissed her pretty forehead.

'Of course you are very dear to me,' the Prince would say, 'for you have the best heart, you are the most devoted to me and you remind me of a young maiden whom I saw but once, and will probably never see again.

I was on a ship that was wrecked; the waves carried me ashore near a holy temple, where young maidens were taking part in a religious service. The youngest one found me on the shore and saved my life. I only saw her twice. Her, and her alone can I love. But she belongs to the holy temple, that is why good fortune has sent you to me for consolation and never will we part!'

'Alas! He does not know it was I who saved his life,' thought the little mermaid. 'I carried him across the sea to the wooded shore, where the holy temple stands. I sat, hidden by the rocks, watching to see if anyone would come. I saw the pretty maiden, whom he loves more than me!' And the little mermaid sighed deeply. Cry she could not. 'But the girl belonged to the holy temple, as he said. She would never come out into the world and they will never meet again; whereas I am always with him, I see him every day. I will care for him, I will love him, I will give my life to him!'

But the Prince was to marry, and was to take the lovely daughter of a neighbouring King for his wife, or so the people said. That was why he was fitting out a magnificent ship. It was announced, of course, that the Prince was going to inspect the neighbouring land but, in truth, he was going to inspect the King's daughter, and many attendants were going with him — so people said. The little mermaid shook her head and laughed for she knew the Prince's thoughts better than anyone else.

'I must go!' he had said to her. 'I must see the beautiful Princess, for it is my parents' wish. But they will never force me to bring her home as my bride. I cannot love her for she cannot resemble the beautiful maiden from the temple, as you do. If I were to choose a bride, I would be more likely to choose you, my little dumb foundling with the speaking eyes!' And he kissed her red lips, played with her long hair, and laid his head on her heart, whereupon it filled with dreams of human happiness and an immortal soul.

'You are not afraid of the sea, are you, my dumb child!' said the Prince, as together they stood on the splendid ship, which was to take him to the lands of the neighbouring King. And he told her of storms and calm seas, of strange fishes that dwelt in the deep, and of the things the diver had seen. The mermaid smiled at his words, for she knew better than anyone else what went on at the bottom of the ocean.

In the clear, moonlit night, when everyone on board was fast asleep apart from the helmsman, she sat by the rail, gazing intently into the water, imagining that she could see her father's palace below, and above it her old grandmother with a silver crown on her head, looking up towards the ship's keel through the foamy currents. Then her sisters appeared above the surface, looking sorrowfully at her and wringing their white hands. She waved to them and smiled at them, and wanted to tell them that everything was going well; but then the cabin-boy came along, and the sisters plunged under the surface, which made him think that the white he had seen on the sea was nothing but foam.

The following morning the ship sailed into the harbour of the neighbouring King's splendid city. All the bells were ringing, and from the tall towers trumpeters were blowing trumpets and trombones, while underneath soldiers stood with banners flying and bayonets flashing. Every day there was some kind of a celebration. Balls and parties were held one after another, but the Princess had not yet appeared. They said that she was being educated somewhere far away in a holy temple, where she was being taught all the royal virtues. At long last she arrived.

The little mermaid was anxious to see her beauty, and she had to admit that she had never before seen such a beautiful girl. Her skin was so clear and delicate, and beneath long dark eyelashes smiled faithful eyes.

'It is you!' cried the Prince. 'You who saved me, when I lay almost dead on the shore!' And he clasped his blushing bride in his arms. 'Oh, how happy I am!' he said to the little mermaid. 'The very best, what I had not ever dared hope for, has come true. You will surely rejoice in my happiness, for you love me more than any of them!'

The little mermaid kissed his hand, while it seemed to her that her heart was breaking. For the Prince's wedding morning would bring death to her, turning her into foam upon the sea.

Again the church bells rang, and heralds rode through the streets, announcing the coming marriage. Fragrant oils burnt on every altar in precious silver lamps. The priests swung their incense vessels, and the bride and bridegroom joined hands, and were given the bishop's blessing.

The little mermaid, clad in a robe of silk and gold, stood there holding the bridal train, but her ears were deaf to the ceremonious music, her eyes blind to the holy ceremony; she thought only of the coming night, which would bring her death, and of all she had lost in this world.

That same evening, the bride and bridegroom went on board the ship. Cannons were fired, flags waved in the wind and, in the middle of the deck, a royal tent of gold and purple was erected, with the most beautiful, soft cushions for the newly-weds to sleep on in the cool, still night.

The sails swelled in the wind and the ship glided lightly and gently across the clear sea.

When darkness fell, coloured lanterns were lit and the sailors danced merry dances on deck. The little mermaid was then reminded of the moment when she rose from the sea for the first time, and saw the same splendour and merriment. She joined in the dance herself, fluttering lightly, as a swallow flutters when being chased. Everyone cried out in admiration, for never had she danced with such grace. Although it was as if sharp knives cut deep into her feet, she did not feel them; the pain in her heart was far greater. She knew this was the last evening that she would see the one for whose sake she had forsaken her home and family, for whom she had sacrificed her beautiful voice and suffered daily the most unbearable pain, without him having the least idea about it. This was the last

night that she could breathe the same air he breathed, the last night she could see the deep sea and the dark blue sky beset with stars. An everlasting night awaited her, a night without memories and dreams, for she had no hope of winning one. Everyone on the ship rejoiced and made merry long after midnight, and the little mermaid laughed and danced with the thought of death in her heart. The Prince kissed his lovely bride, and she played with his black hair and hand in hand they then entered the magnificent tent to rest.

All was now silent and still on the ship, only the helmsman stood at the helm. The little mermaid leaned her white arms on the ship's rail and looked towards the east for the dawn, for she knew that the first sunbeams would bring her death. Suddenly she saw her sisters rising out of the sea, deadly pale, as she; their lovely long hair no longer streamed in the wind — it had all been cut off.

'We have given it to the witch, so she would help you and save you from dying tonight! She gave us a knife, see how sharp it is? Before the sun rises, you must plunge it into the Prince's heart; when his warm blood flows on to your feet, they will grow together into a fish's tail and you will be a mermaid again. You will be able to come down below to us and live the full three hundred years before turning into salty sea-foam. Hurry now! Before the sun rises, either he or you must die! Our old grandmother is so grief-stricken that her white hair has fallen out, as ours fell to the scissors of the witch. Kill the Prince and come back to us! Hurry, hurry! Do you not see the red streaks in the sky? In a few minutes the sun will be out, and you will have to die!' With these words the sisters gave out a strange, deep sigh, and disappeared in the waves.

The little mermaid drew aside the purple curtain of the tent and saw the lovely bride asleep, her head resting on the Prince's chest and, bending down, she kissed his forehead. She looked up at the sky, and saw the morning dawn grow brighter and brighter. She looked at the sharp knife, and then again turned her gaze on the Prince, who in his sleep was calling the name of his bride, for he thought only of her, and the knife in her hand trembled.

Then all at once she tossed it far into the waves, which glittered scarlet where it fell, as though drops of blood were spurting from the sea's surface. Once more she glanced with her fast fading eyes at the Prince, then plunged from the ship into the sea, and felt her body slowly melt into foam.

The sun rose from the sea, and its beams fell softly and warmly upon the deadly cold foam. The little mermaid had no feeling of dying, for she still saw the glorious sun, and over her head hovered hundreds of transparent, beautiful creatures; through them she could distinguish the white sails of the ship, and the red clouds in the sky. Their voice was a melody, so light and so fine, that no human ear could hear it, just as no human eye could discern their forms; their own lightness allowed them to glide through the air without wings. The little mermaid then saw that she too had a body like theirs, and felt herself rising higher and higher out of the foam.

'Where am I going to?' she asked, and her voice sounded just the same as the voice of the other creatures, so ethereal, that no earthly music could match it.

'To the daughters of the air!' they replied. 'The mermaid has no immortal soul, and can never have one, unless she wins the love of a man! Her everlasting life depends upon an unknown power. Neither do the daughters of the air possess immortal souls, but they can create one themselves by good deeds. We fly to hot countries, where the sultry, plague-spreading air kills human beings; we spread through the air the scent of flowers, and bring health to men. And if we thus strive for three hundred years to do all the good we can, we shall win an immortal soul and a share of the eternal happiness of human beings. And you, poor little mermaid, you have striven with all your heart for the same thing; you have suffered and been deprived, and have now raised yourself into the world of the aerial spirits. Now you yourself can create an immortal soul by doing good deeds for three hundred years.'

The little mermaid stretched out her transparent arms towards God's sun and, for the first time in her life, felt tears.

On the ship there was much noise and bustle again, and she saw the Prince and his lovely bride looking for her, then gazing sadly at the foam on the waves, as if they knew, that she had plunged into the sea. Invisible now, she kissed the bride's forehead, smiled at the Prince, and then, with the rest of the children of the air, she soared to the rosy cloud which was sailing above.

'In three hundred years time we shall sail like this into God's heaven!' whispered one of the daughters of the air. 'We fly unseen into the dwellings of men, where there are children, and for every day, when we find a good child, who gives his parents joy and who deserves their love, God shortens the time of our test. No child ever knows when we fly through the room; nor that whenever we smile with joy at seeing such a good child, a year is struck off the three hundred. But when we see a naughty, wicked child, we must weep bitter tears of sorrow, and every tear prolongs our time of trial by one day!'

Ole Close-Your-Eyes

There is no one in the whole world who knows so many stories as Ole Close-Your-Eyes. How he can spin those tales!

In the evening, when children are still sitting quietly at the table or on their little stools, Ole Close-Your-Eyes usually comes along. He climbs up the stairs very softly, for he walks about in his socks. He opens the door so very gently and—swish! he squirts sweet milk into the children's eyes, not very much, but enough to make them shut their eyes, so they cannot see him. Then he creeps up close behind them and breathes lightly, so lightly, upon their necks. Straightaway their heads become very heavy, oh, so heavy! But it does not hurt the slightest bit, for Ole Close-Your-Eyes means it kindly and only wants them to be quiet, and quiet they are most of all when they are in bed. They have to be quiet, so that he can tell them his stories.

When at last the children are asleep, Ole Close-Your-Eyes sits down on their bed. He is smartly dressed, with a coat made of silk, but it is impossible to say what colour that coat is, for it shines now green, now red, now blue, according to the light and how he moves about. Under each arm he holds an umbrella. One, which has pictures painted on it, he opens over good children, who afterwards have the most delightful dreams all night long. And the other umbrella, which has nothing on it, he opens over naughty children, and then they sleep rather heavily and wake up in the morning without having dreamed at all.

And now let us hear how Ole Close-Your-Eyes visited a little boy called Hialmar every night for a whole week and what stories he told him.

MONDAY

'Just you wait,' said Ole Close-Your-Eyes in the evening, as soon as he had got Hialmar into bed. 'Now I will decorate this room!' And, all at once, all the flowers in their pots grew into large trees, with long branches that spread right up to the ceiling and along the walls, so that the room looked like a beautiful arbour. The branches were full of flowers and every flower was more beautiful than even a rose, and had a wonderful smell. Moreover, if you were to eat one, you'd find it sweeter than jam. Fruit glittered like gold and there were cakes full of currants. It was truly delightful! But all at once, something started to moan and to complain most awfully in the table-drawer, where Hialmar's school books were kept.

'What is the matter?' wondered Ole Close-Your-Eyes, as he went up to the table and opened the drawer. It was the slate who was rather distressed, for a wrong figure had got into the sum on it and the other figures were pressing and squeezing together, till the whole sum nearly fell to pieces. The pencil was hopping and skipping about like a little dog, he really wanted to help that sum, but he could not! And Hialmar's copybook was there too and it moaned and groaned in a most unpleasant manner! On each page at the beginning of every line was a capital letter

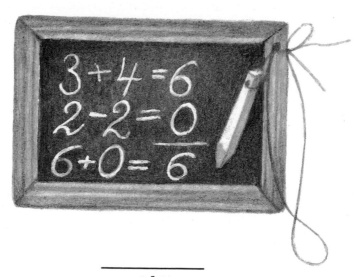

with a little letter next to it; this was the example. And by its side were other letters intended to look like the example. Hialmar had written these, but they seemed to have fallen over the lines upon which they should have been standing.

'Now this is the way you should hold yourselves,' said the example. 'Slightly slanting, like this, and turning round sharply and smartly!'

'Oh, we would like to do that,' said Hialmar's letters, 'but we can't, we are just not up to it!'

'In that case you need the powder medicine!' said Ole Close-Your-Eyes.

'Oh no,' the letters cried, and stood up so straight they were a joy to behold.

'Well, I can't tell any more stories now,' said Ole Close-Your-Eyes, 'for I have to drill those letters! Left right! Left right!' So he drilled the letters and they looked so straight and healthy, as if they were the examples themselves. But when Ole Close-Your-Eyes went away and Hialmar looked at them the next morning, they were just as badly formed as before.

TUESDAY

As soon as Hialmar was in bed, Ole Close-Your-Eyes touched with his little magic wand every piece of furniture in the room, and they all started to chatter and they all chattered only about themselves, with the exception of the spittoon. He was standing there quietly, annoyed at their vanity talking only about themselves, thinking only about themselves, without even remembering him, who stood so modestly in the corner and had to put up with being spat upon.

A large picture in a gilt frame hung over the sofa. It was a landscape. In it you could see tall old trees, flowers in the grass and a big lake with a river that flowed round the wood, passing many palaces on its way to the stormy sea.

Ole Close-Your-Eyes touched the painting with his magic wand and immediately the birds started to sing, the boughs of the trees swayed to and fro and the clouds actually moved, you could see their shadows flitting over the landscape.

Ole Close-Your-Eyes lifted little Hialmar up to the frame, and Hialmar put his legs right into the picture; there he stood in the tall grass and the sun shone down upon him through the branches of the trees. He ran to the lake and sat down in a little boat which was anchored there. It was painted red and white, with sails glittering like silver. Six swans, all with golden garlands round their necks and shining blue stars upon their heads, pulled the little boat along, past the green woods, where the trees were telling stories about thieves and witches and the flowers were talking about the pretty little elves, and of what the butterflies had said to them.

The most beautiful fishes with scales like gold and silver swam behind the boat. Every now and then they leapt above the surface, splashing the water. And birds red and blue, big and small, flew after him in two long rows; the gnats danced and the cockchafers mumbled, 'boom, boom'. They all wanted to go with Hialmar and every one of them had a story to tell.

A voyage it was to be envied! Now the woods were dense and gloomy, now like the most beautiful gardens filled with sunshine and flowers and in those gardens there were big palaces built of glass and marble. Young Princesses stood on the balconies, and they were all little girls whom Hialmar well knew and with whom he had often played. They all stretched out their hands to him, each holding a pretty little sugar pig, like those sold in sweet shops. Hialmar seized the end of one of the sugar pigs as he sailed by and, as the Princess was holding on tight, each got half, the Princess the smaller, Hialmar the larger. At every palace little Princes were keeping guard, they had gold swords at their side and they were throwing raisins and tin-soldiers all around — they were true Princes!

Hialmar sailed sometimes through woods, sometimes through large halls or the middle of a town. He also passed through the town where his nurse lived — one who had looked after him when he was just a little boy, and who loved him dearly. Now she nodded and beckoned to him as he passed by, waving and singing the pretty song she had herself composed and sent to him:

> 'How many times I think of you,
> My Hialmar, my boy!
> How I'd kiss your cheeks, your lips,
> You were my pride and joy!
> Your very first words I heard you try
> But then time came to say goodbye.

May the good Lord be your guide
And stay always at your side.'

And all the birds sang with her, the flowers danced on their stalks, and the old trees nodded their heads, as though Ole Close-Your-Eyes were telling the stories to them as well.

WEDNESDAY

Oh, how hard it rained, how it poured! Hialmar could hear it in his sleep. And when Ole Close-Your-Eyes opened the window, water came in over the ledge. There was quite a lake outside, with a magnificent ship right by the house.

'Do you want to sail with me, little Hialmar?' asked Ole Close-Your-Eyes. 'We can visit foreign lands tonight and be back here again first thing in the morning!'

And so Hialmar found himself standing on deck, dressed in his Sunday clothes. The weather had cleared. The ship sailed through the streets, cruised round the church, and soon they were on the wide, wild sea. They were sailing for such a long time, that there was no land in sight, only a few storks, who had also left their home and were travelling to warmer lands. The storks flew one behind the other and had been flying thus for a long, long time. One of them was so weary, his wings could hardly keep him up. He was the last in the row and was soon far behind the others. He sank lower and lower, his wings outspread; he managed to move them a few more times, but it was no use. His feet touched the ship's rigging, he slid down the sail and, plonk! there he was, standing on deck.

The cabin-boy picked him up and put him in with the hens, ducks and turkeys. The unfortunate stork stood among them quite confounded.

'What a funny fellow!' babbled the hens.

And the turkeycock thrust out his chest as hard as he could and asked the stork who he was. The ducks waddled backwards, nudging each other and quacking: 'Move over, move over!'

The stork told them about warm Africa, about the pyramids and the ostrich, who races the desert like a wild horse. But the ducks did not understand him and only nudged each other, remarking: 'Don't you think him stupid?'

'Yes, indeed, he is stupid!' said the turkeycock and began to gobble. With that the stork lapsed into silence and thought of his Africa.

'What beautiful, slender legs you have,' said the turkeycock! 'How much did they cost you per yard?'

'Quack, quack, quack!' laughed the ducks, but the stork pretended not to hear the question.

'You should have laughed with us!' said the turkeycock, 'for it was a very witty joke! Or was it, perhaps, slightly common for you? Oh, oh! You're not that grand yourself! Come on, let's keep ourselves to ourselves!' With that he turned and gobbled on, and the ducks quacked on: 'quack, quack, quack!' It was indeed the most horrible noise, but they probably thought it pleasant.

Hialmar went over to the hen-house, opened the door, called the stork, and the stork immediately hopped out on deck. He had rested enough and bowed his head to the boy, as if to thank him. Then he spread his wings and flew away to warmer regions. The hens cackled, the ducks quacked and the turkeycock turned purple.

'Tomorrow we'll make a soup out of you all!' Hialmar threatened but then he awoke, and found himself in his own little bed. It was indeed a strange journey that Ole Close-Your-Eyes had taken him on that night.

THURSDAY

'I'll tell you what,' said Ole Close-Your-Eyes. 'Don't be scared and you'll see a little mouse!' And he held out his hand with the tiny, pretty little animal in it. 'She has come to invite you to a wedding. This very night, two little mice here intend to enter into matrimony. They live under the floor of mother's pantry. Apparently it is the most beautiful apartment!'

'But how am I to get through a little mouse-hole?' asked Hialmar.

'Leave that to me!' said Ole Close-Your-Eyes. 'I'll make you small!' He touched Hialmar with his magic wand and Hialmar started to shrink and shrink, till he was no bigger than a finger. 'Now you can borrow the tin soldier's clothes. I think they will suit you, and a uniform looks so imposing when in company.'

'Agreed then,' said Hialmar and in a trice he was dressed like the smartest tin soldier.

'Would you please be so kind as to sit in your mother's thimble?' asked the little mouse. 'I would consider it a great honour to be allowed to pull you!'

'Heaven forbid that a young lady would go to such trouble!' Hialmar protested. But they were already on their way to the mouse wedding.

First they came to a long passage under the floor, which was only just high enough for the thimble to be pulled along. The whole passage was lit with lighted tinder.

'Isn't there a lovely smell in here?' said the mouse who was pulling the thimble. 'The whole passage has been rubbed with bacon-rind! There is nothing in this world to beat it!'

And now they were in the bridal apartment. On the right hand side

stood all the lady mice, gossipping and whispering and cracking jokes. On the left hand side stood all the gentlemen mice, stroking their whiskers with their paws. In the middle of the floor were the bride and groom.

They stood in the scooped out rind of a cheese and were ardently kissing each other before everyone's eyes. They were, after all, betrothed, and were to be married straightaway.

More guests arrived every moment. The mice nearly trod each other to death and the bride and groom had placed themselves right by the door, so no one could go in, nor out. The whole apartment, like the passage, had been rubbed in bacon rind. That was all the refreshment they had but, as a dessert, a pea was exhibited, in which a little mouse who belonged to the family had bitten out the names of the bride and groom, or rather their initials. It was something quite extraordinary.

All the mice agreed that it was a truly memorable wedding.

Hialmar then rode back home. He had certainly been in the most distinguished company. Though he felt slightly abashed at allowing himself to become so small and wearing the uniform of one of his own tin soldiers.

FRIDAY

'It is truly incredible how many old people want my company,' said Ole Close-Your-Eyes. 'Particularly those who have done something wicked. 'Dear, good Ole,' they say to me, 'we can't sleep a wink all night. We lie awake and see all our bad deeds sitting like ugly goblins on the edge of the bed, sprinkling scalding water over us. If you would be so kind as to come and chase them away, so that we could have a good sleep!' And then they sigh deeply, 'We'd be happy to pay you! Good night, Ole! You'll find the money behind the window!' 'But I don't do anything for money!' said Ole Close-Your-Eyes.

'What are we doing tonight?' asked Hialmar.

'Well, I am not sure if you would like to go to yet another wedding tonight. But it will be quite different from yesterday. Your sister's big boy doll, Herman, is going to marry the doll Bertha. Besides, it is Bertha's birthday as well, so there'll be a lot of presents.'

'I know this very well!' said Hialmar. 'Whenever the dolls need new clothes, my sister lets them celebrate either their birthday or their wedding. It must have happened at least a hundred times already!'

'Yes, but tonight they will be married for the hundred-and-first time. And this hundred-and-first marriage has to be the last. So this is sure to be a special wedding. Come on and look!'

Hialmar looked upon the table. A little doll's house stood there, with lighted windows and tin soldiers at the door presenting arms. The bridal pair were sitting on the floor, leaning against the leg of the table and looking somewhat worried. They probably had their reasons. But Ole Close-Your-Eyes, dressed in his grandmother's black gown, was marrying them! When the ceremony was over, all the furniture in the room started to sing this pretty song, written specially by the pencil:

'We sing fond farewell
To the bridal pair
With kid-leather skin
Yet straight and so fair.
For beau and belle hurrah, hurrah!
Let our song echo near and far!'

Now the presents were brought to them. Nothing edible, of course, would they accept. They had enough love to live on!

'Shall we live in the country, or go abroad?' asked the bridegroom. They consulted the swallow, who was well-travelled, and the old hen, who had hatched five broods of chickens. And the swallow spoke of beautiful warm regions, where bunches of grapes grow large and heavy, where the air is balmy and mountains are tinged with colours here unknown!

'But they haven't got our cabbage!' said the hen. 'Once in the summer I lived with all my chicks in the country, where there was a gravel-pit in which we could dig and scrape about, and from there we had access to a garden full of cabbages! Oh, how green they were! I can't even imagine anything more beautiful!'

'But surely, one head of cabbage looks exactly like another!' said the swallow; 'and then the weather here can be so awful!'

'Yes, but we are used to that!' the hen argued.

'But it is so cold here. It freezes!'

'That is good for the cabbages!' said the hen. 'And as for the heat, we have it too! Did we not, four years ago, have a summer which lasted five weeks? It was so hot, it was impossible to breathe! Besides, here you won't find all those poisonous animals which they have in foreign countries! And we don't have to fear robbers! Who doesn't consider our country the most beautiful of all, is an idiot! He doesn't deserve to live here with us!' And the hen burst into tears.

'I too have travelled. I've covered twelve miles in a coop! There is no pleasure at all in travelling!'

'Oh yes, the hen is a sensible woman!' the doll Bertha declared. 'I don't like travelling in the mountains, because one is always going up and down! No, we will go to the gravel-pit and stroll in the cabbage garden.'

And so it was settled.

SATURDAY

'Are you going to tell me another story?' asked little Hialmar, the moment Ole Close-Your-Eyes put him to bed.

'We've no time for that this evening!' said Ole, spreading his beautiful picture umbrella over him. 'Just look at those Chinese pictures!' The whole umbrella looked like a large Chinese plate with blue trees and pointed bridges, on which stood little Chinese men and women, nodding their heads. 'By tomorrow morning I must put the whole world in order,' said Ole. 'It is, after all, a festive day, a Sunday. I've got to examine the church tower, to see if the little goblins have polished the bells to make them ring nicely, I must look at the fields to see if the winds have swept the dust off the leaves and the grass. And the hardest job of all, I must take down all the stars from the sky and brighten them up. But first I have to number them; and the holes up there, into which the stars fit, have to be numbered too, to make sure the stars will return each to his proper place. Otherwise they wouldn't sit firmly and we would have falling stars tumbling down one after another!'

'Now listen to me, Mr. Ole Close-Your-Eyes,' said an old portrait, which hung on the wall near Hialmar's bed. 'I am Hialmar's great-grandfather. It

is only fitting for me to give you my thanks for telling the boy stories, but you must not confuse him. Stars cannot be taken down and polished! Stars are heavenly bodies, same as our earth, and that is the good thing about them!'

'Thank you kindly, old great-grandfather', said Ole Close-Your-Eyes, 'many thanks indeed! You are, after all, the head of the family, its very oldest head! But I am older than you! I am an old heathen; the Romans and the Greeks called me the God of Dreams! I have visited the most distinguished families, and I visit them still! I know how to deal with great and small! Now it is your turn to talk!' And with that Ole Close-Your-Eyes went away, taking the umbrella with him.

'So one is not allowed even to speak one's mind today!' muttered the old portrait sadly.

And then Hialmar awoke.

SUNDAY

'Good evening!' said Ole Close-Your-Eyes. Hialmar answered his greeting with a nod, jumping up at the same time to turn his great-grandfather's portrait to the wall, so he would not interrupt them as he had done so the night before.

'Now tell me stories—about the five peas who all lived in one pod, about the proud cock courting the hen, and about the darning-needle, who was so conceited she fancied herself a sewing-needle!'

'That is too much at once!' protested Ole Close-Your-Eyes. 'I would actually rather show you something else! I will show you my brother, he too is called Ole Close-Your-Eyes, but he never visits anyone more than once. And whomsoever he calls on, he takes on his horse and tells him stories. He knows only two; one is wondrously beautiful, such as no one in the world can imagine; the other is so terrible and dreadful — indescribably so!' And Ole Close-Your-Eyes lifted little Hialmar up to the window, and said, 'Now you will see my brother, the other Ole Close-Your-Eyes! He is also called Death. You see, he is nowhere near as frightful as he looks in picture books, where he is all bones! See his clothes, they are embroidered with silver. He is wearing the most magnificent uniform! His cloak of black velvet flies above his horse. See how he gallops!'

And Hialmar saw the other Ole Close-Your-Eyes ride on, taking with him on his horse folk young and old. Some he placed in front of him, others behind, but always he asked first, 'What kind of a report have you?' 'Good!' said one and all. 'Very well, but let me see it!' he said, and so they had to show him their reports. And all those who had 'very good' or 'excellent' written on theirs, were allowed to sit in front and to listen to the lovely story. But those who had 'fairly good' or 'bad' inscribed, had to sit behind and had to listen to the horrid tale. They trembled and cried, and tried to jump down from the horse but that they could not do, for they were as firmly fixed as if they had grown there.

'Why, Death is the most beautiful Ole Close-Your-Eyes!' Hialmar cried. 'I am not afraid of him!'

'And neither should you be,' said Ole Close-Your-Eyes. 'Just make sure you have a good report!'

'Most instructive indeed!' grunted the great-grandfather's portrait. 'It must help, after all, to give one's opinion!' He was now content.

So this is a story about Ole Close-Your-Eyes. This evening he may tell you more himself!